# Live, Local,
## and
# Dead

Also available by Nikki Knight

The Ella Shane Mysteries
(Writing as Kathleen Marple Kalb)

*A Fatal First Night*
*A Fatal Finale*

# Live, Local,
## and
# Dead

## A VERMONT RADIO
## MYSTERY

# Nikki Knight

CROOKED
LANE

NEW YORK

Published in the United States by Crooked Lane Books, an imprint of The Quick Brown Fox & Company LLC.

Crooked Lane Books and its logo are trademarks of The Quick Brown Fox & Company LLC.

Library of Congress Catalog-in-Publication data available upon request.

ISBN (hardcover): 978-1-64385-945-3
ISBN (ebook): 978-1-64385-946-0

Cover design by Rob Fiore

Printed in the United States.

www.crookedlanebooks.com

Crooked Lane Books
34 West 27th St., 10th Floor
New York, NY 10001

First Edition: February 2022

10 9 8 7 6 5 4 3 2 1

For all the pros.

# Chapter One

## Frosty Bites the Dust

I shot the snowman. But I did not kill the guy inside.

Sounds kind of familiar, doesn't it?

I didn't catch the echo—or a lot of other things—at first. It was only later, after the state police and the locals and the medical examiner had done their work and I was back to doing mine that I played "I Shot the Sheriff" for the Marley Dude, and there it was.

*I shot the snowman . . .*

You're welcome.

I love to share a good earworm.

I don't love snow, and I don't love small towns, and I really don't love running a radio station.

Too bad for me, because here I was, stuck in this frigid corner of East Hell, trying to make live local radio work and not go bankrupt. So it was all-request love songs at night, brought to you by the hardware store, the mini-mart, and the town legal notices. The one thing I can promise you is that it's a damn good show.

Sorry not sorry, I happen to think the occasional sappy love song adds to the general positivity of the world.

Lord knows everyone needed some freaking positivity. We'd returned to the frozen tundra because David survived the cancer but our marriage didn't, and it seemed like a good way to give our daughter two parents close enough for her, but separate enough for us.

It was probably a good thing he wasn't there to try and talk me down, considering I was armed and all.

He'd taken over the English department at the community college just across the river in New Hampshire, moved into his parents' house, and started work on a decent memoir and an impressive list of hookups. I'd taken the buyout from the new overlords of the New York City station where I'd been your happy and friendly workday DJ pal for most of the last decade, and gotten a deal on was left of WSV, the place where I had my first on-air job when it was still a real radio operation.

Master of words that he is, David had convinced me I could make a go of it, and I didn't fight him nearly as hard as I should have. Did I suspect that his uncles, both town leaders, had meddled a little to make it happen? Well, they'd fixed us up in the first place, so it was possible.

Anyway, the station was doing okay, thanks to lots of goodwill, good friends, and good hard work.

Mostly goodwill anyway. We had a couple of deadenders who could not accept that music had replaced their man-crush, not that this crew would tolerate an even mildly homoerotic reference without running screaming into the night.

With all the other drama in my life, I damn sure didn't need Harold the TruthTeller and his silent buddy Howard marching around like militia wannabes because I dropped the second-rate, hate-mongering satellite talk shows they loved for light rock and love songs.

But they were what I got. Every Tuesday at the former air time of the *Edwin Anger Show*, they appeared in full costume to demonstrate, straggling back and forth in front of the station with muskets that had started unnerving but were now just stupid.

And that's how I ended up standing on my recently painted but sagging porch that frigid February evening listening to five o'clock Harold chant: "Bring back Edwin Anger . . . Edwin is angry and so are we!"

Howard doesn't chant. I'm not sure he can. Didn't matter. Everybody's got their limit, and I'd just hit mine.

You really want to talk angry with me, boys?

I stomped off the porch and wrenched the muzzleloader out of Howard's hands. "Here's what I think of Edwin Anger."

That college summer of hanging out with the cute reenactors was finally going to pay off. I took careful aim at the ten-foot snowman left over from last weekend's Winter Carnival, making sure no live humans were remotely close, and fired.

Full disclosure: I wasn't even sure the thing was loaded. But Frosty's icy white head exploded with a satisfying boom, spraying bits of snow and slush everywhere. It looked like white fireworks in the single streetlight. Pretty impressive, actually.

A few people passing by, safely out of range in the Plaza, cheered. That'll get your attention.

Got my attention, too. The muzzleloader had a good kick, and I was going to have a nice bruise on my shoulder. Still worth it.

My friend Alicia Orr shot me a thumbs-up from her car in the bank parking lot and yelled "You go, Jaye!"

Her husband the police chief might see it differently, but that was his problem.

"Thanks." I handed the musket back to a gobsmacked Howard. "You might want to clean that before you reload. Looks like it hasn't been oiled in a while."

Harold and Howard stared, their faces now pretty much the same grayish-yellow shade as the Gadsden flag shirts they wore under their costume-sale greatcoats, even though the Tea Party was probably too trendy lefty for those two.

"Understand," I said calmly. "I respect your First Amendment right to protest. But you can do it over there in the public square where you're not getting in the way of my business or the restaurant's. Right about where I left a nice pile of slush while exercising my Second Amendment right."

The snowman just stood there, headless and basically intact, mutilated but still giving no hint of the disaster to come.

Harold and Howard picked up the shreds of their dignity and marched off toward the parking lot. It would have been plenty more formidable if they could've stayed in step, and if they hadn't been wearing New Balances and tube socks with their baggy breeches.

They might also have been plenty less docile if they'd known what—and who—was in that snowman, but all bad things in their own good time.

I walked back up to the porch, to high-fives from my daughter Ryan and her new best friend Xavier.

"Nice one, Ma."

"Yay, RyansMom."

It was comforting to know that my name was the same whether we were in New York or Vermont. Her old school friends had called me that too, and it always made me smile. Partly because of the way kids talk to adults—but also because of the name. Ryan's Hebrew name is Rina, for David's late grandmother, and I love the echo.

None of Ryan's pals back home had been as good a running buddy as Xavier. They shared most of the same interests, mainly space and electronics, plus they acted, and even looked, almost like sibs, both dark-haired and tall for their age.

"Jaye, what the hell did you just do?"

My former boss and morning show partner Rob Archer walked out of his restaurant next door, running his bony hands through his brown hair, his light blue eyes glowing with the exact exasperated look he used to have when I asked one of the town worthies too hard a question.

Ryan and Xavier snickered. The only thing ten-year-olds like more than seeing things get blown up is seeing their parents unhappy about it.

"Just making a point," I said with a shrug.

"And pretty damn magnificently, if you ask me."

Everyone turned in the direction of the voice, which I recognized, and not just from the occasional sound-bite over the last couple of decades.

Will Ten Broeck, the once and current governor, political unicorn and actual Knickerbocker—as in descendant of Old Dutch settlers, not free throws—walked past the decapitated snowman into the circle of light cast by that single streetlamp. He looked as good as ever, the blond hair maybe a little silvery now, the face a bit thinner, and a few crinkles at the corners of his deep blue eyes as he smiled at me. But damn, that smile.

Reporters call it That Thing, the charisma some natural politicians have. He'd never used it on me, since I was just a kid coming through on her way up, but it sure felt like he was turning it on now.

"Governor." Rob's tone was cool, but his left brow was twitching, which is his tell. "The Chamber mixer isn't for a few minutes yet."

"I was running a little early. Figured Fortescue might enjoy a cup of coffee." He nodded to his state trooper, all the security a governor of Vermont usually needs. "Just happened into the show."

I shrugged, only slightly sheepishly. I'm sure I was blushing, not that it would've shown in the half-light.

"Well, Jaye lost her temper a little," Rob explained. "She's had a rough patch lately."

"I'm just glad she's on our side." Will Ten Broeck smiled at me again. It wasn't a mistake. It felt a lot like chemistry, but surely not.

"You're safe, guys." I managed a smile too. "I need to set up my studio and get these two little angels off to their next posting—"

"I'll take care of that." Rob favored our giggling children with the intense glare that had once failed to motivate me, with about the same success. "Tim is taking them over to Claremont for some dreadful fast food."

Ryan and Xavier exchanged some sort of special secret handshake as they dashed down the stairs. I should have known that Rob would enlist his husband, the adorable and easygoing half of the partnership, into keeping the kids busy during the mixer.

"Thanks," I said. "I'll see you and the dignitaries in a while."

Surprisingly, I had the feeling the governor's eyes were on my back as I headed into the station. So yeah, I'd had a crush back in the day. Everyone had, even half the straight guys, but that didn't mean anything.

I took a glance back at the snowman, *not* Will Ten Broeck, as I went inside. It was just standing there. Well, the bottom two-thirds, anyway. No reason to think it wouldn't be there until spring, looking sad and silly, as a reminder of my little tantrum.

Sure would have made my life easier if it had.

In addition to setting up the studio for my show, I went upstairs and neatened myself up a bit. Ryan and I live above the station, in a third-floor apartment that had borne a distinct resemblance to one of your more poorly organized ancient Egyptian tombs when I bought the place. The previous owner hadn't quite been a hoarder, but he hadn't been a minimalist either. After we mucked out, we found two cozy little bedrooms, plus a small but adequate bathroom, a galley kitchen, and a mini-living room we almost never used because we were usually downstairs.

It was just fine for us. Ryan happily filled her walls with planet posters and the ceiling with an astronomically accurate display of glow-in-the-dark stars. I didn't want to sleep alone in a big bedroom anyway.

As for the neatening up, I freely admit my fashion statement, to the extent there was one, was a lot different than it would have been back in the day. In my first hitch in Vermont, I'd tried for as professional a look as I could afford, with wool blazers and indestructible dress pants over the required long johns that added unneeded bulk to my pudgy post-college form, the businesslike style undercut by flaming red hair because at some level I was desperate for attention.

Over here! Notice me! I'm great!

I don't have the energy for that anymore.

These days my look was a lot less professional and a lot more DGAF. I'd gone back to my natural black hair after Ryan was born. Well, except for the new addition of a wide platinum streak at the side part, a midlife-crisis gesture I made when David filed the papers.

It wasn't my only midlife middle finger to dressing for success. Instead of the ladylike business separates I'd worn in the city, I had my Uncle Edgar's vintage black leather moto jacket, a real James Dean one that had sat in Uncle Edgar's closet and storage boxes for decades, until I found it when he and my mother were getting ready to pool their pensions and move to a retirement village in Florida. He was going to throw it out, but I scooped it up.

Too bad for him, because he and Mom were now the brother-and-sister rebel act of Palm Fountains, a surprisingly happy ending for a couple of hardworking kids from western Pennsylvania glass factory country. He'd asked, only half-jokingly, if he could have the jacket back to impress the ladies, and I informed him it was no longer available.

It was a part of my personality now. I'd also spent thirty whole dollars at the consignment store on jeans that fit. Three pairs, amazingly, all vintage men's styles with the slim hips that showed off the only good thing about a couple of years of being too stressed to eat much. Finish off with a warm long-sleeve sweater or a smart-alecky tee, and the floral print Docs that David had always hated, and I had a pretty badass uniform. Still needed the long johns, though these days they were pretty nice, and thin, black pointelle ones.

For mixing with the Gov, I swapped my gray *Titanic Swim Team* tee for my best red cashmere V-neck, a gift from David so long ago that he'd actually taken it off me the night he gave it to me, not that I needed to remember that. Never mind David, it's really fine cashmere, and you'll pry it out of my cold dead hands.

All good, if possibly a touch informal for a schmooze with the town worthies; RyansMom wears combat boots, but maybe not for this. I traded the Docs for a pair of black Chelseas that looked a lot more expensive than they were.

Not bad. Except that I'm so pale I turn blue when I'm tired, and I'm tired most of the time. Time for a smack of makeup.

I started with the usual: a good schmear of undereye cover, tinted sunscreen moisturizer to give me a little color, and the red lipstick that Ryan had nagged me into buying, telling me I needed something bright. The clincher for me was that if I wore lipstick, I didn't really have to think about doing anything else—unless I wanted to.

That night, I did want to. I told myself it was for the Chamber. Black eyeliner and mascara to play up my gray eyes, and some nice pearly strobing powder someone had given me at the holidays.

As I shook extra highlighter from the brush, my wedding ring fell off. For a second, I just stood there holding it. The divorce had been final for months, but I hadn't been able to make myself take off the ring. Guess life just did it for me.

Neither life nor anything else was going to make me part with my remaining piece of jewelry, a stylized silver starfish necklace that recalled a Star of David. I didn't feel observant enough to live up to a full-out one. Still, I'd converted and I meant it, and the star was staying, no matter who I was—or was not—married to.

The thought also occurred that I might need to deal with that no-eating-from-stress thing. Or maybe just have a damn sandwich.

No time to process any of that, though. I dropped the band in my grandmother's old daisy-print china cup on the bookshelf and ran downstairs, past my office and the little reception area, taking a second to listen and be sure that the satellite music was still playing. All good. I'd have an hour or so before I had to get back here and jump into my request show.

For starters, we were only really live and local at night. For the morning, Rob voice-tracked some music, and I taped some news headlines, with the idea that if there was ever enough money to really pay him, we'd start doing a proper AM drive show again. At that point, though, he was willing to accept the pathetic sum I could offer for the hour it took to track the show for the sheer pleasure of being on air again.

My hand was on the door when I heard the howl of outrage. This time, not an angry listener, but a much more serious contender.

Neptune, our giant gray cat, was standing in the foyer with an expression of absolute indignation. How dare the humans go gallivanting off without paying tribute?

It will not surprise you that Ryan named him for her favorite planet at the time, because the shelter people told us he was part Russian blue, and Neptune the planet is blue. So is Neptune the cat these days. It's been a rough few months for him, and he's made sure that all of us humans pay. Usually in tuna.

As canny as Neptune is about scamming his loyal staff for treats, it is the only real sign that he is in fact a cat. Mostly, he behaves like a golden retriever, which is to say not especially bright but exceedingly loving to his people.

All two of us. Anyone else is beneath notice.

David was merely another potential food source Before, and now Neptune blames him for the fact that he no longer has his cozy window seat in the suburbs. So he tries to nip at his ankles when he comes to pick up Ryan.

While Neptune is nominally my cat, he is actually Ryan's adoring protector, and I usually get the privilege of serving as lady in waiting. The exception to this is during the nighttime request show, when Neptune sits on the old turntable cabinet, because it's near the heating register, mostly napping, and periodically awakening to disparage the locals' taste in music.

I may jokingly call myself the Queen of the Night, but there's only one actual royal in this house.

"Here to serve, Your Majesty." I ducked in my office and grabbed a bag of treats, giving him a handful and a pat. "Try not to destroy anything of mine while I'm gone."

He gave me a glare and a ruffle as he crunched away on a Tuna Greens Surprise, and I made my escape before he could ask for more.

The Plaza was quiet as I zipped across, moving fast so I didn't feel the cold, and the snowman just stood there. It was full dark now, and Frosty didn't look pathetic anymore. More menacing.

Seriously? After everything I've faced down in the last year and change, I'm worried about a pile of snow?

You really can't fix stupid.

I wasn't stupid at all, though. What I didn't know then was that my life was about to be turned upside down again—this time thanks to the body in that snowman and the Knickerbocker.

# Chapter Two

## The Don Quixote Discount

I'll admit to being a bit wound about the mixer; I knew I had to get serious about schmoozing if I wanted to bring in more local ads, and that's just not me. But I guess it's me now.

Steeling myself for the awful social stuff, I walked into Janet's, the only real restaurant in town, named for Rob's mother. His building was once a blacksmith's shop, and the main floor still has the huge hearth, and a rabbit warren of brick-walled rooms that were once used for work and storage, and now make lots of nice little alcoves for dining and talking. The food wouldn't even have to be good, but it is, in that very simple, satisfying way you hope for in a small-town restaurant.

Inside, the hearth was roaring away, and I saw a few people I knew, nodding and smiling to them. Maybe start with the woman with the phone company nametag; my friend Maeve's husband must work with her —

"So, since you're unarmed now, I figure it's probably safe to welcome you back to our great state."

Will Ten Broeck grinned up at me. He was still maybe three inches shorter than my six feet, and still completely unaware of, or unconcerned by that fact, which is very rare. Most guys are either bothered by it or way too into it. David had been into it.

"Yep. I'm at WSV again." I managed a wry smile as I held my hand out for a shake. Please don't ask me to explain. "Welcome back to you too."

"Oh, I never really left." He took my hand and held it a fraction too long with a wry smile of his own.

I assumed that the little crackle of current I felt from the touch and eye contact was just because I hadn't been around an eligible man in more than a decade. Never mind *this* eligible man.

It wasn't just That Thing; Will Ten Broeck was objectively hot, especially in a sharp midnight-blue suit and French blue oxford, the serious politician look diluted just enough by a tie featuring Champ the Lake Monster. He'd been known for the cheeky ties, and that hadn't changed any more than the smile.

"I know how I ended up back here, but why you?" I asked, quickly moving on. I'd heard he ran and won again, but it didn't make sense then or now.

He shrugged. "Wanted to do something constructive. Kids are in college, ex-wife is long gone, sure not waiting for a phone call from D.C."

We smiled together at that. He'd been the interior secretary almost ten years ago, the token red in a blue administration, taking the job out of what sure sounded like genuine patriotism even though a lot of people suspected he'd been offered it to keep him out of the presidential politics game in the next cycle. He actually lasted a couple of years before he left for a blink-and-you-missed-it appointment as national GOP chair, during the elephant's little flirtation with moderation and diversity. Whatever the panjanadrums had promised him, he learned very quickly that being smart, sensible, and open-minded was not an asset in the party of Tea.

Even less so now.

Now, of course, he was a unicorn, one of the few remaining New England Republicans. His last name marked him as a unicorn in another way: a genuine Knickerbocker. The original Willem Ten Broeck had been one of the first Dutch settlers in New York, buying up land that still kept the family coffers full, and a later William had been a pal of Alexander Hamilton's.

This one had come for college (UVM geology—yes, an interior secretary who actually understood the Grand Canyon!) and stayed. He'd never been closer to Hamilton than a road company of the hit show, pronounced the name Ten-*broke*, one word, and joked that nobody could spell it. Certainly nobody who said nasty things about him online could.

And there were plenty of them, if only because a lot of people don't like unicorns, of whatever variety.

None of my business why he was still red. I knew he hadn't gone orange; there'd been a very funny and high-profile exchange a few months before David and I moved up here. The former president, frosted by some imagined slight, had tossed a few lame insults about moose and maple at the Gov, whose name he seemed to think was Ten Bucks. Ten Broeck brushed it off by allowing as how he was happy to be called a Syrup Sucker by someone who looked like Tang.

I'm sure he knew I was thinking about that as I nodded and smiled. "Understandable."

"Besides, this is a fun job."

"Nice to do something for fun," I said before I thought.

"Rob said something about family issues?" he asked, looking sharply at me. "You had a great job in New York, right?"

"Um, yeah." I pushed a stray strand of hair back, and realized he was marking my newly bare left hand. "Long story. Enough to say that I'm here at the radio station with my daughter, and her dad is over in Charlestown."

"Ah." He held the eye contact, assessing. "Well, it's good to see you again, and hear you."

"You listen?"

"Sure. Heard one of your commercials every once in a while, or caught you when I was in New York. Hard to forget that voice. Queen of the Night now, huh?"

"Yeah, well." It's one thing to resurrect an ancient nickname for fun, another entirely to have your old crush use it.

All right, old crush. Back in the day, I'd had a huge, completely unrequited, late-adolescent crush on Will. Appropriate because I *was* a huge late adolescent; I graduated early and I was a young twenty-one when I got up here for my first on-air job after a year in a big Pittsburgh newsroom.

Not a kid anymore, though.

We stood there for a second, just watching each other. It would have felt like the eighth-grade dance if we weren't both well into our second acts.

"Hey, Jaye!" Rob called with a bad-big-brother gleam in his eye. "You hit the Gov up for a couple bites yet?"

"What? Oh, yeah." I nodded. "I could use a little tape for the morning news updates."

"Doing news again too?"

I laughed. "Somebody's got to."

I'd been the news director, read entire news department, when I was first at WSV, and had been sure I was *called* to be a journalist. Still think like one.

But I'd started as a teenage DJ in my tiny Pennsylvania home-town, calling myself the Queen of the Night so I could keep my real name for Serious Journalism. That precious pretension lasted until my first news job after Vermont, when a program director in Hartford had taken one listen to my voice and sent me right back to the board—with a raise.

A couple years later, a PD at our sister station in the city scooped me up. That job also led to a nice little sidelight in com-mercials and narration, which, thanks to the magic of technol-ogy, still brings in the occasional check to help keep Ryan in cool sneakers and pizza.

As a pro, I know that I have an extraordinary instrument, low and distinctive, with an unusually wide expressive range, but I don't think much about it. It's just me.

"If she doesn't do it, it doesn't get done." Rob smiled at the Gov, and then turned to me, twinkling. He was having much too much fun with this. "And you could give him the fifty-cent tour while you're at it."

"You can stay here, Fortescue." Will Ten Broeck called to his trooper, who was enjoying Rob's excellent coffee in a warm spot by the bar and gave no sign of wanting to leave. "Ms. Jordan is an old friend."

I didn't correct him. I'd never used David's name on the air, any more than I used my real first name, Jacqueline, though I was legally Mrs. Metz and answered to it most of the time. I was still thinking about whether I wanted to go back to Jordan, but it seemed like a lot of paperwork, and I had plenty of that already from running the station.

"You're not a snowman, so she's probably harmless enough, and the coffee's great." Fortescue, an amiable, slightly puffy older guy, raised his cup with a smile.

Once upon a time, I'd have made some snappy comment about how I might not be harmless at all, but I wasn't really that girl anymore. What I was now was mostly business, briskly walking the few feet to the station, determinedly ignoring the snowman, which seemed to be starting to disintegrate. I told myself the creepy feeling about the snowman was nothing as I guided the Gov inside.

He was not, by the way, the only unicorn in the neighborhood. WSV is one of a handful of radio stations with three-letter call signs, marking it among the first in the nation. Until the last five years or so, it was an acclaimed and beloved heritage station in southern Vermont. Then somebody decided they could make a lot more money with a satellite drone than they could with a real local operation.

See, for a small fee, or even just trading commercial time for content, you can run a radio station without having to pay actual people. Put up whatever the service sends, and collect your ad revenues. Why inform and enlighten the community when you can have Edwin Anger screaming about Those People?

It happens every day in the business, but it's not supposed to happen to a three-letter call heritage station.

That's why I got a deal on the place. The old owner had enough respect for the station's history to offer anyone fool enough to try live and local a break. Call it the Don Quixote discount.

Yay for the Knight of the Woeful Countenance. Tilting at windmills and shooting snowmen is a little too close for comfort.

I may have felt like an amateur production of *Man of La Mancha*, but I've always been good at being an absolute pro, and I held onto it that night. Quickly closing my office door to hide the mess and keep the now-sleeping Neptune safely penned, I waved the Gov into the foyer, where the old awards, recently polished by Ryan, still hung. Even a few with my name on them.

Then I showed my VIP visitor around the station, turning on every light in the place, and very coolly walking him downstairs to the old bomb shelter where the actual work got done. It was the same place he'd been dozens of times, of course, just a lot quieter and a little sadder.

No reason to acknowledge that, though, and he didn't, as I sat him down and started the interview. I wobbled a bit on the consent to tape because it had been years since I'd done one in person, but other than that, I was right on my marks.

I'm sure he knew the ferocious professionalism was cover, but he played along.

I would have pulled it off if not for the music. We were still in the main studio maybe ten minutes later, the boilerplate interview about this week's business in the legislative session duly taped, sitting on opposite sides of the board, me at the mic, him in the guest spot. After a quick double-check on the sound—no point doing an interview if you don't get the bites—I brought the monitor back up.

And that effing Tim McGraw song was on.

You know the one. About how life-threatening illness improves your life.

I cursed, not quite under my breath, and quickly turned the speaker back to mute as I looked down at the board, hoping he wouldn't see my reaction.

"Want to tell me about it?"

I should have known I couldn't put anything past a guy known for reading a room better than anyone short of Bill Clinton. I tried for wry. "For the last two years, I've been promising myself I was going to write Mr. McGraw a nasty letter."

"Why?"

"Cancer doesn't make you nice. It makes you mean and angry and drives knives into the sore spots." My eyes were full, but not spilling over.

"Whoa." The genuine concern in his face stunned me more than the earlier flirtatiousness had. "Your husband?"

"Ex. Remission divorce." I took a breath. "Look, just forget this, all right?"

He shook his head a little, and stood, taking the few steps over to me. "Are you okay?"

"I'm always okay."

"Right."

"Okay is my job."

He very carefully put a hand on my shoulder. "How's that working out for you?"

I looked up at him.

"Yeah." He nodded. "Okay isn't a job. It's a default setting."

"That's pretty good." I managed a small smile.

"I know a little something about not-okay."

The way he said it closed off any further discussion, which was fine, because I was getting back to my usual balance, and it was really enough to know that if he wasn't exactly in the club nobody wants to join, he'd sure been to some of the meetings. "Just gotta keep walking."

The Gov nodded and smiled a bit himself. "Better than standing there in the headlights waiting for the car to hit you."

"Got that."

He hadn't moved his hand from my shoulder. "None of my damn business, but your ex is an idiot."

"He can't look at me without seeing the chemo suite. I understand it."

Now he ran his hand down my arm, waking up every damn nerve ending on the way, his fingers finally resting for a second where my wedding ring had been less than an hour ago. An entirely innocent gesture that felt anything but. "That's sure not what I see when I look at you."

I stared at him.

"I'm probably a first-rate creep for even thinking it at this exact moment, never mind saying so, but you've grown into a beautiful woman, and I'm not at all disappointed that you're single."

*Hey, now.* Unless my sexual radar had gone completely dead, he was thinking about a lot more than which box I checked for marital status, and *I* wasn't at all disappointed about that. Not that I was even remotely sure what to do about it. I played it off. "Thanks. My self-esteem needed that."

His smile and voice were cool, but his eyes weren't, as he replied. "Glad to help."

I had no idea where to go after that exchange, and I turned up the volume on the speakers again for a subject change, figuring the awful song was over.

It was. The up-tempo Spanish beat of "Despacito" filled the studio, and the governor of our great state grinned and held out a hand. "May I have this dance?"

"Sure."

He wasn't bad, actually, and neither was I, thanks to years of Latin cardio discs. It was a cute, funny way to acknowledge whatever was going on here, without explicitly acting on it. But it sure wasn't dance class. Even though he was holding me at a very respectable distance, his hand in an entirely neutral spot on my back, I could feel the heat of his skin through the cashmere sweater, hear his breathing, and catch a faint scent of aftershave, something clean and mineral.

It would have been pretty damn sexy if he hadn't started chuckling at the hook.

"What?"

"Did you really go all *WKRP in Cincinnati* when you took over?"

I shrugged, trying to cover my blush with a laugh. I hadn't quite reenacted the famous scene where the rock and rollers took over a beautiful-music station with a loud metal riff, but I had indeed cut off Edwin Anger mid-screed with the Latin hit. The Spanish-language version, of course. "I meant to start at the top of the hour with U2's 'Pride in the Name of Love.'"

"But?"

"I couldn't stand another second of 'Those Evil Dirty People coming to take over our Sacred White Nation.'"

"Yeah, I'm pretty sick of hearing that too."

"And I can do something about it now. My air. No hate speech."

"Fine by me." He gave me a shy smile. "I'm kind of sensitive to the illegal immigration thing, since nobody was offering old five-greats Willem a visa."

"You guys turned out okay."

"I like to think so." He pulled me a fraction closer, but still well within decent distance. "Anyway, nice choice of songs. Let 'em know who they're dealing with from the jump."

"Go hard or go home, baby." I could not believe that came out of my mouth.

"That's what I always say." His impish grin diluted the insanely filthy subtext.

We didn't talk during the last chorus. Didn't need to. Then:

"A lovely dance, miss."

"Thank you, sir."

We shared a very neutral smile, both knowing that there really was a hell of a lot going on here, as the song ran into its final few bars. At the end, he spun me back to my seat and bowed gracefully, still holding my hand. "Very nice. What would I have to do to get another spin around the floor sometime?"

He seriously just asked me out. The twenty-one-year-old who still lived in some carefully hidden corner of my soul was squealing and jumping up and down.

Grownup me managed a very cool reply. "Probably just ask nicely and tolerate a little back and forth with calendars and baby—er—kid sitting."

"I can do that."

We just gazed at each other for a moment, and I had the definite feeling he was thinking about making some kind of serious move. Hell, if I'd had the faintest idea what to do with someone so far out of my league, I might have made one myself if we hadn't heard the sirens.

"What the hell?" We weren't trying for unison, but it worked out that way. We both took off for the stairs, he a few steps ahead, and clearly happier to be in front of me. I let him have that, even though I'm taller, tougher, and probably more adept with weapons.

Outside, most of the Chamber of Commerce crowd and a bunch of other folks were gathered around the snowman. An ambulance, Simpson's two fire trucks, and the police chief's cruiser were all screaming into the parking lot.

Fortescue, who had seemed like a bored older functionary just putting in his last days before retirement, was half-kneeling in the snow and taking notes, with the cool command presence of an experienced detective.

Rob walked over to us, looked from the Gov to me and smiled a little, then nodded to the Plaza. "I think you may have done a public service in more ways than one."

I followed his eyes to the snowman, which was now really falling apart in big chunks, revealing something in the middle.

Actually, someone.

# Chapter Three

## No Popsicle Jokes

"Honestly, you two. I was trying to watch a Big East game," Police Chief George Orr said, fixing Rob and me with an irritated glare as he walked up to the scene.

A former NYPD lieutenant, he came up here after he put in his twenty-five years, bringing a level of professionalism Simpson had never seen, not to mention the town's first African American family in a long time, if ever. His wife Alicia works at the bank and has become a fast friend of mine, bonding over the shortage of good coffee and a shared hatred of snow.

"Sorry." Rob and I hung our heads like bad little kids.

"Oh, I don't mind so much. I got my degree at CUNY. You can explain to Alicia. She did her grad work at Seton Hall, you know."

"Eeek." I shook my head. This was never a concern for me either way. Pitt almost never fielded a decent basketball team, or any other kind of team for that matter, not that I really cared.

Rob, the proud Syracuse alum, just nodded wisely. "I'll send you home with some muffins."

"Peace offerings always help." He looked at the remnants of the snowman, and the remains inside. "State police and the ME

24

are on the way. Guess the Gov's guy called them. I'm assuming you didn't know anyone was inside Frosty when you blew his head off, Jaye?"

Chief George gave me a watered-down version of the NYPD hard look, because he had to.

"Nope. I was just making a point about boundaries with the TruthTellers."

"Next time, maybe you just paint a line?"

"Right." I took my medicine like a good little girl, which was a lot easier because the corner of the chief's mouth was twitching.

He turned to Rob. "Seen anything weird in the Plaza lately? The ME will give us a better idea of how all this went down, but I've got to wonder if he's been in there all along or what?"

"There are probably some pictures from the Carnival. We might be able to figure out when it was built."

"Might want to ask the paper, too," I suggested.

Chief George's face tightened a bit. "All reporters aren't as friendly with the authorities as you, Jaye."

I sighed. Little stuff often became big in a small town. "Anyway, there's also a surveillance cam on the porch here. I'll get you the memory stick."

"Thanks."

We returned to staring at the snowman in moody silence. I'm sure we were all thinking about various thoroughly inappropriate popsicle references, but as long as we didn't say them, it didn't count.

"This is entirely unacceptable."

"Ayuh."

The comments announced the presence of Oliver and Orville Gurney. Oliver is the select board chair, owner of the hardware store, and probably the single savviest local pol I have ever seen. His twin Orville is my business lawyer, and a power in his own right, not that Oliver ever acknowledges it. They've been fighting since Orville arrived three minutes after Oliver, and I'm sure it won't stop till they're buried next to each other. Maybe not even then.

They also happen to be David's uncles, thanks to their younger sister's running away to college in New York and marrying Alan Metz of the Bronx, making them Ryan's and my sworn protectors. I tend to prefer Neptune's brand of chivalry, but I don't have any real choice in the matter.

They consider themselves responsible for us, since they'd suggested David look me up when he ended up in the same state as me a few years after I left Simpson, because, as they said, "We know she's a nice smart girl and he needs one."

I choose to take it as a compliment.

Chief George, Rob, and I all turned in the direction of the twins.

Oliver looked annoyed. Orville looked amused. This was about as usual. Oliver's a much nicer guy than he reads, and Orville's a lot less easygoing, but it's all in the presentation.

"Well?" Oliver asked.

"I shot the snowman," I admitted. Oliver's eyes narrowed. Orville choked back a snicker. "But I did not kill the guy inside."

Rob shook his head.

Chief George sighed.

"Please explain?" Oliver's eye was twitching, and I knew he was holding back a snicker of his own.

"The TruthTellers were protesting, as they usually do at five PM on a Tuesday," Rob started. His aunt Sadie Blacklaw, the town clerk, is the real power in Simpson, so he has some pull that the rest of us don't. He also has a very good understanding of my situation with Orville and Oliver. Sadie is worse.

"And Jaye decided to discourage them from coming onto her property," Chief George continued.

"With Howard's muzzleloader," I continued. Might as well get it all out there.

Orville smiled. "I didn't know you could fire one."

"Been a while." Didn't seem fair to explain I'd learned while chasing hot men in tight breeches, none of whom I'd ever caught, by the way.

Oliver made a sound like a sneeze, which I knew was a stifled laugh, and then pulled back to his serious face. "What about the body?"

"Well," Chief George said, "that's what we're trying to figure out."

Oliver nodded. "Reckon you've got it under control."

"Sure do," the chief agreed.

"Good enough." Oliver took one more look at the scene and shook his head.

"Maybe we skip the sculpture contest next year," Orville said. His voice wobbled on the last word, and we all carefully stopped looking at each other to avoid collapsing in gales of unbelievably inappropriate laughter.

"All okay here?" Will Ten Broeck just suddenly appeared, the way Neptune sometimes does. I thought he'd left, but of course Fortescue wouldn't release the scene till Chief George got to him.

"Yes, Governor." The chief's voice was NYPD formal. "Just getting a little insight on the scene."

"Will. Chief Orr?"

"George is fine."

They shook hands as Orville and Oliver walked up to take their turns, and for a few moments, everyone focused on completing the social formalities.

Once all hands had been shaken and appropriate greetings exchanged, the governor nodded to his trooper, who was studying what he could see of our victim: a stiff arm in a snow-covered fleece. At the wrist, I saw a logo I recognized—of an expensive "athleisure" brand. Not something you'd see a lot around here. Maybe not a local.

"Fortescue's been keeping everyone away." The Gov nodded to his man. "He was a detective for twenty years before he took the security detail."

"Excellent," Orville said.

"Nothing better than a trained eye, Little Brother," agreed Oliver.

"True." Chief George gave us all a small farewell bow. "I'm going to go take over the scene. I know where to find you if I need you."

We all nodded and watched him go.

"Well, so much for the schmooze," Rob observed. "Sorry, Governor."

"I imagine the poor guy in the snowman has some complaints about the evening." He shrugged, and his eyes moved to me. "But I don't."

"Got a request?" I asked.

For a long second, he stared at me. Then: "Oh, a song."

"Yeah."

"Maybe I call you later."

"Lines are always open."

He nodded, and put his hands in his pockets, making me wonder what he wanted to do with them. "Mine too. You call me if you need anything."

It wasn't a come-on, though there was plenty of that there. It was a stand-up guy looking out for a lady, and I understood it as such. It would have been a warm and fuzzy moment if not for the supporting cast; Orville and Oliver nodded approvingly, and Rob cut his eyes to me.

This really did feel like eighth grade.

"Thanks." We smiled together for just a second, and the others pretended not to notice. Then I pointed to the bank clock, which said five minutes to air. "I'm out of time. Maybe you can all salvage a little mixing in the Plaza."

They laughed. I felt Will Ten Broeck's eyes on me again as I went in, but didn't turn back this time. I wasn't sure what I wanted to do about any of this.

I didn't get a lot of time to think about it, because for whatever reason, it was a busy night for anniversaries, happy and otherwise, which meant I had to really work to provide a listenable show between the power ballads and the weepies, and prevent the entire audience from either turning off the radio or just lying down on the train tracks.

Fortunately, I had no such temptations. Ryan, as is her habit, brought her books and sat down in the studio with me, doing homework and rolling her eyes extravagantly at the music, and sometimes the calls, joining forces with Neptune for an impressive chorus of disdain. Tweens and cats have very little tolerance for drama, unless of course it's *their* drama.

Comedy won out shortly after eight, though, when the Marley Dude called in that request for "I Shot the Sheriff."

Everywhere I've worked, I've had a few regulars with very specific wants. In my first job in Punxsutawney, it was a guy who wanted "White Rabbit." You can supply your own joke about rabbits and groundhogs. In Connecticut, there was a lady who had to hear "I Will Always Love You" a couple of times a month. And in the city, there were several of them, but my favorite was the lady who asked for Mary J. Blige on the last Friday of every month, giving me an excuse to play a song I absolutely love.

The Marley Dude sounds like a standard Old New Englander, with a good thick Vermont accent. But he likes his reggae, and it's mostly well within the range of stuff I play, so why not? If I can make my listeners happy, I will.

That night, though, he made Ryan and me as happy as we'd been in a long damn time. During the first chorus, she looked up from her homework, and I looked up from the log, and it hit us.

"Ma shot the snowman!" Ryan sang out.

We danced around the studio, laughing like fools and singing along until I had to seg into the next thing.

The Marley Dude gets his requests for life.

A few hours later, Ryan was tucked in upstairs with Neptune asleep on her feet, and the camera monitor I hoped she didn't know about running in the background on my phone. She always read for a while when she was supposed to be down, and she'd fallen asleep holding her book, her silky dark hair spilling over the pages, her face softer and younger. I'd stayed up late reading too when I was a kid, and I didn't see any need to make an issue of it.

Or to make an idiot of myself by going upstairs and hugging my baby.

Shortly before eleven, Will Ten Broeck had called in a request for Shana Gilbert's "Never Saw You Coming," a surprisingly romantic choice, and one I didn't even think anyone remembered, since she was an R&B singer who had that one crossover hit when her label tried to turn her into the next Whitney. Lucky for her, it didn't work. Will gave me a shy laugh when I admitted that it was one of my favorites too. I played it without talking it up or saying who'd requested it. Nobody's damn business.

# Live, Local, and Dead

At almost midnight, I was wrapping up the show with some Barry White extravaganza for a guy who'd clearly been looking for a good end to his evening, and hoping his heart was up to it, when the doorbell flashed. It was another small-town thing I was getting used to again. In the city, you had a receptionist and a staff between you and the outside world. Here—just a doorbell light to let you know someone is there without a sound that would interrupt the show.

Not to mention a reminder that you're on your own at night. Late at night.

Way too late for almost anyone. Except Maeve.

The Reverend Maeve MacKay Collins, to be precise, Episcopal priest, makeup maven, and generally terrific buddy. She was standing on the porch in her shiny green puffer jacket, which echoed her hazel eyes, perfectly lined even at this hour, and holding a bottle.

While the bottle was new, the visit wasn't. We often had a late-night cup of tea or coffee at the end of our busy and demanding days. One of the best things about the move up here was renewing our old friendship and becoming really close.

"Thought you might need some pastoral counseling." Maeve grinned at the irony, knowing that I'm at least a little bit observant in my scrambling informal way. She held up the bottle, which looked to be some kind of whiskey, Irish like her husband. "And a drink."

"Just not in the studio. FCC rules."

"Damn feds. Finish up downstairs, and I'll pour us a couple."

Five minutes later, we were settled in my office sipping actually very good whiskey (Niall wouldn't tolerate bad poteen!) from coffee cups.

"So what happened out there tonight?" She stretched out on the couch while I put my feet up on the desk. There are some perks to being the boss.

"I was making a point about boundaries and put a load of Howard's buckshot in the snowman."

"'Bout time you did." She laughed. "But that didn't kill anybody."

"No," I agreed, "but it did unearth the body that someone had left in it."

"Well, that's going to be fun."

"Not for the guy . . . and probably not for me."

Maeve shook her head. "I'm sure Chief George knows you didn't do it. But we do have someone out there killing people and burying bodies in snow sculptures—which isn't exactly soothing."

"Not at all."

"Any idea who the guy was?"

"None. Not a local, I think. He had one of those expensive athleisure fleeces."

Maeve giggled, and it wasn't the whiskey. "Not like us woodchucks and our cheap stuff."

"Cheap and hard-wearing, thanks. I've had some of mine since my last hitch."

"Yeah."

After the laugh ebbed, we drank in silence for a moment.

"Aside from that, how was the play, Mrs. Lincoln?" she asked finally.

"No new clients at the Chamber mixer, but I snagged a few bites from Will—Ten Broeck, for the morning updates."

Maeve's eyes widened a touch at the slip, and she smiled. "Oh?"

"You know, gubernatorial stuff. Land use, legislative session, whatever."

"Uh-huh. He's been divorced a while, you know."

"I haven't."

"But there's nothing like a nice hot rebound man to reset all the dials."

"Reset the dials?"

A tiny blush crept up her cheeks. "I'm not good at all that blunt girl talk. You know what I mean."

"I know. I'm not sure scoring the governor wouldn't get me anything but a whole lot of trouble, though."

She laughed. "Your point is?"

"Yeah, well."

"Sooner or later, you have to start dating again."

"I do?"

"Unless you want to spend your waning years alone with a succession of giant cats, yes."

Well, that's a pleasant thought. "Maybe."

"It doesn't have to be the Gov, but he's really not a bad choice."

"How you figure that?"

"Well, as long as you can overlook the Republican thing." Maeve sipped her whiskey and thought for a moment. "Maybe the Knickerbocker thing balances it out. I don't think I've ever met anyone else whose great-great-grandfather partied with Alexander Hamilton."

"I think a couple more greats in there, but I'm not thinking about a relationship with his family tree."

"You aren't thinking about a relationship at all at this point." She smiled as wickedly as a woman of the cloth can. "You can get your old crush and your rebound out of your system at once. You don't expect or—I think—want much from this but a little fun, right?"

"I don't even remember fun. And somehow, I suspect my idea of fun and Will Ten Broeck's are far different."

She almost did a spit-take, and then took a moment to regain her ministerial mien. Maeve knew I'd been the next thing to a cloistered virgin when I married David, and obviously I hadn't had any chance to up my game since. "You'll figure out the fun part when you get there. I'm just saying, he's pretty well perfect. You don't want to keep him, so he can't hurt you, and he's universally acclaimed as nice, hot, and fun. Ta-da."

"Ta-da?"

"Technical term from seminary."

"Ah."

We giggled together.

"Anyway, give dude a chance . . . if you don't all get arrested first."

# Chapter Four

## Look Back in (Edwin) Anger

I don't dream a lot, at least not good dreams. But that night I was Joanne Woodward with my brand new Oscar, and my very hot husband Paul Newman was explaining to me how he was going to help me celebrate. Don't ask me where that came from; maybe flirting with Will Ten Broeck made me think of blond men with naughty smiles and good principles. Always liked Newman.

Anyway, there I was with an incredibly appealing man who was as happy for my success as I was, and not shy about showing it. Yeah, I should have known it was a dream. It was all pretty great until the tongue that was flicking at my ear moved to my nose, I heard the sound of a little bell . . . and realized that I was actually waking up to Neptune.

Worse, that it was 4:44, and I might as well get out of bed.

I muttered one—okay, a couple—of the Seven Dirty Words, grabbed the fleece I kept on the nightstand for this very moment, and stuck my feet into the little ballet slippers I usually wear around the station. Yay for another fun morning at the ranch.

No Butch or Sundance for me.

I chuckled as I headed downstairs. If I'd told that story on the air in New York, which I would definitely have been tempted to do, I'd have had to change Paul Newman to Brad Pitt. My next-to-last program director didn't want us mentioning anything that millennials might not get. Because of course they're too stupid to have the old movie channels and streaming services.

Typical desk jockey move. Assume your audience is dumb instead of giving them a chance to enjoy a little extra. Not me. I went along to get along as much as I could in the city, but I always treat my listeners like they're as smart as I am, and more importantly, like we're all in it together. Because we are.

And not for nothing, everyone knows Paul Newman . . . and anyone who's seen a picture of him from his early days would have wanted some of that. A good fantasy crosses all demographics.

After Neptune was fed, and Paul Newman and other hot blond men pushed from my mind, it was back to what had become my new routine: check the machines to make sure the voice-tracked show was running properly, then a dance DVD in the tiny gym area I'd scavenged out of the old sales offices on the empty second floor—before on to the mom chores: packing lunch and snack and getting Ryan off to school.

On good days, she walks up the hill with Xavier to Madeleine Kunin Elementary, named, of course, for Vermont's first woman governor. When it's too cold, though, they pile into the back of my vintage red Wrangler for the five-minute drive. I'd taken over the school run in late fall because it was something I could do for Rob and Tim; as an assistant district attorney, Tim had to leave before eight to get to White River Junction for court, and morning was Rob's heavy food prep time.

By nine, I was cleaned up and at my desk in the old station manager's office, doing whatever paperwork I had, lining up a little voice work online, and looking for ideas to bring in advertising. At some point, I'd have to get more serious about sales, but so far, the return of live and local programming had generated enough ads through word of mouth to let us scrape along with the evening show, and wherever I went I kept my eyes open for potential sponsors.

I was on my third or so cup of coffee when Chief George appeared on the porch at about ten thirty, as low-key and unobtrusive as a six-foot-three African American man in a leather trenchcoat and Indiana Jones hat can be in the middle of a small Vermont town.

I'm familiar with the concept. Even though I'm just a scruffy kid from Punxsutawney, after my years in the top market, I've learned to carry myself like a New Yorker, and some people, amazingly enough, find that a little threatening. Probably a lot more threatening when it's the chief, of course, but I immediately recognized the carefully wry smile intended to defuse any concern caused by his impressive presence.

"Come on in. I just made a new pot of coffee if you'd like."

"Sounds good."

He chuckled at my tee, today faded red tie-dye with coppery script reading *Be Kind or Get Out*, and followed me inside.

We got settled in my office, and then he dropped it on me.

"So we've identified our homicide victim."

"You have?"

"And we may have a problem here."

"We me?"

"Nope. Surveillance video of your door was pretty clear. And I bet you've got security system records to show you go in and stay in every night."

"Yes, the exciting life of a deejay."

He smiled a little. "Yeah, well."

There was no way he could not be aware that my girls had been urging me to start dating again, since at least one of the conversations took place at a slightly boozy ladies' brunch at his house (Alicia made sure Maeve, Sadie, and I all stayed and dozed through a couple of episodes of *The Crown* till our blood alcohol was back to zero). But this was on duty.

"Anyhow," the chief continued, "the issue isn't any possible suspect."

"No?"

"It's the victim. One Edwin MacGillicuddy of Atlanta."

I stared at him. "Okay?"

"Works under the name of Edwin Anger."

"Oh, hell."

"Something like that. His producer—who's staying at the Telescope Inn up the hill, by the way—says he was planning to do a remote here in protest of your decision to take him off the air. They were coming to town yesterday after a long weekend at some resort or other."

"Work a little skiing in with your righteous fury."

"Yep. Producer, one Spencer Lyle, claims they split up for a while Friday because Anger had a new lady friend. Expected to see him yesterday afternoon."

"Figured he was still busy trying to charm the locals?"

"That's his story." The chief's voice left no doubt as to his opinion of the producer's credibility. "Claims he was getting a bit worried, but had no idea where Anger might be until he turned up in the snowman, having, as they say, met with some kind of mishap."

"Any idea what kind?"

"The ME will rule once he's thawed out, but it looks a lot like the ever-popular blunt-force trauma to the skull."

"Ouch."

"Yup."

"I wouldn't put a lot of weight on the lady friend."

Chief George nodded. "I'm not. Based on the photo and atti-tude of his online presence, I doubt he's a chick magnet."

I snickered at that.

"Anyway," he continued, ignoring the snicker, "what I am hoping to get from you is some background on Mr. Anger and his beef."

"Mr. Anger had a beef for every day of the week. He was a lower-rent version of the big names on the Gadfly Network. Sta-tions that couldn't afford the major satellite services would buy the one that carried him, and he gave them basically the same bile for the buck."

"Did he lose a lot of money when you dropped him?"

"Probably little if any." I thought for a second. "After I bought the place, I called the satellite service and renegotiated my deal to change from talk to music for off-hours."

With a little help from Orville. He talked me through the negotiations, having me put the exec in charge on speaker and then silently guiding me along. It's too bad nobody caught that on camera; it was probably one of Orville's best moments ever.

There are times that my protectors can be annoying, but the sat service negotiation was not one of them. Orville helped me drive a very good bargain without burning any bridges. The satel-lite company still got their ads on the air and I got music instead of hate speech. Everyone ended up happy, except Edwin Anger's few fans, and, I now had to assume, the host himself.

"So?" Chief George asked.

"So I don't know. Even a second-rate host can't care much about losing an affiliate as tiny as we are. I'm sure whatever his deal was with the service, the financial impact would've been minimal."

"Which leaves ego."

"For sure. How dare you drop me?"

"How dare you particularly drop him. I bet the fact that you're a woman running a radio station on her own is part of it."

"You'd lose no money on that." I'd only heard Edwin Anger refer to women on the air twice during the couple of weeks I was getting the station ready to go live. Once was the moldy oldie "lock her up," the other a reference to some "uppity woman" member of Congress who had the temerity to sponsor a childcare bill.

"So you figure this was a stunt."

"I'd guess it was supposed to be."

Chief George drank his coffee and contemplated. "Sure didn't turn out that way."

Things got dramatically weirder as the day wore on, starting with word that the late Mr. Anger's producer would be taking over his planned remote.

Sadie Blacklaw, Simpson's town clerk and Rob's aunt, tipped me off, stopping by at the station on her way to lunch at Janet's with a visiting colleague. She's basically who we all hope to be when we grow up: elegant, graceful, and beautiful in the way women are when we live healthy and purposeful lives, and take a little pride in our appearance.

Today she wore a red plaid blazer under her heavy black down stadium coat, and matching red reading glasses, nicely setting off her amber eyes and blonde hair, this season in a shortish cut that had not looked nearly as good on the Oscar-winner who popularized it.

Sadie's real secret is her face, which glows without benefit of highlighter, though she uses a touch. Her skin's just healthy, with only a light coat of some kind of protective moisturizer. She doesn't try to hide her few lines, and why should she?

After turning down coffee, she took a hard look at me. "Rob's right. You really do turn blue when you're tired."

"Yeah, well."

"Seriously, Jaye." She shook her head. "Ryan's with David every weekend. You should spend it in bed."

"Um . . ."

"Sleeping." Her eyes twinkled. "At least for now. The talent pool in this town isn't worth losing sleep over. And then you'll be all rested up when someone who deserves you comes along."

I just laughed. Not much I could to say to that.

Sadie nodded. She'd made her point. "Anyway, you should know, that weaselly little radio man is planning a show today."

"What?"

"Took out a permit for the Plaza. I had to sign off, of course."

"Ugh. It's going to be Howard and Harold squared."

She shook her head. "Not unless he brings in reinforcements. Most of town is really happy to have a real radio station again."

"I hope so."

Sadie, privy to all manner of conversations I would never hear, gave me a smile that would not have been out of place on a sphinx. "Don't worry, we are. A lot of folks would like to see Rob back for a real show too, but there probably won't be money for that for a while."

"No. But I'm glad people appreciate what we can do."

She gave me a definite nod, firmly ending that part of the conversation. "Now about that strange little man and his show."

"Yeah."

"Will he bring protesters?"

"I don't know. I guess we're about to find out if anyone cares about Edwin Anger."

"How does this work?"

"I assume he's got a decent remote unit, so all he—or his tech—has to do is set up a table on the Plaza, and his friends will come cheer him on."

"Do you want me to call Chief George?"

"Maybe just let him know there's a permit for a broadcast."

"I'll tell Francis, too. Perhaps some of the firefighters will take advantage of mac and cheese night at Rob's."

Francis, Fire Chief Frank Saint Bernard, yes, his real name, is officially a friend of hers. Unofficially, he is far more, but that is absolutely none of you young things' business, as she has told Rob on occasion. Whatever their relationship status, a word from her would bring him, and a shift change's worth of friendly, and burly, smoke-eaters to the Plaza.

"Mac and cheese night is a good thing," I agreed, knowing that Chief Frank and the boys would be providing a little informal protection from whatever weirdness the remote might bring.

Never mind the mac and cheese; backup, especially Sadie's kind of backup, is a very good thing.

# Chapter Five

## Charlemagne the Magnificent

M ac and cheese night happened to fall on the same day as one of my other weekly duties, which was how I remembered it: the check of the transmitter shack.

Soon after Sadie left, I climbed back into the Wrangler, which I really loved. After most of a decade of suburban-mom sedans for the school and train run, I hadn't minded trading in for the little Jeep. I couldn't afford anything bigger or newer, and that was just fine by me, since I'd always wanted a Wrangler.

It came in really handy for the drive up Quarry Hill to the shack; the hill seems nearly vertical in spots and if there's the least bit of snow or ice, the narrow road can be pretty dicey. Since it had been more than a week since the last storm, it was a quick and easy trip that day.

Many small radio stations have their studios at the transmitter site, inevitably known as the shack because when the radio geek boys started playing with Mr. Marconi's invention a century and change ago, they often worked in the family woodshed or shack. WSV had evolved with studios in town because the family that started the station owned the building there.

So the transmitter was at a separate shack, at the highest available point in town, and it really was a shack. Corrugated tin around the base of the stick (transmitter tower) with meters and dials and such that I don't begin to understand. Ryan and Xavier, thanks to those STEM toy Snap Circuits boxes and having the run of the studios, probably would know a lot more than me. That's exactly why I usually do the transmitter check while they're at school.

Still, I make sure to bring Ryan, and Xavier if he's around and allowed, out to the site once in a while for other reasons. One big one.

As I locked up the shack after I finished my weekly look at the inside, I heard my buddy. Even if he's in a relaxed and friendly mood, he makes a racket in the underbrush.

I reached in my pocket for the hard maple candy Rob had reminded me to bring the first time I came out after I bought the station, and stepped into the clearing, far enough away from my Jeep to give him space. The crashing sounds had stopped, and it was absolutely silent, not even a ruffle of wind in the dried-out dead weeds. The crinkle of the candy wrapper seemed as loud as it would in a darkened theater.

I put the candy in the palm of my hand, held it out, and waited. Not long.

Charlemagne stalked slowly out of the woods, something like seven feet and a couple thousand pounds' worth of bull moose, complete with imposing antlers, his big brown eyes taking in the candy, and me, with his usual curiosity and affection.

"Hey, fella," I whispered. I don't know how sensitive moose hearing is, but somehow, the presence of such a magnificent animal hushes most people. Even the kids just stand and stare. I don't let them offer candy because Charlemagne is still a huge wild animal, even if a very sweet and friendly one.

He loped slowly to me, looming over my head for a moment, I swear almost smiling at the sight of his treat. Then he bent and daintily lipped it off my hand, tickling my palm with his fuzzy mouth. For a second, he stood there, just happily crunching away, enjoying the sweet and tolerating the human who gave it.

Then he seemed to bow in thanks, and turned, first slowly, then more quickly heading for his deep woods home.

I let out the breath I always held but didn't notice, and smiled. "Bye, big guy."

Ya don't get that in Midtown.

Back at the Plaza, I swung into Janet's for a second to give Rob a heads-up on the evening's festivities. He was sprinkling crumb topping on two giant casseroles of cheesy mac, and humming along to whatever nebulous background music the sat service provided at midday.

"Looks like it will be a good mac and cheese night."

"I think so." He looked at me and laughed. "Shack day?"

"How can you tell?"

"Pine cone in your hair."

"Oh, hell." I took it out. Just a tiny one. "Jeez. Good to see Charlemagne, though."

"Yeah. Maybe I'll come out next time you guys go."

"Just bring the candy."

"Yep. See anything weird out there?"

"Didn't see anything at all other than Charlemagne. Why?"

"Aunt Sadie says someone's been taking an interest in the adjacent land. Parcel maps, got permission for a survey, all kinds of odd stuff."

"It's out in the middle of nowhere."

"Yeah—but it's apparently over a giant aquifer. Be good for a water company . . . or maybe beer."

"We could all use a good drink," I teased.

"You'd be surprised at the environmental impact of a brewery." His eyes stayed sharp and serious. "Somebody looked at it years ago. It would've been a mess because there's no easy way to get rid of the wastewater at that site."

"Probably bother Charlemagne too."

"Ruin his habitat." Rob put the dishes in the oven and wiped his hands on his chef's towel. "It might have happened, though, if the company hadn't lost financing because of the recession."

"Trying again now that the economy's better?"

"Maybe." He shook his head. "I doubt it."

"Why?"

"They'd have to get a state land use change for it, and I can tell you without even asking that Will Ten Broeck would never sign off on it."

"Former interior secretary and all."

"And all." Rob gave me a significant little grin. "He's all right for a guy who went to the big leagues. Can't say the same for the lieutenant governor."

"Charity Slater, right? I saw the name on the state website but I don't know anything about her."

"She's from the Chester Slaters, next town over, one of those nouveau retrogrades. Tim can't stand her. She plays in a brass band in the summer parades. He calls them the Aggressively Straight Horns."

"Love that."

"Don't love them, though. There were just enough knuckle-draggers to get her in because the Greens ran someone with name recognition."

"Ugh."

"Yeah. The usual ugly orange cocktail of prejudice and venality. She'd let them put a nuclear waste dump on Quarry Hill if they offered her a buck and made the right noises about Those People."

"Sounds like a sweetheart."

"Yeah." Rob checked the coffeemaker. "How 'bout your sixth cup of the day? I need to get rid of this and start fresh—and there are exactly two cups left."

"Works for me."

"You know, if the brewery did try again, you'd probably get something out of it."

"What?"

"The shack parcel has road access."

"No way. I can always do another commercial for generic Viagra if I get desperate."

He laughed as he poured. "That *was* you."

"Oh, hell, yes. *Guys, are you tired of paying too much for the little blue pill?*"

Rob almost dropped the mugs, but managed to hand me mine and sat down at the prep table. "Nice."

"Nice money anyhow. Look, I didn't just come over here to enjoy your excellent company and coffee."

"The protest this evening?"

"What?"

"Sadie was here for lunch, remember?"

"Right, she was."

"That's why I'm making two pans of mac. It sounds like the whole fire department, not to mention the rest of town, is coming for the show."

"Yay."

"Might want to touch up your lipstick."
I just shook my head.
"Or not. Probably won't get the Gov."
"You going to tease me about him forever?"
"Yep."
"Just needed to know."

# Chapter Six

## Speaking of Stunts . . .

When did young conservatives stop looking like Alex P. Keaton and start looking like Gollum?

That was the first thing that came to my mind when I saw Edwin Anger's producer and heir apparent, or at least apparent heir, setting up his show in the Plaza. The guy looked like the angry, cranky types who hung around together at lunch because nobody else would have them. Of course, it's everyone else's fault for not recognizing their innate superiority and wonderfulness. Yeah.

It was tough to tell from the way his face was crunched up in a scowl, but from the speed of his movements, and the fact that what hair he had was brown, I got the sense that the dude wasn't much more than a kid. That was despite khakis and a brownish fleece in a cut and style that wouldn't have been out of place on Orville . . . except topped by an aggressively puffy olive-colored parka that, even from the porch, I could see had the same logo that had been on the wrist of Edwin Anger's top.

Somebody had spent a bunch of cash gearing up for this little expedition.

A tired and bored-looking engineer in an old but indestructible navy parka and jeans was helping him set up the table and connect cables, and I noticed that the tech looked familiar.

"Is that it?" Ryan asked, looking up from her nightly reading, this time the *Who Was* biography of Sally Ride. She sniffed and returned to space.

"We'll have to see."

I felt bad for the tech. They always get stuck in the middle of whatever crap the front office wants to do. I smiled a little as I had an idea. Grandma Daisy always said if you're going to kill 'em, kill 'em with kindness.

"Ryan, sweetheart, go get the big thermos from upstairs."

"What are you—"

"We should always be kind." I grinned. "It's much more fun that way."

My girl returned my wicked smile and ran up to our kitchen, while I brewed a fresh pot of coffee. One of my pals back in the city had signed me up for a fancy coffee-of-the-month club as a going-away gift, and I decided to share the good stuff.

It was okay. I'd already socked away a voice work check to renew the membership. I might have to make the long johns last another season, but hell if I would give up good coffee.

By the time the coffee was done and the thermos properly heated with hot tap water, our visitors had finished their setup, with the host at the table with his feet on a space heater and the engineer standing there shivering. You can tell everything you need to know about somebody by how they treat their crew.

I picked up the thermos and a couple of old WSV mugs from the promo closet, where several decades' worth of leftover swag lives, and walked out to the setup.

"You look like you could use some coffee," I said to the tech, handing him a mug.

"Thanks," he replied gratefully, taking a good look at me as I poured. "Jaye Jordan?"

"Yep. You were at RadioStar for a while, right?" I didn't remember his name, but I remembered the friendly smile, and I knew I'd seen him at the cluster of stations where I had worked in the city.

"Yep. Pat Neely." We shook with our free hands. "You took the buyout, too?"

I nodded. "Family stuff."

"Offer I couldn't refuse." He shrugged. "This gig isn't IBEW, but I don't need as much. Two years till the pension and it's cheaper to live in Atlanta for now."

We exchanged tight smiles. Radio, even at the highest levels, is a tenuous business on a good day, and then there are the bad days. "Just gotta do."

"Hey, Neely, the mic's not working!"

Pat Neely shook his head. "Have you had the privilege?"

"Suppose I'd better."

"I'll check it." Neely nodded to the guy, and motioned to me. "Jaye Jordan, meet Spence Lyle."

With as friendly a smile as I could manage, I held out the thermos and the other mug. "Nice to meet you. Want some coffee?"

Spence Lyle glared up at me, which he would have had to do even if he weren't sitting at his little card table. "What's in it?"

I laughed. It was impossible not to, this close to his crunched-up face with its pursed mouth and weird, reptilian eyes regarding me with comically over-the-top suspicion. From my vantage point I had a great view of his deeply receding hairline too, a peculiarly perfect half-moon across the top of his head.

"Nothing but ethically sourced beans from Costa Rica. Dark roast if you care."

"I don't. I'm not taking anything from you." He spat the words with a little actual spittle, fortunately out of my range. "If Neely's dumb enough to let you poison him, that's his business."

"I wouldn't bother poisoning you, Mr. Lyle. It's not worth it."

Lyle's scowl went slack as he gazed at me for a second, his oddly full lower lip hanging down in classic mouth-breather fashion. Then his eyes dropped to my shirt.

For a second, I thought he was staring at my less-than-bodacious endowments. Then I realized he'd read the tee. I'd changed to a special one for some good energy:

REFORMED SHIKSE GODDESS in hot pink on black, with a big silver Star of David.

Rabbi Liz Goldsmith had given it to me as a gag gift when I finished my formal conversion. David never liked it, but I loved it.

"You're Jewish?" Lyle asked, with a tone and expression that made my skin crawl.

"By choice." I smiled. "Converted when I married."

For a moment he stared at me. I returned the stare long enough to let him know I don't run.

Then Neely turned back after checking a cable, and I handed him the thermos. "Here. Stay warm."

I put the other WSV mug down on the table by Lyle. "Have a little souvenir."

As I walked away, I heard Neely stifling a laugh with a cough.

"Did they like the coffee, Ma?" Ryan asked, looking up as I stepped inside.

"One did. Let's watch until showtime. I can't listen to his remote downstairs, but—"

Ryan put her book down and gave me a pitying stare. "Ma, we can stream it online."

"Right." I should have thought of that.

"I'll listen in Production while you do your show." She took my laptop from the old receptionist's desk.

"Good luck with that. If he says anything that bothers you or you don't understand, we'll talk—"

"Ma," she began with one perfectly quirked brow, the tween sign of disdain for foolish parental units, "I can probably do his show for him, not that I would. Immigrants bad, white people good, the more guns the better, women need to stay in their place any way we can put them there, and oh, yeah, climate change is a hoax."

We laughed together. "I think you got it."

"Well, let's see if he gets anyone for his little protest." Ryan watched the Plaza.

Howard and Harold marched up a few seconds later, in costume as always, but significantly sans muzzleloaders, and arranged themselves on either side of Spence Lyle, while Neely stepped back, shaking his head.

And that was it.

No, really.

Harold tried his standard chant, forcing Neely to turn away to hide his laughter. A half dozen people heading into Rob's restaurant did stop and laugh too, enjoying a little entertainment before their mac and cheese.

A couple of minutes later, an old Jimmy and the fire SUV pulled up, and four burly guys plus a smaller, older man walked toward the restaurant. Chief Frank and the firefighters. They lined up between Spence and the station for a few minutes, just watching and looking formidable.

Even from inside, I could see Spence tensing, nervous or angry or both. Good for him.

After they'd made their point, the fire crew nodded among themselves and proceeded in for mac and cheese night. I didn't have to ask to know that Rob would put the guys in the window table. Sadie was probably waiting inside with a Manhattan, and one for Chief Frank.

The Simpson Police SUV drove slowly past the Plaza, but kept going.

"Almost airtime, Ma," Ryan said, pointing to the clock.

"Yep. I think it's going to be a pretty good show."

She grinned. "You *always* do a good show."

"Gotta give people their money's worth."

While I, with the support of an unusually annoyed Neptune, did indeed give people my best work that night, the same could not be said for Spence Lyle. Or, if that was his best, we had a bunch of other issues. About an hour in, Ryan came into the studio during a song, carrying the laptop.

"What?"

"He's just awful. Hasn't hit one break clean yet. He has a clock, right?"

"Yes, but timing is a lot tighter on a satellite show. Don't be too hard on him." It was a matter of honor for me to hit the end of each hour on the second, as it is for any good jock, but everyone doesn't have that level of training.

"He also can't talk, Ma. Listen."

Spence Lyle appeared to be inveighing against the big media conspiracy to silence the late Mr. Anger and himself, but it was hard to be sure, since I did not hear one complete sentence in five minutes. Worse, Lyle needed a good voice coach. He probably didn't start with a great instrument, but he was at the top of his range, brittle and nervous, and not helping himself with his phrasing.

I had a hard time imagining that even a second-rate sat service would put that on the air for long.

"Whew." I closed the laptop. "Enough of this for the night."

"Okay."

"Cocoa and a little downtime for you, young lady."

"Double shot?"

I sighed. Once, she'd made one cup with two packs, and the resulting thick, nutritionally horrific mess was now a rare and beloved treat. "You didn't get dessert, so okay."

Ryan was back to Sally Ride with her mug of evil when the doorbell lit up just after eight. I told her to watch the board and fire the second song if necessary, leaving the show in her capable hands for a moment while I ran up to see who was there.

Sadie and Chief Frank, holding the thermos, stood on the porch.

"Come down for coffee?" I asked.

"Nope, don't want to fight with the nightcap," Chief Frank said, smiling a little at Sadie. She lives in an old Victorian on a side street. He lives on the old family homestead outside of town.

I knew they'd both kill me if I acknowledged what he'd just let slip, so I just kept going. "Fair enough. Thanks for sending in reinforcements."

Chief gave me a Jimmy Stewart shrug.

Sadie smiled. "Glad to. And it worked."

"Really?"

"Oh, yes. He finished his little show just now and blew out in a huff."

"Ah."

"Said something about going back to Atlanta to finish the mission," Chief added, handing me the thermos. "His tech was nice, though. Wanted to make sure I gave this to you and said thanks."

"Neely's a good guy. Just running with that jerk till he gets his pension."

Chief Frank nodded. "Guy's gotta make a living. Even if he's stuck with some fool on a mission."

"As long as he takes his mission somewhere else, right?" Chief George joined the two of them on the porch. "I didn't see any need for extra security."

"Nope," Chief Frank agreed.

"And we don't need to give that nasty little man anything to complain about," Sadie said with a sharp nod. "I suppose you have to let him leave town?"

"I *want* him to leave town," the police chief observed. "It's not like we can't find him if we need to charge him with something."

"Spewing live from Atlanta," I agreed.

"Not that we're listening," Sadie put in, with a cool look to me. "Especially not you, Jaye."

"No way."

"Good." Chief George nodded to us all. "Just came by to make sure you were okay, Jaye. You call me if there's anything weird. Even if you think it's no big deal."

"I will." The only possible answer to his steely tone and concerned gaze.

The rest of us watched him go. From the speaker behind me, I heard Ryan make a textbook-perfect seg into the next song as the police chief reached his SUV.

"Great guy. I'm glad we were able to get him," Chief Frank observed. "Best thing we ever did, hiring him."

"Best thing I ever did, finding him." Sadie smiled. "If I hadn't put the ad in the Commanders' Union journal . . ."

"Yes, Sadie, you are always right." The slight edge in the words was more than softened by the way he said her name.

I swallowed a grin.

"Anyway, thank goodness that creep is gone," Sadie said with a relieved eye roll. "You've got more than enough on your plate without him."

"Something like that."

She gave me a hard look. "And you'd better start letting Rob feed you up a little, girl."

"Not now, okay? Let's just be glad tonight's over."

"We can all agree on that." Chief Frank nodded. "Good to be done with this mess."

I suspected their optimism had much to do with mac and cheese and accompanying libation, not to mention the way their night was likely to end. As I walked back down to the studio, I had a hard time believing we were done with anything.

# Chapter Seven

## Me Jock, Me Spin Records

Around noon the next day, I was crossing the Plaza from the bank, where I'd been depositing one of those nice little voice work checks, and not incidentally having a good talk about weather, kids, and moisturizer with Alicia, when I heard a voice that didn't belong here.

"Hey, Jackie Jordan!"

I didn't turn at the shout, because literally no one in the world calls me Jackie.

"Mizzzzz Jordan!" the voice tried again. Male, near the top of his range, not a New Yorker, but trying to sound like a tough guy from Brooklyn—and somehow managing to make a perfectly acceptable title sound like something insulting. I hadn't realized until that exact moment that there was anyone left who had trouble with Ms.

I stopped. Standing at the other corner of the parking lot was the nasty frat boy type the Gadfly Network employed to ambush Democrats and other whipping-persons of the red—orange?—world. He'd swathed his beer gut in another of those overpriced parkas, this one red, what else, topped with the athleisure version of those comical earflap hats. I hoped an actual elk hadn't died for it, but I wasn't optimistic.

# Live, Local, and Dead

I was vaguely aware of the smarmy creep's existence b
David's hundred-and-three-year-old grandfather watche
Gadflies all the time, driving his liberal parents crazy. Tha
a lawsuit against Frat Boy for his harassment of a town
cil member in a New York suburb who'd called for a reso
deploring a high-profile white supremacist march.

He'd spent the better part of a week at the woman's hous
his camera and his questions, until her husband the white
lawyer had enough and let the dogs out his way.

I was pretty amazed that anyone thought I was impo
enough to come after, to tell you the truth.

If you made me guess, I'd say creepy little Spence Lyle
buddy at the net, and the Gadflies had nothing to do on a
news day. Maybe Frat Boy wanted to work in some skiing wit
moral outrage too.

Anytime something freaky happens in Vermont, you ha
remember that. A lot of people come here to ski or vacation,
if many of the locals have never seen a ski lift from anywhere
the ground. I know I haven't.

Somebody sure needed a hobby if they were coming all
way up here to harass one little local station with maybe ten th
sand listeners on a really good day. I wasn't sure whether to
impressed with my importance or their stupidity. Considering
source, stupidity was a better bet.

"May I help you?" I asked coolly, wondering exactly what I
Boy's mentally constipated fans would make of me, in the us
jeans, boots, and Uncle Edgar's jacket, my hair trying to escap
big clip. I'd left my long down coat at the station because the ba
was just a short sprint across the Plaza lot. It was only as he turi
the camera on me that I remembered I was wearing my rainbo
flag *Love Love Hate Hate* tee too.

That'll work.

"Why are you denying the good people of this town their free and unfiltered news?"

"I'm sorry?"

"Why are you enforcing your liberal agenda on these fine New Englanders?"

I burst out laughing. "Honey, I'm a jock."

"What did you say, a jock? Is that some kind of lesbian feminist—"

I just shook my head. Sometimes you have to laugh because you can't let yourself cry at what an idiotic world it is. "A jock. A deejay. I play music. I bought the station and took it live because there's no station around here doing local programming."

"Edwin Anger was bringing good conservative information—"

"If it's conservative, it's not information. It's opinion. Would be if it were liberal, too. I'm playing love songs at night. Happy little request show." I dipped my voice into an exaggeration of my air delivery. "You're listening to the Queen of the Night on WSV."

He stopped for a moment, clearly trying to figure out what to do with someone who didn't lose their temper or just fold. After half a year in the chemo suite, I don't fold, and I damn sure don't lose my temper in public. I was perfectly calm when I shot the snowman, after all.

"Hey, want me to play you a request?" I grinned evilly. "Bet I could find something good for your girl—or guy."

"Trying to subvert small-town values with the gay agenda?"

"Nope. There *is* no gay agenda, honey. Just offering to play something for you. None of my business who it's for unless you make it my business."

"What about Edwin Anger? Did you kill him?"

Cool and careful, I reminded myself. Everything looks different on TV. "Of course not. I have no idea what happened to him, and I'm sure it's a terrible loss for his family."

Frat Boy scowled. He knew he had nothing good—bad for me—so far. "Come on. You're not disappointed that he's dead."

I looked straight down the barrel of the camera then, and spoke slowly and carefully. "I don't wish death or loss on anyone. There's too much of it in the world already."

"Mizz—"

"We're done here." I turned back toward the station.

"Jackie!"

I kept walking.

"Come on, Jackie! You have to answer the allegations!"

He kept yelling as I kept walking. At the door, I did look back at him. "My name is Jacqueline."

"And a very nice name it is."

I wasn't sure which one said it: Orville and Oliver were on my doorstep.

They had no doubt changed clothes any number of times since Tuesday night, but they looked exactly the same: khakis, plaid shirts, and fleeces under heavy, serviceable parkas, Orville's in shades of blue, Oliver's in green. My guess: Mother Gurney dressed them in different colors to tell them apart three score plus ago, and they never saw any reason to change.

It's sort of cute in a bizarre way. Like the bickering.

"Hey. I'm just about to start a new pot of coffee. Want some?"

"Wife is trying to get me to cut down on caffeine," Orville said.

Oliver smiled. "That good club stuff, right?"

"Sure thing."

"You'll skip a cup at home, Little Brother."

Inside, Oliver handed me a small package. "New book for Ryan. They just put out a *Who Is* book on Mae Jemison."

"Who?" Orville asked, betraying the fact that he had only one young female space expert in his life, unlike Oliver, who had two granddaughters in addition to his great-niece.

"First black woman astronaut, Little Brother. Keep up."

I swallowed a chuckle and got the guys settled in my office while the coffee brewed. I hadn't seen them in a couple of days, and I suspected they were just checking on me in the wake of all of the unpleasantness.

By the time the coffee was poured, I knew I was right. Both inquired carefully and cautiously as to what Ryan had been up to, and how business was going, while closely watching my face.

Yes, it was patriarchal and a little intrusive, but it was also stand-up guy and pretty adorable.

Soon enough, the coffee was gone and pickup time fast approaching, and they went on their way, once again bickering, this time about the forecast, and whether we would see any warmer weather this week.

I shot the last of my coffee and picked up my car keys. Ryan and Xavier spar sometimes too, but on them it's a lot cuter.

That night, dinner and the appropriate thank-you note for the new Mae Jemison book (my mother trained me to write thank-you notes, and I make sure my daughter does too!) were done, and I was setting up the show when Ryan blasted down into the studio in a panic.

"Where's the report outline?"

"What?"

"Ms. Featherstone sent home an outline for the history report yesterday? I have to fill it out and bring it back tomorrow?"

"I thought it was just a letter telling parents—"

"Where is it?"

"I tossed it. We have so much paper—"

"MA!" Ryan wailed. "I need to turn in my outline tomorrow!"

I thought for a minute. It was probably in the studio trash, which I had taken out to the dumpster that morning. In a pile of coffee grounds, gum wrappers, and who knew what else . . .

We still had fifteen minutes to air.

"All right," I assured my anguished progeny. "I will go check the trash. You come get me when it's five minutes to air."

"Okay. Find it, Ma. Please?"

I wanted to brush it off for the drama it was, knowing that if I threw myself on the mercy of Ms. Featherstone, a fellow Saturday yoga enthusiast, Ryan would come out just fine. But the simple fact is that everything matters so much when you're ten. Especially when eight and nine had been so hard.

So I grabbed one of my snow-shoveling gloves in hopes of avoiding complete revulsion, and a milk crate to climb up on, and headed out back.

It was cold as hell and mostly dark except for the tiny motion-sensor LED I'd installed so I wouldn't fall over something on the way to the Jeep. The only mercy was, we were the only people using the bin, so it didn't take long to find the bag, and the necessary paper, which was indeed splattered with coffee grounds, and redolent of slightly decayed strawberry yogurt from Ryan's evening snack the night before. But it was still readable, if damp.

"Ma? You've still got ten minutes, but . . ."

"Success!" I waved my prize. "We're good, sweetheart."

"Um, what's that?"

She pointed to the back door of the station, where someone had scrawled in black spray paint "Edwin Is Angry and So Are We."

"A message," I said quickly, shepherding her in with my clean hand.

Her brows pulled together, and her round little face was suddenly sharper and older. "It's that weirdo and his friends, isn't it?"

"Probably. We just keep going, kiddo. All we can do."

"Okay."

"C'mon. I have to find the hair dryer and smooth out this paper." And wash off my dirty glove, ick. "And you have work to do."

After that, it was the Marley Dude ("One Love" this time), a spate of "Will You Still Love Me Tomorrows" that made me wonder what people had been doing on this night in 1960-whatever, and a couple of giggling girls who sounded a lot like Ryan who wanted to hear a hot new rock song. I didn't have it, and I also knew that it featured language their parents would have rightly complained about to the FCC. I suspected I recognized one of the girls' voices as Ryan's school Welcome Buddy, but decided it wasn't worth pursuing.

Just another fun evening in the studio. I played "Mama Said There'd Be Days Like This" for "my young friends from Kunin," and went on with my night.

Who says I don't have a sense of humor?

My impish sense of fun had also apparently had an effect on the Gadflies and their viewers.

David called me later in the shift, an hour after Ryan's bedtime and just after I seg'd into Meat Loaf's "I'd Do Anything for Love (But I Won't Do That)."

"Got a request?"

"You're not going to play classical." He had always liked old-school symphonic stuff, and it had somehow spoken to him during the illness. I'd never been big on it, and now I was only slightly fonder of Beethoven than Tim McGraw.

"Not ever."

"Well, my grandfather told me to call you."

"Really."

"Did you have some kind of run-in with the Gadflies over that dead talk show host?"

"Nothing serious."

"Grandpa says you're a pistol. Wants to know what the hell I was thinking trading you in for a bunch of empty-headed blonde things, even if they have—quoting here—great gazongas."

I laughed. "He doesn't get that the empty heads and the gazongas are all you can handle right now."

David let out a little snort.

"Maybe I should have chosen a different verb."

We shared another genuine laugh.

"Let's just leave the verbs and gazongas out of it."

"Better that way," I agreed. We were turning out to be much more comfortable as friends and co-parents than we'd been as a couple in the last few years.

"Seriously, Jaye, are you okay?"

"Takes more than a little frat boy harassment to shake me."

"Okay." His voice turned serious. "You need anything, you call me."

"I'm fine, babe." By the time he saw Ryan I would be able to tell him I'd reported the graffiti, and I didn't want to talk about that mess right now. "Give Grandpa a kiss for me. I'll make sure I see him to say hi when I pick up Ryan Sunday."

"He'll like that."

Another half hour or so later, just after I talked up some Dan Fogelberg for somebody's milestone anniversary, the phone lit up again.

"Why did I not know your name is Jacqueline?"

Will Ten Broeck pronounced it the French way, *Zhak-leen*, which no one had ever done. My mother occasionally called me by my full name when she was worried or annoyed with me, as a reminder that I had been named for a legendary lady, but this didn't come out parental. It came out hot. Really hot.

"You probably assumed it was Jane, like most people do." I tried for a cool reply, glad that he couldn't see my blush.

"I never assume anything."

"Well," I took a breath. "I never liked being called Jackie, and Jaye Jordan sounded good on the air."

"It is a good name for a jock." He chuckled. "The Frat Boy was way out of line, but most people really don't know that deejays call themselves jocks."

"Anyone who watches the Gadflies does now."

We laughed together.

"Nice job today. That guy is really good at upsetting people and you didn't give an inch."

"Thanks."

"My son says you are trending on YouTube."

"No."

"Apparently, 'there *is* no gay agenda, honey,' accompanied by that shirt, have turned you into today's cool mom with young gay men."

I had known Alex Ten Broeck was out, but not that his dad was so comfortable and matter-of-fact about it. Good on him. "Well, better than losing my temper with that creep."

He chuckled. "Safer for snowmen everywhere."

I laughed too.

For a second, we were both silent. There was an awful lot in the room here, and I probably didn't know the half of it.

"Got any Motown?" he asked finally.

"Can't run a music show without it."
"Gladys Knight, then. 'Midnight Train to Georgia.'"
"Damn. I love that one."
"I love women with voices."
"Well played, Knickerbocker."

# Chapter Eight

## Digging Out and Digging In

Next morning, Ryan headed off to school with her outline, still splotchy, but at least not reeking of old coffee and rancid yogurt because I'd been smart enough to make a copy of the paper and let her work on that. After drop-off and clearing the usual e-mail and paperwork, I headed over to the cop shop.

The dispatcher was drinking coffee and studying for her EMT test, and barely nodded to me as I walked in and knocked on the chief's door.

"Hey, Jaye! Did Alicia tell you Maya got the fellowship?"

"I haven't seen her yet today. That's great!"

Chief George scowled a little. "As long as I don't mind my twenty-one-year-old daughter being in Italy for a year."

"You were on the street when you were twenty-one, right?"

"So were you. You want Ryan going to gas explosions and house fires when she's twenty-one?"

We shook our heads together. "I get you. But I think Italy's pretty safe these days."

"Safer than Bed-Stuy in the '90s for sure." He nodded to the side chair and shrugged. "Just being a dad."

"I'm sure I'll be the same way when it's my turn."

"Yours is going to want to go to Mars."

"Mission Control, yes. Flying the thing, hell no."

We laughed as I sat.

"Why do I suspect you aren't here to discuss our kids' career choices?"

I shrugged. "You told me to tell you if anything weird came up."

"How weird?"

"Not very. Some fool spray-painted 'Edwin Is Angry and So Are We' on the back door. Annoying but basically harmless."

"If that's all it is."

"I don't want to make an official big deal of this, I just want you to know."

"Fair enough. I'll keep an eye." He nodded. "Speaking of eyes, I got the footage from the bank lot camera."

"And?"

"Got a great shot of the snowman from Friday night, with the base they'd built that afternoon, and a short guy in a puffy parka cutting a hole in the top, and then it's Saturday and the team is putting the rest of it on."

"Damn."

"Some kind of glitch in the memory drive. Of course there is."

"Did you get a good look at the guy?"

The chief shrugged. "He's short and slight, and he could be the guy from the remote the other night. He could also be just about any short guy who ever spent too much on down. We didn't get his face."

"Did you get his head at all?"

"Why?"

I squirmed a bit, looking at the chief's bald scalp. I was pretty sure it was either fashion or practicality and not hair loss, and really sure it was none of my business, but I still felt kind of awkward. "Um, Spence Lyle has this really odd receding hairline."

"Would you recognize it if you saw it again?"

"Sure."

Awkward falls before good evidence. The chief beamed. "I'll print up a copy from the video once my tech guy enhances it. Thanks."

"Glad to help."

We smiled and I stood.

He gave me a slightly tense glance. "Are you really busy right now?"

"I have a few hours till the end of school, so not bad."

"Can you stop by the bank and talk Alicia down a little? She's afraid Maya is going to get herself into some kind of trouble over there."

"You're all way too smart for that."

"I know that and you know that, but we all know moms."

"Too true." I snapped a couple of snaps on my big coat and left the police station for the block and a half walk to the Plaza and the bank. It was only about fifteen degrees, so I was glad of another layer over my moto jacket.

Alicia was drinking coffee, scowling at her e-mail, and fiddling with a pencil when I knocked on her office door. "George sent you over, didn't he?"

"You're good."

"Sit for a second." She sighed and bit her lip. I envied her deep pink lipstick and the pink-on-pink wool blazer it echoed. "I made the mistake of expressing a bit of concern about Maya being an ocean away if she had a problem. Now he thinks I'm a paranoid mommy."

"I don't. I'm a mom too. I'm living in fear that Ryan will decide she wants to go to Israel—or Mars."

She smiled. "Yeah. I don't want to stop Maya from flying. I just hope I can deal when she does."

"Exactly."

"George is one of the good ones, but he's still a guy." She fiddled with the pencil. "Every once in a while I forget and say something I shouldn't say to a man because he'll take it the wrong way."

"They do."

Alicia picked up her coffee. "Want some? It's horrible, but it's hot."

"No, thanks. I'm heading for home next."

"That's right. You still have the coffee-of-the-month club."

"I'm re-upping for next year. Thank heaven for voice work." She sniffed her wretched mug and smiled wistfully.

"Make sure you come over for a cup soon. The new box has something from Myanmar with tasting notes that mentioned caramel, cocoa, and spice."

"Hell, Jaye, I'll move in and do your books if you want."

We were laughing as I left.

Out in the Plaza, it was sunny and cold. Colder than it should have been, since the bank clock said we'd gained a whole degree to sixteen. I gave thanks yet again that I'd bought myself a full-length down stadium coat from Outfit Outlet, even though the only color they'd had left by the time I realized I needed it was dark gray. I chose to see it as shiny elegant gunmetal, though it could just as easily be taken as battleship. Battleax maybe.

Rob was chopping at what was left of the snowman with a shovel. The police tape had disappeared a day or so ago, but it had been in the lower twenties and cloudy most of the week. Even though it was really cold today, it was sunny, and it looked like the edges were slushy.

"What?" I asked.

"Got tired of looking at it." He shrugged. "Not what I want people to see from the window seats."

"I'll help."

"You don't have to."

I was already on my porch, grabbing the shovel. It may or may not have been the right thing to do for Rob's business, but it sure was good therapy. Once I got going, I didn't feel the cold as much, and it really was satisfying to knock down big chunks and smooth it over.

"How are you two doing?" Rob asked. "That loser's remote was pretty annoying."

"Annoying was all it was." I smashed the last big chunk of snow with a satisfying crunch. "Ryan's good . . . and she'll have the weekend with her dad in Charlestown, which is a nice break."

"True. Tough on you, though."

"A little." I shrugged, not wanting to go there, even with Rob.

He got it, nodding as he smoothed out a small chunk close to him. "Still, you're on the air every day. Worth a lot."

"You are too."

"Yeah, I am. Sort of." Rob stopped tamping down the snow and leaned on his shovel, smiling. "I love the whole live dance. Dinner service is similar but not the same."

"It's the performance."

"Exactly. I miss it sometimes."

I scraped my shovel over one of the last remaining chunks of snow, and it caught, throwing something up, and making me jump back. "Yikes!"

"It didn't hit you, did it?" Rob asked, picking up the small, bright blue and white thing.

"No. What is it?"

"A box?" He turned it awkwardly in his ski-gloved hands, then held it out to me.

I took it, glad that I was wearing a thinner pair that let me hold the box for a good look. It was clear blue and opaque white plastic, with two segments marked **AM** and **PM** and the word **FRIDAY** stamped on it in black. I knew exactly what it was. "A pillbox."

"Yeah?"

"For somebody who's on a lot of pills. David had one at the height of the chemo. The boxes for each day fit in a holder, and you take your day's meds with you when you leave the house."

"Looks like Edwin Anger may not have been the picture of health."

I nodded. "You'd have to be on more than a couple of things to have one of these . . . or something that has to be very carefully monitored."

Rob looked at the clock. "Half hour till pickup. David's getting Ryan and Xavi?"

"Yeah. I'll run this over to Chief George."

"That's a good idea. You can give him some insight, too."

As I walked over, my phone buzzed. A text, from David.

*"Grandpa Seymour says you scared off the Frat Boy. The Gadflies are apparently running promos about how he's going down south to investigate the CRISIS AT THE BORDER."*

*"And good luck to him."*

*"Us too. See you after pickup."*

I was smiling as I opened the police station door.

I wasn't the only one smiling when I left. Chief George was happy to get the pillbox, happier to know that we'd only touched it with gloves, and happiest when I told him that the receding hairline on the screenshot sure looked like Spence Lyle to me. His tech was still working on a more enhanced version, but now he could start looking for photos of Spence, too—and get some actual evidence.

As I walked back to the station, glad to see the newly flat patch where the snowman had been, I thought about it.

It all felt too easy. Why would Spence put him in the snowman anyway? Make a martyr of him? Pretty weird even for that crowd.

Of course, nobody, not even me, knew I was going to give ol' Frosty what-fer with the musket before it happened. Spence might have seen the snowman as a way to put off the discovery of the body, with the added bonus of making my life difficult when his less than lamented boss finally thawed out. That made sense, as much as anything else in this cuchifrito did.

It was pretty clear that Spence wanted to take over Edwin Anger's spot, but the big question in my mind was: Could he? Based on what I'd heard the other night, he just wasn't broadcast quality. I doubted he'd ever get hired by any conventional means; a program director would hear the first ten seconds of that mess and hit "delete." Even a second-rate sat service would not hire someone who couldn't reliably fire the commercials when they were supposed to. Never mind provide an intelligible show—if not a listenable one.

But if he started as a fill-in? It would give him a chance to worm his way in before the front office really figured out what was going on. Might be the only way he would get his shot.

Once the Great Man surfaced in the spring, Spence would have had some time in the slot, and the listeners would be used to him. That might be enough for a second-rate company that just wanted to move the meters and keep the listeners buying generic Viagra, gold coins, and whatever else the advertisers were selling this week.

It was more than a little nuts. But I'd been in the business long enough to know that the need to be on the air makes people more than a little nuts. Sometimes even dangerous.

Spence didn't fit the type of crazy I'd seen most: the people who were *almost* good enough to make it, but lacked that last little bit of lightning in a bottle. It's maddening to be that close, good enough to work mid-markets, maybe even fill in at the majors, but never get a big offer. Can curdle your soul. I need more than one hand's worth of fingers to count the number of cable and online "media critics" who come from that experience.

Not important now; Spence wasn't good enough for that. But there was another type of crazy that could break just as bad: the ones who are sure they're G-d's gift to broadcasting. It takes a particularly delusional set of mind to hear yourself on the air, and even more so on your audition tape, and convince yourself that you're putting out terrific product when it's really unlistenable. These people do exist, though, and if you're nuts enough to deny the reality of the sound of your own voice, who knows what else you might be able to come up with?

And who knows what you'd do to the woman who messed up your scheme?

Dumping a body in a snowman might be just the beginning of the crazy. What a happy thought.

Neptune met me at the door, squawking and getting up on his hind legs, demanding attention and treats. I scooped him up and giggled as his whiskers tickled my neck. Cat drama was about all I could handle right now.

# Chapter Nine

## Light a Candle or Don't Whine about the Darkness

David picks Ryan and Xavier up at Kunin on Friday afternoons, because it matters to him to be the pickup parent once a week. Makes him feel involved in her life.

Most weeks, Xavier and David talk a little baseball trash, as a boy being properly raised in Red Sox Nation will do with a supporter of the hated Yankees, before Xavier heads off to whatever he and his dads have planned.

Ryan comes home to snack, pack, and light Shabbat candles with both of us before heading over to Charlestown for her usual daddy–daughter weekend. We might stop that in the summer, when it's still way too far from sunset just after four, but none of us is ready to give up the family moment yet.

While I converted with the help of the Hillel rabbi at David's college in New York, we don't belong to a synagogue, and we're not all that observant. I do my best not to take G-d's name in vain, always fast on Yom Kippur, and eat matzoh at Passover, but that's about it.

Except for Shabbat. We always light candles, no matter what. We may do it a few hours off sunset one way or the other, but there is no circumstance under which we do not light them. It's not just religious, but cultural, and not only for Ryan, either.

Knowing who and what you are and celebrating it is good for everyone.

Especially if you've chosen it. For me, it's an honor to be a part of five thousand years of tradition that everyone from the Romans to the Inquisition to the Nazis has tried and failed to eradicate. Not to mention the fact that Reform Judaism just makes sense to me in a way that the vengeful, narrow-minded fundamentalist Christianity on offer in my hometown didn't.

I like that we're expected to think and question. Even more, I like that we're expected to make things right with people, not just apologize to G-d for being a jerk. It's probably a *shikse* thing, but I actually kind of enjoy atoning on Yom Kippur. More than once, it's forced me to admit I haven't been as good a wife, mother, daughter—or friend—as I should, and work to do better. Can't beat that.

When Ryan was small, I lit our Shabbat candles, despite a command of Hebrew that is uneven at best. Since she's been old enough for Hebrew school, first in New York, and now every Saturday midday at the Hillel at David's new school, it's become her responsibility. All I do is bless her, in English, thank you.

David blesses her too. In English, because he doesn't want to show me up. Give the guy credit.

Which I always do.

It's still weird and painful to walk them to the door, knowing that she's spending the weekend with him and without me, and that it's not going to change. But we're all better this way, and all of us—Ryan included—know it.

I made sure to start my show with some up-tempo stuff that night, before diving into the pile of anniversary and special date requests that always flow in on Fridays. I don't have a lot of control over what happened to David and me, but I have plenty of control over what I do about it.

So bring on the Bangles.

"'Walk Like an Egyptian,' really?" Maeve asked when I picked up my cell phone.

"Sometimes ya gotta. Spice Girls next hour."

"You really do need some help." She laughed. "I saw David and Ryan leave, and Niall is untangling some horrific computer virus mess at the office. Want some company?"

"Sure. I might even have cookies to go with the coffee."

"Only if you eat one too."

"Just get over here."

By the time I'd seg'd from the cheerful Bangles to the first of the anniversary requests ("Time in a Bottle," which would be enough to make me run at the altar, not that I'm any authority these days), Maeve was at the door. I let her in, set out a mug, and settled in for a nice visit.

"How are you holding up?"

"Friendly co-parenting is hard, but way better than yelling at each other from across the abyss."

"I didn't mean that, but I'm glad you're adjusting." She sipped her coffee, as Neptune raised his head to cast a disdainful eye her way. Maeve and Niall have a genuine Irish wolfhound, Brigid, who is actually taller than Maeve. She's a rescue; her first family knew she would be big, but not THAT big, and had no idea what to do with her. Neptune has never met Brigid, but he can smell her existence, and doesn't like it one bit. "Hey, fella. You ever going to get over hating me?"

Neptune snorted and curled up again, making sure she got a full view of kitty posterior.

"I'll take that as a no." Maeve chuckled. "Just as well. When Brigid smells another animal on us, she sulks for days."

"Neptune's bad enough. I can't imagine having something that big unhappy with me."

"Oh, she just sits around looking wounded. It's actually pretty funny, if you know it's only drama."

"Drama I know. Cats and tweens are masters of it."

"Too bad that's the not only kind of drama you've had lately."

"Ah, yes. Spence Lyle and the TruthTellers. All three of them." She giggled. "If somebody throws a protest and nobody comes . . ."

"They had an engineer, too, so I guess four." I took a slug of my own coffee and checked the commercial log to be sure I was on track. "I'm not bugged by Lyle, I'm worried about the local contingent."

"Howard and Harold are just harmless crackpots."

"But somebody scrawled 'Edwin Is Angry and So Are We' on the back of the building. It could have been there since the protest, but maybe not."

Maeve shook her head. "You told Chief George."

"Sure did."

"I wouldn't worry too much then. We really don't get a lot of that crazy hard-rightie stuff around here, whatever Charity Slater is spewing these days."

"The Lieutenant Gov?"

"Yeah. Rob probably told you about her, right? Tim even does an imitation."

"The Aggressively Straight Horns." I couldn't help smiling at that. "I haven't seen either the real thing or the parody, but it's hard to take a fanatic with a brass band too seriously."

"Whatever the soundtrack, homophobia, racism, and venality are still bad."

"No argument."

We nodded together, and I did the break, talking up a couple more anniversary requests, including the mandated playing of "You're the Inspiration," which I refused to spin more than once a night.

"I get why Rob and Tim can't stand Charity Slater. Why you?"

"Every once in a while she gets onto that whole God's law thing, and I want to smack her." Maeve looked like a tiny little avenging angel as her perfect brows knit and her eyes narrowed. "We don't get to invoke God to abuse other people. And we sure don't get to judge."

"Got that." I shrugged. "Rob said she got in because the Greens ran somebody with name recognition?"

She laughed. "Some half-baked former reality star who's now running a goat farm outside Manchester."

"Bet they feel stupid."

"Nah. People like that never do. Got her clicks, and now she's tweeting about goat cheese again."

"Ugh."

"It's not even good goat cheese. And we get Charity Slater, who doesn't seem to do anything except hold a news conference every few weeks to yap about the lack of values and the burdensome regulations on the poor dear job creators."

"Tell me how you really feel." I joined her bitter chuckle. "I wonder if I'll get the privilege."

"Oh, you will. Especially now that you've ticked off the Gadflies." Maeve's eyes widened a bit. "You may hear from her sooner than later because of all of this mess."

"Hell."

"Sadly, there's some question as to whether there is a literal hell these days." Maeve sighed, a habit she picked up from Irish

Niall. "But Charity is probably busy with the legislative session right now."

"There's that." I tried to drink a little more coffee, only to discover that my mug was empty. Crap. "Well, if you have to have someone like that around, Lieutenant Gov's a good place for them."

"Maybe."

"Think about it." I toyed with my empty cup, telling myself I didn't need to lie awake all night. "Keeps her visible but basically out of the way since the legislature isn't close enough that she'd get to break a tie."

"No. And your pal isn't that kind of Republican so she's not moving his agenda."

"I'm not sure he even has an agenda."

"In the legislature," Maeve said, watching me very closely.

"It's the only agenda I care about."

"You were never a good liar, and you still aren't. It's one of your better qualities."

"Yeah, thanks. Not tonight, okay?"

"Fair enough." She heard it in my voice and let me go. "You're going to yoga tomorrow, right?"

"Yep."

"Excellent. We can hide in the back with Alicia."

"Yeah. Let Sadie have the attention."

# Chapter Ten

## One Night in Simpson

S aturday nights are the worst. Sure, I'm alone all weekend, but somehow the second night is lonelier. It's probably a function of the sad-sack callers who crawl out of the woodwork at about ten. You don't want to know how many requests I field for "Hard to Say I'm Sorry," and "Faithfully," by those who've been neither sorry nor faithful until they found themselves alone that night.

Even if I start in a good mood from yoga with the ladies, this week even extended to a big salad and gossip at Janet's, a couple of hours of helping the full range of human misery find expression in embarrassing power ballads takes a toll.

More than usual that night, since it wasn't breakup wails, but death songs.

About the only good thing in the shift had been a call from Will Ten Broeck at about nine. He requested "Despacito," because of course he did, and we spent a few minutes talking, both admitting to being alone and maybe not too happy about it.

He sounded a little off balance; apparently he'd had some kind of minor mishap that afternoon, stepping out onto solidly iced-over steps from his office in Montpelier and almost taking a very bad fall. Somewhere a maintenance person was in serious trouble because I'm sure those steps were supposed to be kept clear, even on a Saturday, never mind allowed to accumulate a coating of ice like somebody had soaked them.

At least he had someone to blame. If I end up face-down at the bottom of my stairs, it's my own damn fault.

Maybe it was the near miss that made him sound vulnerable and actually approachable. Or maybe I needed to just admit that I wanted the guy, even if I wasn't sure what I would do with him if I got him.

I felt kind of like the dog closing in on the car.

There was definitely something there, however uncertain I was about it. Problem was, I genuinely had no idea how to handle this.

Despite meeting every pol in the state in my early years here, I'd never dated any of them, in part because none of the cute ones were available or offering—but also because it was an ethical minefield. Still is, even though I'm a jock and not a journalist. Not to mention one helluva rebound.

But the Knickerbocker seemed to want to play, and it might just be fun.

I didn't remember fun.

After the call, though, it was just another lovely night in deejay purgatory. Even the Marley Dude was in a dark mood, asking for an obscure B-side I didn't have and musing about the general misery of life. Sometime after eleven thirty, I'd given in to the poor girl who choked out a request for "My Heart Will Go On," against my better judgment, and was shooting the last of my current cup of coffee with a couple of Advil when the doorbell lit up.

Standing on my porch, impossibly alone, was the absolute last person I'd have expected to see.

Will Ten Broeck.

He had on a midnight-blue barn jacket over a dark sweater and khakis, hands in his pockets, hair ruffled by the wind. He looked a little uncertain, and about as hot as any man I'd ever seen.

"Do they even let you out by yourself?" I asked, opening the door and waving him in.

He laughed. "It's Vermont, remember? I usually only have a security detail when I do official stuff. I'm kind of expected to tell somebody where I am, but that's all."

"Come downstairs. I only have a couple minutes left on my song."

"Thanks. I like the shirt."

My tee was a gift from Ryan: charcoal heather with the words *We'll See* in tiny rhinestones. "My daughter made it."

"Smart kid."

"Smarter than me." We exchanged a parental smile on the stairs and I waved to the kitchenette. "There's still some coffee."

He poured his own cup, black, both of which spoke well of him, and followed me into the studio to take the guest spot, where he'd sat a few days ago, just watching me while I did a break and seg'd into the next song, "Separate Ways."

He cringed a bit.

So did I. "Not a Journey fan?"

"Um, no." He winced again. "Mostly, I like jazz or R&B."

"Hence Shana Gilbert."

A sheepish, almost shy, smile. "Yeah. Gorgeous voice. Always liked that song."

"Me too."

"Takes one gorgeous voice to know one, maybe." Before I even caught the compliment, he nodded to the speakers, breaking the moment. "You don't like this stuff . . ."

"Somebody does." I shrugged. "I do actually like a lot of pop music . . . but if I have to hear 'You're the Inspiration' more than once a night, I get a little nuts."

"Good thing you don't have a muzzleloader in the studio."

We laughed together.

More silence with overwrought guitar and vocals in the background.

"So all right, I just wanted to see you," he said finally.

"I let you in, didn't I?"

"You did, at that." He gave me a close, appraising look. "Why?"

I played it off because I didn't have a good answer. "You seem harmless enough."

That got me a laugh. "God, am I safe? The kiss of death."

"Not that kind of safe." It was, now that you mention it, pretty stupid to just let any random person, even the random governor, into my studio this late. Except that I did feel safe with him. The good kind of safe. The kind I'd felt in the Plaza the other night when he told me to call him if I needed anything. "Safe is a very good thing sometimes."

"You haven't had a lot of that lately, have you?"

"Haven't had a lot of things lately." I picked up my commercial log and checked off the last spot. "I manage."

"You do a lot more than that." His gaze was warm and appreciative. "Y'know, I like the dark hair a lot better—even with the streak. Not the kind of thing I'm usually into, but on you it works."

"Thanks. Midlife crisis, you know."

"Kid, if you're midlife these days, I'm a damn dinosaur."

"T-Rex?"

"Velociraptor. The one you don't see coming till it's feasting on your entrails."

I laughed. I probably should've been at least a little shocked, maybe even troubled, but the dark sense of humor I'd developed as a journalist had never left me, and it had saved me in the last couple years. "Heads you win, entrails you lose."

Will—I guess I should call him that—laughed too. "Damn, you're good."

"If you can't laugh . . ."

"You're much prettier when you smile." He held my gaze. "Really, you're beautiful now, smile or not. Awfully thin, though, but I bet your neighbors are working on that."

Game? Probably. Did I even care? "Thanks. You're not so bad yourself, Knickerbocker, but I bet you know that."

"Everyone likes a compliment." The grin he'd flashed at my comment faded as he toyed with his coffee cup. "I remember you as a kid. The voice, of course, smart and talented, and funny—but a kid, and I was never into little girls."

"I was never a *little* girl." And he wasn't as old as he played. The fifteen years between us had been an impossible gulf in experience then. Now? Not so much.

He chuckled. "Yeah, well. The point being, I was kind of curious to see how you'd turned out."

I shrugged. I was a lot better a couple of years ago, but I didn't want to bring that up.

"And we pull up and there you are, like some kind of avenging goddess blowing away that stupid snowman."

"Um, yeah. I have a temper. You probably never saw it when I was up here before."

"I wonder what else I didn't see before."

Our eyes held over the console. No question what was in the room—the only question left was what we'd do about it.

86

My song was running down. I quickly made the seg, without doing a break because I didn't trust my voice.

The next song was "Piano in the Dark." I'd lined it up an hour ago in hopes of breaking up the dirges, just because I like it. But it also happens to be one of the sexiest songs in recorded history, which I hadn't thought about until it started threading around us.

Oh, holy hell.

Any jock, every jock, has elaborate and filthy fantasies about the studio. It's a universal radio thing, and anyone who tells you they haven't thought about it is lying through their damn teeth or doesn't know you well enough to tell the truth. Maybe both. Everyone will also tell you that they've never actually done it, because you don't admit something like that without getting yourself fired. Or at least in big trouble with the FCC.

I really hadn't, though. And my professional code would have stopped me under any normal circumstances.

I kept my hands and eyes on the board for a moment.

"Jacqueline?"

He pronounced my name the French way again, *Zhak-leen*, and it was probably the hottest come-on I'd ever heard.

I looked up. Will was right beside me.

He reached over and brushed a stray strand of hair off my face, his thumb lingering on my cheek. There was no way he could know about the studio thing, but he surely knew vibe when he saw it and felt it.

We both froze for a moment, eyes locked.

"I should go," he said, the low, thick tone of his voice betraying what he really wanted. What I really wanted, too.

The only sound in the studio was the song, and our breathing. His hand was still on my cheek, the warmth of his skin soaking into mine.

"Really. I'll go."

He didn't move, and neither did I.

There's a button on the board that turns on the satellite music service. Two hours before, it would have been a very big deal, because I had my few local spots. But in the last hour on a Saturday night? If anyone was still listening, they might not even notice.

I didn't make those calculations in the moment. That came later.

At the time, all I did was hit the button.

"Stay."

It was the last coherent thing either of us said for a while.

I probably didn't actually pounce on him like Garfield on lasagna, but I sure felt like I did. Only this time, the lasagna pounced back.

The usual awkward first kiss thing wasn't even a consideration. I was at the board, and then a breath later, we were tangled together in an embrace so hot the old soundproof foam should have caught fire. Somehow he ended up against the wall, his hands moving down my back, pulling me to him like he couldn't hold me tight enough. I'd been a little worried about keeping up with him, but in the moment, all I had to do was go with it, and enjoy it. That I could handle. Oh, hell yes.

I really doubt "Rock Me Like a Hurricane" was playing in the background, but it might as well have been.

It was pretty much every good deejay fantasy, ever.

Just in case anyone from the FCC is out there, we took it upstairs. Barely.

And just in case you think I am not a responsible adult, I took a second to grab the Green Mountain Safe condoms that had been languishing in a corner of the old newsroom since we got the

World AIDS Day press packet a couple of months ago. The state health director, an extremely earnest woman who had exhorted everyone to make safe sex fun while doing her best to take the play right out of it, probably would have fainted if she knew.

As for the rest, let's just say that Will Ten Broeck knows how to show a girl a good time. A very good time.

A lot later, he was toying with the streaked strand of my hair and studying my face in the patch of moonlight from my bedroom window, both of us probably a little stunned at how we'd ended up there—and how good it was. I hadn't remembered that my body could do that. I wasn't a hundred percent sure it ever *had* done that before.

He looked a lot more troubled than happy, though. "This wasn't what I had in mind."

"Right. Because you showed up at my doorstep at eleven o'clock on a Saturday night to talk about tax policy."

"Really. I'd have been glad to just talk. Maybe even about taxes."

"Well, you are a Republican." Which is when it hit me. "Holy hell, I just slept with a Republican."

"New England Republican, please. We are a different animal."

"That's one way to put it." Somehow, I doubted that he'd picked up his skills at a party conference.

"Anyway," he said, his eyes turning serious again, "I did not come here expecting to get you into bed. I have a lot more respect for you, and us, than that."

"You don't have to lie, and you don't have to do anything else." I meant it. Really. "If this was some kind of one-time thing, it was pretty damn terrific for me, and I'm not going to be weird."

"You really don't know much about me, Jacqueline."

"Yeah?"

"Yeah." He ran a hand down my arm, the way he had that first night in the studio, then laced fingers with mine, not breaking the eye contact. "I've done a lousy job of showing it just now, but my intentions, for lack of a better description, are honorable. I haven't met a woman I wanted to be with in years. Till you."

"All that for shooting a snowman?"

"It was a good opener."

I didn't know how much weight to put on all of this. David had been my only really serious adult relationship, because I'd been so busy building my career. I suspected Will was feeling guilty about the way the evening had turned out.

I wasn't. At some level, it was exactly the reminder I needed that I was still alive and attractive, and I wasn't sure I wanted to get serious about anyone anyway. "You had a pretty good opener yourself."

"Yeah, but I can do better." He pulled me closer. "I'm not usually the trail of clothes across the living room guy."

"What guy are you, Knickerbocker?"

"Ah, well played." Will smiled slowly, wickedly. "I'm the take my sweet time guy."

"Well, as it happens, I don't have to be anywhere till morning."

# Chapter Eleven

## Back to Reality

The weekend always ended with picking up Ryan at the Metzes' in Charlestown and a big bag of mixed feelings: thrilled to get my girl back and return to our normal routine, glad to see Alan, Sally, and Grandpa Seymour, and weird to still be part of the family without being inside anymore. Now, add some morning-after glow and yes, all right, a little bit of western P-A good-girl guilt over the previous night.

Gonna be an interesting Sunday.

Will left when I got up at six to start the public affairs shows, giving me a goodbye kiss that he definitely meant, and a "see you soon" he may or may not have. I watched him walk down the porch stairs, then turned away, firmly reminding myself that I was cool with a one-time thing and I didn't need anything serious anyway.

Would have been easier to hold that line if I hadn't found myself thinking about the look in his eyes after that last kiss and wondering if he was actually serious about that honorable intentions stuff. If I even wanted him to be serious about it.

Man, was I a mess.

However that was going to spin out, I had a busy day ahead of me.

It started with Neptune, who was not satisfied with the usual morning offering of wet food and attention, and followed me into the studio complaining. I was just glad he hadn't appeared at an inopportune moment the night before, and in the spirit of that gratitude, I gave him an extravagant handful of his favorite Tuna Crunchie treats.

Bribery is bad in politics and essential in pet—and human—parenting.

After the shows, I cleaned myself and the apartment up, making sure there was nothing that would suggest to Ryan that I hadn't spent the last night reading the new book on the San Francisco earthquake I'd picked up on our most recent trip to the library.

Yeah, I have a thing for historical disasters. Always did, and somehow, reading about horrible events that happened long ago became soothing while dealing with our real-time mess. Probably doesn't make any more sense than David's new love for classical music.

Once the house and I were back in some kind of order, though I could see a suspicious glow to my skin despite my heavy charcoal wool sweater, I spent an hour recording some narration for what could only be described as stupid money for the effort, cleared the paperwork from my desk, and printed out the next day's commercial log. All stuff that had to happen, and once done, I could just enjoy my afternoon and evening with Ryan.

I also sifted through the station e-mail account, and the phone messages to make sure I didn't miss any requests, or possible sponsors. That's when it got ugly.

Maybe two dozen e-mails, all starting with exactly the same wording, from what looked like real accounts, demanding I give them back their *Edwin Anger Show*. A few had thrown in some invective and low-grade obscenities at the end of the messages, but there didn't seem to be anything actively threatening.

Since I doubted there were enough people in Simpson to care, I suspected that the charming Mr. Lyle had taken his grudge back to Atlanta with him. Several of the e-mails were signed, and others had names on the accounts. I didn't have anything better to do, so I got out the phone book (yes, we still have White Pages here!) to see if they matched any local listings. With the exception of a J. Smith and a T. Francis, none did—and I'd be willing to bet that just about every town in the U.S. has those.

It was harder to brush off the phone message. A woman with a nasty shrill voice informing me that it's "Adam and Eve, not Adam and Steve" and I'd better stop playing songs for those perverts or God will get me too. What bugged me wasn't the repulsive and timeworn content, but the fact that it was delivered with a definite, even slightly exaggerated, New England accent.

That one might be worth a little concern. The voice sounded vaguely familiar, but I couldn't place it. I'm pretty good; if I hear someone speak a few sentences, even once, I remember them. But I didn't have enough.

My cell phone alarm beeped just then; it's programmed for pickup time at Kunin because once in a while I can score a nap in the afternoon and I don't want to be late. I've never bothered to change it to weekdays only. It was a good cue to get moving now too, instead of being distracted by one stupid voicemail. Whoever the caller was, she'd still be mad once we got back from Charlestown.

Driving over always makes me think about how it all fell apart.

*It was a little over three months after his last clear scan, a couple of days after a wedding anniversary that had felt more like valediction than celebration. David had just come to join me in bed, but we were as far apart as it was possible for two tallish people to be in a queen-size. I was finishing a chapter in a book about the Cocoanut Grove fire in Boston, and he'd just switched on a rerun of that old comedy where the guys grunt about power tools.*

*"Are you happy?" he asked.*

*"At this exact moment, I'm just tired."*

*"No. I mean happy with our life. Our marriage."*

*I put the book down. At some level, I knew this was it. I still don't know if anyone was convicted in the fire. I never got back to that particular disaster because I was too busy with a more immediate conflagration.*

*"It's not working anymore, Jaye."*

*"What?"*

*"Life's too short not to be happy. We know that."*

*"Is there something you need that I—" I started. I had no idea what he was looking for. Never mind what I could do about it.*

*"No. You've done everything you could and more. Nobody could have been more supportive or loving."*

*He took my hand, and for the first time in more than ten years together, I recoiled from his touch. "Then what?"*

*"I need to do things, and be things, and I don't think I can be a good husband anymore."*

*"What does that even mean?"*

*David squirmed and sat up, his face tight and uncomfortable. "I've got enough ethics left that I don't want to cheat on you, Jaye. But I don't have enough left to be a real partner right now."*

*"Which means . . ." I had a pretty good idea where this was going, and I wanted to make him say it.*

*"I just want to have some fun. To not answer to anyone. To just . . ."*

*I shook my head. "And what do you suppose I want?"*

*"I don't know, Jaye. I know it's been terrible for you—you're so thin and tired and—"*

"I'm still here," I said pointedly.

"I know. And I'll never be able to thank you enough for standing by me, but I need something different now."

"Some one different."

"Yeah. I'm sorry I can't be good for you."

I wanted to cry and throw things, but I wasn't going to give him that. I swallowed the tears, and tried to keep my mind on what really mattered here. Ryan. "Can you still be a good father?"

"As long as there's breath in my body."

"Then we'll figure it out."

I didn't cry until he got up and went into his office, probably to start looking for blondes on a dating site. Or maybe just to give me some space because he knew me well enough to know I was close to losing it. I made damn sure I was quiet enough that he didn't hear me.

A week later, he brought me word from Orville and Oliver that the current owner of WSV was looking to sell and would give me a break if I promised to bring back some local programming. I wasn't at all sure, but since my program director in the city had just told me to take the buyout because the new owners were thinking about a format change, I figured it was the best of a bunch of bad options.

It was the right call, by the way. Two months later, the station went sports talk, and my program director went back to school for her teaching certificate. Speaking of making something good out of bad options.

As for Team Metz, we landed in Simpson in time for the start of school, so David and Ryan could get a clean beginning. It took me several weeks to finalize the sale and get the station back on the air, but soon enough we were settling in.

Dirty little truth of life: you can handle almost anything if you impose a routine on it. So once we had a pattern for our days, it was basically manageable. Sometimes even happy.

*That said, I probably did need to stop the part of the routine where I reflected on the events that brought me here while driving over to pick up Ryan.*

It was only as I turned off the Connecticut River Bridge into Charlestown that it occurred to me that it would have been a lot more relaxing to spend the last fifteen minutes reviewing the highlights of the previous evening. Whether or not there was going to be a replay.

How often does a nice girl from Punxsutawney get to score the exceedingly hot governor of the great state, after all?

By the time I had that thought, though, it was quite literally neither here nor there because I was turning onto David's street.

# Chapter Twelve

## Meet the Metz

The Metz clan lives in a sprawling old Victorian near the river that divides New Hampshire and Vermont. David has taken over the turret, which used to be Grandpa's territory until he turned one hundred, decided he didn't want to climb the spiral stairs anymore and moved into the mother-in-law apartment over the garage. The turret is also a separate apartment, but it sat empty until David returned.

Now he lives with his parents, but without being in their business, and without them all up in his. I know, because he's made oblique references to it, that David's been taking full advantage of the space, to Alan and Sally's mild, but rarely expressed, disapproval.

They're wrong on that, by the way. He never brings the blondes around Ryan, so it's nobody's damn business, including mine. I do my best not to judge because I know we made the right decision. Even if it hurt like hell. Ryan deserves parents who can focus on how much they love her, and not on how much they hate each other.

We were smart enough to call the game before that happened.

All due respect to Alan and Sally, one of those couples who were meant to be from the second they met at twenty, none of us gets to criticize David for living the life he wasn't sure he'd have, as long as he's treating his daughter right. And the one unshakable certainty in my life is that David Metz is a good father. It makes up for everything.

At this point, David doesn't really need to live with his parents, either for health or financial reasons, but they like having him around, and they *love* having Ryan on weekends. David, like me, is an only, and Alan and Sally were never thrilled with having their grandbaby so far away.

They also weren't thrilled about the split, but they understood it. I think at some level they still hope David will come to his senses and we'll all move into the turret for good one fine day. Everybody needs a rich and interesting fantasy life.

As for Grandpa, he's also very happy with the current situation. Despite his great age, he requires little extra care, except for the occasional ride to the doctor or downtown. Mostly, he lives very independently, thanks to good health, cool determination, and a surprising level of tech savvy—including a mastery of ride-hailing apps that New York club kids can only envy.

Independent or no, he likes family dinner with the clan, especially when he can torment Alan, a retired DOT engineer, and Sally, a social worker, with whatever he's heard on the Gadfly Network that day. He's definitely not a knuckle-dragger in any real sense of the word, but he *is* a commonsense, old-school guy who knows the world is a good bit scarier than it used to be. Of course, the Gadflies do their best to make it seem scarier to him, but he thinks they can't put it on the air if it's not true.

I lost that argument once. It was enough.

"Well, if it isn't the feisty one!" Seymour Metz greeted me when I arrived, opening the door and smiling up at me, a wicked sparkle in his light-green eyes, just like David's and Ryan's. "You gave that little creep what for the other day, JJ."

Grandpa Seymour and I have a special relationship. A stand-up guy like my Uncle Edgar with a few more decades of perfecting the art, he is the only person in the world allowed to call me JJ. He can watch all the Gadfly Network he likes, and I will still love him.

For his part, I am the woman who birthed his only great-granddaughter, the one who keeps the name of his late, adored wife Rina alive. It's Ryan's Hebrew name, of course, and she more than lives up to the queenly meaning, as I'm told the original Rina once did. As for me, I'm the *shikse* who insisted on converting because I actually wanted to be part of five thousand years of tradition. That makes up for a lot of what he considers touchy-feely liberal nonsense.

Now, I shrugged a little and gave him a careful hug, amazed as always at how wiry he is despite his wizened appearance. "I don't like ambushes."

"I don't like the Gadflies," Alan Metz said, walking in from the kitchen, a scowl pulling his salt and pepper brows together and diluting his usual friendly expression.

The scent of browning butter and spice filled the house, which suggested he'd been at work. In retirement, he's taken up baking, and become spectacularly good at it, specializing in traditional Jewish treats, but branching out when he's in the mood. "Nice job keeping your temper, Jaye."

Alan and I hugged too, and the rush of footsteps announced the return of my girl. Ryan tackle-hugged me, and I gave her a kiss on the top of the head.

"Pop's making strudel. We've been working on it all day."

"Wow. That's a project."

"Keeps me from telling Dad what I think of his Sunday news shows."

"You could do with a little truth, son." Grandpa Metz cut his eyes to me. "You liberals don't want to admit it, but—"

"It is Sunday, and we are going to have a little peace in the house," Sally announced, reaching the bottom of the stairs a good ten seconds after her granddaughter. Sally and Alan are one of those couples who make the rest of us believe it's possible. When their eyes meet, you can just feel the world turning in a slightly better direction.

It happened now, Alan returning Sally's smile, defusing whatever confrontation Grandpa had been hoping for, not that the patriarch minded. He adores Sally as much as everyone else does.

Not only do Alan and Sally just bring good energy wherever they go, they're practically an advertisement for long-term monogamy. While they may look like a couple of cute older folks, you can also tell that they still have a very happy and fulfilling relationship, in every way. I used to hope that David and I would be like that someday.

Of course, long-term monogamy only works when both people sign on. When both people *can* sign on. I try really hard not to be down on David for his new hobbies, and mostly, I manage it.

As we stood there in the foyer, Sally's perceptive hazel eyes rested on me, and she picked up something. "Ryan, honey, why don't you go help your grandfather check the strudel while Jaye and I get your bag."

"Sure. Dad was getting ready to start grading midterms—he should be over in a minute."

"Cool," I said, as Sally took my arm.

"I'm curious about this strudel business too," Grandpa Seymour allowed, following them toward the kitchen. "Certainly smells good."

Ryan's bag was already packed, sitting in a corner of the foyer, and I picked up her jacket—a shiny blackberry-colored puffer that set off her coloring, so much like mine, except for the Metz eyes.

"Just tell me he's a nice guy," Sally said with a smile.

"Wha—"

"Honey, I know that look. I hope he's sticking around, but if he's not, you definitely needed something to get you off square one, so it's still a good thing."

I dropped the jacket. Sally laughed.

"I'm not going to say anything, and the boys in there wouldn't notice unless you smacked them across the face with the new guy's boxers. I'm just saying go, girl."

"Oh."

She hugged me. "We all know what happened, Jaye."

"We sure do."

"Nobody blames you." Her eyes were level, square on my face. "You gave him—and the marriage—everything you had, honey. If you've got a chance with someone new, go for it."

"Yeah?"

"Yeah. We're all going to be family for life, no matter what, and if there's a guy, we'll figure it out."

"I'm not sure there's a guy,"

Sally blushed. "You mean you're rethinking your orientation—"

"No—Jeez—no," I stammered. "I mean, that's fine for people who are wired that way—but it's a—he's a man . . ."

She laughed. "Sorry. I misunderstood."

"I was trying to say I'm not sure what's up with the guy." I was beginning to wonder if I was imagining this entire conversation. Maybe to hope I was. "He says he's interested in a relationship, but I'm not sure he is, and even if he is, I'm not sure if I want—"

As I babbled, Sally patted my arm and smiled. "You don't have to be sure."

"Yeah?"

"Does he know what you've been through?"

"He knows enough."

"Then if he's worthy of you, he'll give you the space you need." Her kind smile turned more than a little wicked. "And if he's not worthy, well, at least you got something you needed out of the deal."

"Ma! Grandma! Strudel!"

Saved by the strudel.

# Chapter Thirteen

## Honorable and Deadly Intentions

By Monday afternoon, it was very clear that Will Ten Broeck wasn't kidding about the honorable intentions. Also that my trouble with Edwin Anger's spiritual heir had just begun.

The fun part first. A bouquet of huge roses, the kind that shaded from white at the heart to red at the tip, with a distinctive spicy scent, arrived that morning, accompanied by an invitation to Saturday night dinner at the Old Grist Mill in White River, half-way between Montpelier and Simpson, and universally acclaimed as *the* place couples went for important nights out.

If I took him up on it, I would also be officially taking him up on a relationship, and we both knew it.

Maeve, who had been dropping off PSAs for the church's late-winter food drive, grinned as the florist van pulled up, and just laughed at me when I told her I wasn't sure.

"Because you're such a one-night-stand girl." She reached up and patted me on the head. "You made your decision when you hit the satellite button on the board and you know it."

"Maybe." I'd given her a PG-13 summary of events before the van arrived, because I was more than a little confused by everything. "I do like him."

"I figured that out. Let dude buy you dinner, for heaven's sake. It doesn't really mean—"

"It's a very public dinner at the Grist Mill with the governor. It sure does mean that."

"Yeah, probably," she conceded. "Just warn David, then, and enjoy. This doesn't have to be rocket science."

"I wish it were rocket science. Ryan could explain that to me."

"What are you going to tell her?"

"Dinner with an old friend?"

"She won't buy it any more than the rest of us do, but give it a shot. I'll get my sister to raid the beauty closet for date stuff."

Trust her to throw in a treat. Maeve's sister is a beauty editor, and throws away more great swag than most people ever see in a lifetime. "Well, if I get a good highlighter out of it . . ."

She gave me a very wise smile. "You're getting a lot more than that."

After Maeve left, I took one more long look at those roses, probably the first flowers I'd gotten since Ryan was born, and asked myself exactly who I was kidding.

Then I sent Will a text: *Sometimes you just need to say yes, thank you.*

*"I like that. See you Saturday."*

Now I just had to find something to wear.

Edwin Anger's successor was a much bigger and less pleasant issue. Of course I don't listen, and since Spence Lyle had gone back under his rock in Atlanta, I didn't care. I was not, however, able to maintain that posture after the midday mail.

Jerusha, the mail carrier, parked her Jeep in front of the building and dragged out a big plastic box with a laugh that lit up her round face. "Who did you tick off? I've never seen so many postcards in one place."

"At least it's just postcards." I smiled at her as I took the box. Her son is in Ryan's class. Probably a hundred or so cheaply printed cards on the lightest stock allowed, all with the *Edwin Anger Show* logo on the front with a black border, and "Continue the Mission" on the back, with signatures scrawled on them. Even to a casual eye, the writing looked similar.

Something said intern with a Sharpie. Or maybe ol' Spence himself.

There were a few legit ones, I realized as I combed through, taking note of sad shaky hands and even yellow crayon. Bet some of the same folks who sent those hate e-mails over the weekend.

And then I got to the bottom of the box.

A padded envelope that just felt weird and heavy. I picked it up gingerly, and felt something vaguely cylindrical inside. It was addressed to "Jackie Jordan, SWV Radio."

Didn't even get the call letters right.

"Jerusha," I said slowly, as the thing seemed to double or triple in weight in my tenuous grip, "I think we need to call the cops."

I didn't even realize I was praying in my terrible Hebrew until I had very carefully placed the envelope back in the box and Jerusha looked at me funny as I stepped away.

"You don't think . . ."

"I don't know. But the cops will. Let me get Neptune, and we'll wait next door."

Rob, G-d love him, didn't turn a hair at the sight of us on his doorstep. He just welcomed us in, poured coffee, and offered Neptune a plate of chicken scraps.

Neptune was the only one who had a good day.

Chief George walked into the station, took one look, and walked back out, calling the state police bomb squad as he went.

They called in the fire department, and by the time Chief Frank joined the coffee klatsch, the feds were on the way too, not to mention a good crowd of spectators.

It took hours. Jerusha and I told the same story to at least three different law enforcement agencies, not counting Chief George, each time getting the same grim nods and little else. The fed, an older woman from ATF, did at least offer some reassurance. Sort of. She told me that if the thing hadn't blown when I picked it up, it probably wasn't going to.

I chose to take that as evidence that it was not dangerous, not that I had been within one breath of death. I have to be able to sleep.

Maeve came over to check on us three times in between working on her sermon. She informed me that she was going to offer a meditation on the importance of getting along with people you disagree with . . . which her congregation probably didn't need, and the person who sent me that package wouldn't understand anyway. I didn't point that out.

At two thirty, with the device finally out of my building, and the single fed it merited following it to Boston, Chief Frank insisted on driving me to Kunin to pick up Ryan and Xavier. He claimed he wasn't much good at the scene, but he could at least help with this. Of course, his quiet, confident presence was a whole lot of reassurance on its own as I explained everything to the kids on the drive home.

They also thought it was cool as hell to ride in the fire department SUV.

"It *is* cool," Chief Frank agreed with an impish little smile as he pulled up at the Plaza. "You kids want to do a ride-along, just ask your parents to call me."

"When can we go, RyansMom?"

"Yeah, Ma!"

"Rob and I will consult," I said, waving the cherubs out of the SUV. "Thanks, Chief. Hope you don't regret that."

The smile widened. "Never would. Happy to have either of them one day if they belong to you and Rob."

We both laughed, knowing how it sounded.

"Yeah, well. You know."

"I do. Thanks again."

"Just doing what I can. Do what the cops tell you, okay?"

"Doing the best I can."

Chief Frank narrowed his eyes a little. "This isn't just slipping a couple feet past the line to get a better look at the fire."

"You knew I did that?"

"Yep. Never called you on it because you're a smart, good kid."

I nodded, suddenly having a hard time finding words.

"Have a good night, Jaye. It'll get better."

"Yeah. Thanks again."

Back at Janet's, Ryan and Xavier headed for the bar TV and grabbed the remote to change it to PBS Kids for the one show they were allowed before homework. Most of the authorities were gone, and Chief George and the twins were drinking one last cup of coffee at the bar, clearly waiting for me.

Rob was behind the bar, stacking glasses for the night and looking grim.

"Here's how this goes, Jaye," Chief George said. "Now that the feds have taken the thing and gone on their way, you can go back to your business."

"So everything's fine for showtime," Rob added, handing me another mug.

"And the dinner rush." I took a generous swig. "Thank you for—"

"Glad to. I'll be over to track my show in half an hour or so—once I get Eddie set up."

"Good." I motioned to Ryan, who ignored me. "I'll go get ready to do my show."

"Of course you will," Orville agreed firmly as I downed some more coffee, giving me the northern New England no-nonsense look, just in case I'd needed it to stiffen my spine.

I didn't. "Damn right."

The chief and the twins gave me a sober nod.

"Just right, Jaye," Oliver said. "You don't give these bastards an inch, pardon my French."

I nodded solemnly, biting back a smile.

"Whether you like it or not, acting as if it didn't happen is the best thing you can do," Chief George added. "I'll give you an officer for tonight, just in case, and the feds will probably hold and check your mail for a while."

"I won't complain."

Chief George sipped his coffee. "It really is probably nothing but a very bad prank, but I don't like this."

"Neither do I," Oliver said.

"Or I," chimed Orville.

"I'd be worried about you if you did, Little Brother." Oliver's comment to his sib was all it took. They started into their usual bickering session, which was actually very comforting for me, and probably for them too.

If Orville and Oliver were arguing, everything had to be okay.

"I don't like it either," I agreed, shooting the last of my coffee. "But we're here."

"We sure are." Rob shook his head, then glanced over to the kids at the TV. "Ryan can stay with Xavier for a while if you want."

"She should come back and do homework as usual after that show. Trying for normal."

The men nodded.

"Usually best for kids," Chief George agreed. "I'll go call out one of the guys."

Looking at Ryan and Xavier watching TV, I had another disturbing realization. "I'd better call David. I don't want him finding out on the news."

"Yeah," Rob said. "I was going to warn you. I got a call from the paper a while ago."

"Well, yay for old school anyway. If this had happened in New York, it would be live at five and worse from there."

Rob smiled at that as I put my empty mug on the bar.

Orville looked up from his spat with Oliver and put a hand on my arm. "Want me to call David?"

"Nope. It's my job."

David took it better than I'd have expected, and didn't even offer to have Ryan stay with him for a night. He had to know how I'd take that, and I was grateful. He did, though, promise to come over during the show to make sure we were all okay. That was just fine by me.

It turned out to be a little less fine when the other gentleman who thinks he is my protector got into the mix.

# Chapter Fourteen

## Because, Drama

Nothing helps you relax after an attempted pipe bombing like a little family drama.

I told myself this.

My Simpson officer was ensconced upstairs with fresh coffee and the last piece of Alan Metz's strudel by showtime, and Ryan, Neptune, and I settled in for a determinedly normal shift. I had a bunch more requests than usual, some for songs that aren't really in our playlist, so I knew the word was out across town, and people were trying to be supportive. It was sweet, even if there was no way on earth I'd play "Achy-Breaky Heart," not that I had it. Sinatra's "Summer Wind," though, hell yeah.

In fact, it was playing when David walked into the studio, escorted by my cop, who had been warned that he was coming.

"Dad!" Ryan got up and tackle-hugged him, then very quickly backed off, reclaiming the all-important tween cool. "Good to see you."

He cut his eyes to me, and smiled at his girl. "You too. Just wanted to be sure you and Ma got through this okay."

"Nice, Dad."

"Brought a treat too. Cookies from Pop."

David held out a plastic container of hamentaschen, one of his father's best efforts. Alan Metz does a good strudel, but his hamentaschen, the little hat-shaped cookies that celebrate Queen Esther's rescue of the Jews from the evil vizier Haman, are in a class by themselves. "Apricot almond, yet."

"Ma won't have any in the studio," Ryan proclaimed, grabbing the box. "So we'll just go upstairs and make some cocoa."

"Milk, Ryan," I cut in, trying to keep sugar intake down.

She grinned. "I had a very nutritious dinner. Now I can have a treat."

I sighed, knowing that the determined normality of grilled cheese and tomato soup was all for naught, and shook my head at David. "Fine. Not worth fighting over."

"Nope." David bent down and kissed her on the top of the head. "Go start the cocoa. I'll be there in a couple."

"Okay." She shot us both a look. "Talk amongst yourselves."

"Go." I pointed to the door.

Ryan grinned and headed upstairs with her prize.

"She seems to be rolling with it," David said, as we shared an awed smile.

"You know who we're dealing with."

We nodded together. She had announced to us when we came back from the first chemo treatment that she would be going along for the rest of the six-month course: two-day infusions, every four weeks. More, she'd already planned out homework with her teacher so she would be able to keep up, and would have something to do in the infusion suite.

She was eight.

"Let's just hope she still likes us when she runs the world." David grinned. "I'd better go get the queen her cocoa. I'll save you a couple of Dad's cookies."

"Thanks."

Maybe an hour later, after Ryan was safely tucked in with her book, David returned and sat down in the guest spot. More than a year out from the chemo, he looked almost as cute as the guy I'd married, his color good again, his dark hair only a little thinner, his light green eyes as sparkly as they'd been Before. "Just wanted to be sure you guys were okay."

"I'm glad you did." I seg'd into the next song, one of those long Chicago things. "We're good. You saw the officer. That's just for tonight, but the feds will be screening my mail for a while."

He nodded. "I hate this. It was my idea to bring you up here, and . . ."

"Stop it. You couldn't know. Nobody could."

"Okay. I just—I know I didn't do right by you,"

"You did what you had to do. And you lived. That's all that matters for Ryan."

He shrugged. "Okay. I just sometimes wish . . ."

"Yeah, well. How would Uncle Edgar describe your wish?" I asked, setting up a well-trodden family punchline.

"Like looking up a dead horse's backside."

We laughed together. Uncle Edgar still considered David a stand-up guy, and like almost everyone else in both families, put the blame where it belonged, on those effing cancer cells.

"I get it. Did you send me a text before all of this happened?"

The text. I'd asked him to call me so I could tell him about my date with Will. Seemed grown-up and civilized. "Yeah. I wanted to tell you something."

"Okay,"

"Obviously, you've been dating for a while," I started, easing into it with only an oblique reference to the Blonde of the Week.

"Yeah?"

"I have a date Saturday."

He smiled, genuinely happy for me. "Cool. Do I know the guy?"

"Um, Sir—Governor—I don't think—"

The sound of my officer babbling and brisk footsteps told me that he was about to know the guy.

"Jacqueline."

David didn't need to see or hear anything more than Will standing in the studio doorway as he said my name the way only he did. Even if David had ever called me by it (he hadn't, except at the wedding), the tone would have given Will away. For a second, everybody froze.

This was going to be fun. Well, not for them.

I heard the Chicago song winding down, and I'm sorry, but the air product wins all ties.

"Stand by, gentlemen," I said in my coolest professional voice. Neither moved or spoke while I turned on the mic and talked up the next song, which thankfully was a longish Celine Dion extravaganza. No, I have no idea what I said, except that nothing stood out to me, and the phone didn't light up, so it must have been basically okay.

Finally, I turned off the mic, and stepped out from the board. "All right."

David and Will stood there, still sizing each other up as they'd been doing during the break. David was younger and scruffier, in his forest green sweater and khakis, the leather bracelet I'd bought him after the last scan with the silver bar engraved "SURVIVOR," the only sign of what he'd been through. Will had clearly come from governor-ing, because he was in a neat, dark gray suit with a light blue oxford and his usual whimsical tie, today what sure looked like dancing moose.

"Governor Will Ten Broeck, I'd like you to meet Professor David Metz, Ryan's father." That seemed to be the best way to make the introduction, since it was clear without being overly unkind.

Will held out a hand to shake, with an apparently easy smile that suggested he'd moved into politician mode. "Nice to meet you."

David took it, managing a polite smile of his own. "Same here. You and Jaye are old friends, aren't you?"

Considering that David had known, and teased me mercilessly about, my old crush on Will during his disastrous flirtation with national politics, I knew he was having a little fun with it. Not the worst outcome.

"Something like that." Will kept the smile, but his jaw was tight.

"It's okay, guys," I said firmly as Celine soared up to a dramatic high note. "I think we all know what's going on here."

They exchanged wary glances.

"We're good, Ten Broeck," David started with as much of a hard look as an English professor could manage, "as long as you're here to tell her that you're doing what you can to make sure she and Ryan are safe."

Will nodded gravely. "As it happens, Metz, that's exactly why I came. In addition to all of the usual authorities, I have a few friends in various corners of the federal apparatus, and they're taking an interest."

The last-name thing was unintentionally funny; a couple of button-down indoor warriors trying to sound like gangsters. If these two couldn't get along, it would be *Bartlett's Quotations* at dawn, not pistols.

I swallowed a desperately inappropriate giggle.

"Good." David gave Will a nod and another decent effort at a Tony Soprano stare, which was returned in full. "Then I am going to wish you a very good evening and go back to Charlestown, since I've already said good night to my wonderful daughter. If you are going to stay around, I'd suggest you get to know her, but only if you plan to be here for a while."

"I would like that, but it's up to Jacqueline."

Good answer, I thought, as they shared a small, but genuine, smile before David walked out.

"I'll ah—leave you alone."

The stammer from the officer reminded me of his existence.

"C'mon, kid." Fortescue. He gave me a nod and smile, guiding the officer toward the hall. "It looks like there's still coffee."

Of course, as they moved off, Celine started her long fade, and I had to seg into the next song.

"Let me start another record," I told Will, "and then we'll talk."

"Okay."

I bent down and fired the next song, yet another anniversary power ballad, without sitting, and then stepped out from the board. I'm not sure why I didn't just sit safely and professionally back down in my chair, but after hanging on to demeanor through a brutal day and evening, I'm also not sure I need an explanation.

Will didn't hesitate. He just pulled me into his arms.

If I'd had more than four minutes and seventeen seconds, I probably would have really let go and had a good old fashioned crying jag. As it was, I just put my head on his shoulder, and enjoyed feeling safe and protected for a moment.

"You okay?" he asked after probably a minute.

"Yeah. I could use a lot more of that, but I'm okay."

"What are you doing after the show?"

This time, I couldn't stop the inappropriate giggle. "You sound like a groupie."

"I'm with the band, babe."

"Nice, but I'm not going to make Fortescue stay up all night."

"He wouldn't mind. But you're right, it's not fair."

"So I'll put on 'Paradise by the Dashboard Light,' you can hold my hand for a bit, and then Fortescue can see you home."

As I pulled back to look at him, he brushed a loose strand of hair out of my face. "You and your girl are really all right?"

"She's been through worse, and it takes a lot to throw me."

He smiled. "Two tough ladies."

"One tough lady, and one who knows she doesn't have any choice."

Will took my hand. "You don't have to be okay for me."

It was the best thing he could have said. "Thanks. Let me get into Meat Loaf and I'll take advantage of that."

As I loaded the CD and looked at my log to make sure I could run the long song, Neptune, who had somehow slept through all of the family drama, lifted his head and took in the scene. He hopped down from the turntable cabinet, and very deliberately walked over to Will, patting his leg. The two held eye contact for a moment, and then Neptune jumped up into Will's lap.

"There you go, fella," Will said, stroking Neptune's fur as the cat nested comfortably into place. "You're just fine."

"What . . ."

Will grinned at me. "He—he?—knows he's safe with me. My daughter has always had cats."

"Neptune doesn't like anybody but Ryan."

"And me." Neptune shot me what sure looked like a smile as he burrowed into Will. I knew, if he didn't, that kitty was making sure to leave enough hair that the nice suit would need a good cleaning. "Neptune?"

"Ryan's favorite planet."

"Makes sense to me."

I talked up the eight-minute drama with a surprisingly steady voice, and then took the other guest chair, moving it next to Will.

He laughed as he put one arm around me. "The cat's needs always come first."

"Yep."

"Now, c'mere. You know you're safe too."

For a while, the only sound other than the low hum of over-wrought '70s teen angst was Neptune's deep, happy purr. Will didn't say anything, and he didn't have to.

Nice to be the comfort-ee instead of the comforter. I felt like purring too.

By the time Ellen Foley and Meat Loaf had rounded the bases and started bemoaning their misspent youth, I was mostly fine. I got into one more longish song and walked him back up to Fortescue and my cop.

"So maybe one of these nights," he said on the stairs, "I'll be in the south, and my first stop next day will be somewhere close . . ."

"Fine by me, if you don't mind getting up early." Way better than thinking I was waking up to Paul Newman and getting Neptune. And probably about as likely as Newman.

"How early?"

"I have to start the voice-tracked show at five—and I don't really want Ryan seeing stayovers."

"Understandable. I'm not sure I'd want to have that conversation with a very smart ten-year-old."

"But," I continued, sure this was all just theoretical anyway, "I get up before five, and she's not out of bed till almost seven."

"Five?" His eyes widened a little as it hit.

"Working mom. Nothing like a quiet house for getting stuff done."

"My ex worked and she didn't . . ." He broke off, thinking. "You know, I don't know if she did or not."

"Uh-huh."

He gave me a rueful smile. "I think I have a little more of a clue now."

"Better for you if you do, Knickerbocker."

"Point taken." At the top of the stairs, he turned to me. "Are you and your ex good?"

"Never better." I smiled. "He was happy I was seeing someone . . . and I think really glad it's you."

"Why?"

"Safe, for one."

"Oh, safe again?" He looked a bit hurt.

"Safe as in you're a good guy who will help protect his girl and her mom in ways that maybe he can't. It's a good thing."

"Okay."

"And how awesome must he be if the only man who can succeed him is the Governor of the Great State?"

Will burst out laughing. "I hadn't thought of it that way."

"Never underestimate the male ego."

# Chapter Fifteen

## Continue the Mission

Whatever you could say about Charity Slater, she wasn't bothered by tact.

Even a serious right-wing fanatic would think twice about launching a protest about the programming of a radio station that had almost been pipe bombed the day before. But our esteemed lieutenant governor, apparently, was not troubled by such niceties, as I discovered at five PM Tuesday.

Unlike Spence Lyle and the TruthTellers, though, who only managed to get a couple of lines on a blog after the fact, Slater had brought her own media circus. Actually, one puffy and beleaguered-looking multimedia journalist who covered all of southern Vermont for a Burlington TV station, and Marianne Manon, the local reporter for the Brattleboro paper. Local, in the sense that she lived just outside Simpson, not that there was enough news to keep her busy here.

Marianne and her wife have two daughters who go to Kunin Elementary, and we're acquaintances, if not actually friends. So she shot me a sheepish smile when she walked up to the "scene" behind Charity Slater.

Chief George didn't smile; he simply made eye contact when he got out of the police SUV and leaned against it, apparently just happening by.

Other than the media, and Howard and Harold, Slater apparently hadn't been able to recruit anyone in the way of protesters. The scruffy young guy, and the stiff, officious woman who got out of the SUV with her had to be staff, and the woman driving was unquestionably her state trooper. Also unquestionably annoyed.

I watched all of this unfold from the porch; I'd walked out when Ryan asked me if the governor was coming by again, thinking it might be him in the SUV.

That, of course, meant that she'd seen something last night, and I was going to have to have a little chat with my girl about my social life, but I didn't have to think about it right now. I had plenty else to worry about.

"Continue the mission! Bring back the *Edwin Anger Show!*" Harold chanted as an opener, making sure to stay very close to where the snowman had once stood. I noted that there were still no muzzleloaders. It's no fun when the girl knows how to use it better than you do.

The whole Edwin Anger thing was starting to weird me out, though. The guy had been in his eternal reward for more than a week. Shouldn't they be chanting for Spence Lyle? Maybe too hard to rhyme. *Lyle has piles and so do we?*

Obviously, I was getting a little punchy.

But I wasn't stupid. Spence was keeping the focus on Anger for a reason. I'd bet my FCC license it was the same reason he'd put the guy in the snowman: to keep the sat service from filling the slot with someone competent, and give himself a chance to win over the listeners.

Pretty canny for someone evil and/or crazy.

Speaking of which:

"Are you Jackie Jordan?" Charity Slater asked in a pitchy voice with an exaggerated New England accent as she marched toward my porch.

I'd heard that voice before.

I stepped into the center of the overhead light, and presumably the TV shot, hands in my back pockets for warmth because crossing my arms would look defensive or scared. Not to mention hiding my *Mean People Suck* tee. If it looked like attitude, fine by me.

"I'm Jaye Jordan Metz, owner of WSV. Who are you?"

I took a good hard look at her.

In the harsh old-school fluorescent light of the streetlamp, Charity Slater had the hard, desiccated look of your finer Egyptian mummies, if they came in ash white. The brittle cotton-candy blonde hair looked like it belonged in a sarcophagus too. I bet she spent a lot of money on conditioner and moisturizer, to no avail. She should have invested in better lipstick; her unflattering coral red was creeping into the wrinkles around what small line of mouth she had.

Practicality apparently wasn't much of a concern for her: she was wearing stiletto-heeled boots like I hadn't seen since I left the city. Three inches at least. She *might* be able to make it back to her car without a spill. A pencil skirt, too—really silly in this weather—topped by an expensive camel-colored wool wrap coat that probably wasn't nearly as insulated as a sensible puffer. But hey, she had her righteousness to keep her warm.

"Of course, I wouldn't expect a *flatlander* to know." She punched and stretched out the noun, but still her attempted insult landed limply; people can't offend you if you don't take delivery. "I am Charity Slater, lieutenant governor of this great state."

"And a great state it is." I smiled winningly, giving no sign that I'd recognized her voice. She was the Adam and Steve call from last weekend. A little low-rent for a top state official, I thought.

"We agree. Now why don't you give these nice people their show back and we can all move on."

"Sorry, Lieu. Can't do that." I kept my tone cool and friendly.

Charity Slater apparently was not used to hearing no. Her mouth pursed into a tighter little line and her eyes narrowed. Her brow would have furrowed if it could. Yay Botox. "What?"

"I said no. I have plenty of local sponsors for our live night-time request show, not to mention a good number of listeners, and I'm not going back to satellite hate speech."

"Typical liberal lies," she huffed. "The *Edwin Anger Show* is not hate speech. Edwin was a hero, and Spence Lyle is continuing the mission of bringing truth to the masses."

"Well, around here, the masses prefer some nice love songs at night, brought to them by their happy and friendly local deejay." I smiled again. "And that's what they're going to get."

"You will not stop the truth."

"And you won't stop me tonight." I gave her a polite nod. "Thanks for coming by. I have a show to do."

"Some people don't like your show, Ms. Jordan."

"And that's their business. Don't like it, don't listen. Good night." That's when she said it.

"That's a pretty dangerous attitude to take around here, Ms. Jordan. Vermonters don't like people coming in and—"

I saw Slater's trooper wince as she said the first sentence, and Chief George walking toward her as she started the second.

"What did you say, Lieutenant Governor Slater?"

If you've lived or worked in New York, or just watched an episode or two of *Blue Bloods*, you know that tone. We'll assume the

Lieu considered scripted shows the work of Satan, because otherwise she was just dirt stupid.

"I said, Ms. Jordan better be careful of her attitude."

"Are you aware of what happened at this radio station yesterday?"

"Oh, please." She huffed and tried to give Chief George an intimidating gaze. "You can't think—"

"Well, as I'm sure a strong supporter of law and order like yourself is aware, we have to take all threats seriously."

"Threats?" she shrieked, making her face look like it might split open. "I did no such thing!"

"It might have been taken that way, Lieutenant Governor," her trooper cut in smoothly, trying to calm the situation. "The place got a pipe bomb yesterday. They're being cautious."

"Shut up, Murchison," Slater snapped. "I was obviously—"

"I'm sorry," Chief George said coolly, "but I'm going to ask you to leave now."

"That's fine. I have made my point." She turned to me one more time. "You are dependent upon the goodwill of this community, Jackie Jordan, and you had best respect that."

I opened my mouth for a snarky comeback, but Chief George gave me a hard look and I swallowed it.

"Please go now, Ms. Slater," he reiterated with a little more steel.

She shot the chief another poisonous glare, and I wondered if she'd give a fat old white guy so much static.

"Don't be surprised if you get a call from the feds," Chief George told her in a tone as neutral as if he were talking about road construction. "They have to check out every potential threat."

"How dare you?"

"Just doing my job, ma'am." If the chief was thinking anything else, he didn't say it.

Murchison stepped in then, and guided her charge toward her SUV, the staffers trailing, the woman looking as angry as her boss, the guy more than a little embarrassed.

"You have not heard the last of this!" Slater snapped at me.

"Thanks." I smiled. "You can explain that comment to the feds, too."

Chief George narrowed his eyes at me just a tiny bit.

The Lieutenant Gov said something I didn't hear as her staff pulled her in, and I was sure that she'd have to account for every word. I turned to the small crowd that had gathered in the Plaza, and gave them a friendly wave.

"Thanks for coming, folks. Almost showtime. We're happy to take your requests tonight, and every night—at WSV dot com—and 802-555-1212!"

"Yay, Queen of the Night!"

It was probably a fellow school parent coming out of the restaurant who yelled, but everyone who wasn't law enforcement or media joined the cheer and clapped.

I made a lightly over-the-top curtsy and turned for the door.

Ryan shook her head as I walked in. "You're nuts, Ma."

"Probably, but why now?"

"I bet that lady's got some nasty friends." Her little face was tight.

"Oh, honey. We're fine. Cops everywhere, and—"

"I know, Ma. I just hate it sometimes."

I pulled her into a hug, but didn't make any promises I couldn't keep. I hoped the usual reassurances would work, because they were the best I had.

Thankfully, they did. By the time Ryan was tucked away with her book light and the Mae Jemison book from Oliver, the station e-mail box was loaded with encouragement and requests, some of which I could even play. And a few other things, including a very formal statement from the governor's office:

> Lieutenant Governor Slater was not representing the Ten Broeck administration in any way in her outrageous and borderline harassing behavior at WSV Radio this evening. The Governor, like most Americans, strongly supports a free and vibrant local media landscape, and discourages government officials from interfering except in cases of extraordinary malfeasance. He further encourages Lieutenant Governor Slater to apologize in light of her particularly bad timing in staging the event one day after WSV was the target of a bomb attempt that may well have been politically motivated.

The words "don't mess with my girl" did not appear anywhere in the statement, but they were strongly implied.

I wasn't really surprised when my cell buzzed at about eleven.

"Bet you wished you had that muzzleloader tonight."

"Just standing my ground on the free and vibrant local media landscape."

He let out a tight chuckle.

"It was a very nice line," I said. "So was the part about except in the cases of extraordinary malfeasance. Thank your press secretary."

"I already did." Will took a long breath. "Mary Alice is very diplomatic. I am not feeling diplomatic at the moment."

"Slater was just being a jerk. And she's going to get to talk to the feds for the privilege."

"There is that." He was silent for a moment, thinking what to say next. "You and your girl are okay?"

"I'm more annoyed than anything else."

"And Ryan?"

It was probably the first time he'd said her name, and that, and the fact that he was asking after her under these circumstances, stopped me for a second. "Mostly okay."

"My kids sometimes had a tough time with it when they were about her age. And nobody was sending me bombs."

"What did you do?"

"Just kept reminding them that the people out there saying all those things don't know me, and they don't know us, and they don't have anything to do with what happens in our house. Best I could do."

"Might help. Thanks."

"Bought a lot of ice cream too."

I laughed at that. So did he.

"Still like a nice bowl of maple vanilla after I've been singed on Twitter."

"Where on earth do you get maple vanilla?"

"Oh, you were in New York too long." The impish note returned to his voice, taking us very firmly back to slap and tickle. "Place outside Barre makes it once a month. I stock up."

"Good to know."

"If you are very nice . . . or maybe very not nice . . . I will take you there sometime."

"I may take you up on that."

"Good."

"Right now, however, my record is ending."

"Wouldn't want to get in the way of the show. Good night, Jacqueline."

"Thanks, Knickerbocker."

# Chapter Sixteen

## With a Little Help from My Friends

Wednesday was one of those late February days where it feels like winter is putting up a fight: temperature holding around zero with a cutting wind. The doors were already open at Kunin at drop-off, which almost never happens, and the kids just ran right in, trying to stay ahead of the gusts.

Back at the station, there were a few e-mails informing me that I'd gotten what I deserved with the pipe bomb, and several others in my personal account from people I'd worked with over the years expressing sympathy and asking what they could do. I started a file for the nasty ones, figuring I'd send them on to Chief George at some point.

There was also a Facebook message from one AlexTenVT: *"Nice pushback to Charity Slater! You rule, Jaye! How about some Erasure?"*

I replied: *"Thanks! I'll spin you 'A Little Respect' tonight."*

I was sure his dad didn't know anything about the message, and equally sure it would be a very bad idea to make a big deal of it. Since Alex Ten Broeck was at NYU (yes, I read his father's official bio on the state website—don't judge!) he might well have been aware of my existence on his own, if not my connection to Will.

Family drama avoided, I returned to responding to my old friends, enjoying the pleasure of catching up now that the lead line wasn't "My husband has cancer."

Of course, I didn't have a husband anymore, but I did have a decent start on a new life, and so did he. Good enough.

I'd finished the last one when another unfamiliar sender popped up in the station account. LESIrishPat was the address, which you'd have to be a New Yorker to know meant Lower East Side Irish Pat. Probably not a freak.

It wasn't.

It was Pat Neely the tech:

*"You're a nice lady with a kid, so I thought I'd better warn you. Especially after what happened. Spence Lyle isn't done. I don't know what he's up to, but management is doing a search instead of just promoting him. He's worried and looking for attention, and that can't be good.*

*"If I were you, I'd keep your cop and firefighter pals close.*

*"Sorry to make it worse."*

Spence Lyle worried and looking for attention. That's a happy thought. I sent Neely a thanks, and thought about talking again to Chief George.

My phone buzzed. Mom.

This can't be good.

"Jaye, will you please tell your uncle to stop gloating about the Cavaliers . . ."

She didn't know.

Mom and Uncle Edgar were in the middle of some kind of rehashed-adolescent fight, and she flat-out didn't know.

I should probably have been bothered. Maybe even offended. Instead, I was thrilled. One or the other of them always asks me to jump in and referee these weird little disputes, and I was grateful for the distraction.

This one was easy. Mom's NBA fandom had followed LeBron James from team to team. Uncle Edgar is a Cavs fan, world without end amen.

As I talked my mother down, suggesting that the two of them simply agree to disagree on LeBron and perhaps follow college hoops this winter instead, I calculated the odds that she would find out about the pipe bomb. If she didn't know now, more than twenty-four hours later, the odds were pretty slim that it would make the news there.

I was safe enough.

Better to let it slide and hopefully spare Mom the worry.

"What's the temperature today?" I asked her as our conversation wound down.

"Only seventy. Cold snap."

Her relaxed chuckle was reward enough. I've spent a lot of my life protecting my mother from upset, whether in my life or hers, and it always felt good to know she was okay.

I play-growled. "I think I hate you."

"I love you, Jaye." A smile in her voice again. Perfect.

"Love you, Mom."

Despite the wicked cold, Alicia Orr came by toward the end of lunchtime as she sometimes does, just to have a cup of coffee and chat. Considering the timing, I suspected she was actually keeping an informal eye on me for her spouse, and that was just fine.

It's how things work in small towns—and like many things around here, you can either argue about it or go with it. I save the arguing for when it really matters.

We both knew what was up anyhow, and didn't especially care. I'd just made a pot of the good stuff, and we settled in my office with our cups.

"I keep the heat on high here during the day, and turn it up in the studio at night," I said as she took off her long shiny black down coat, revealing a coral boiled-wool jacket that gave a little glow to her deep, creamy-brown skin. Even in wretchedly cold weather, Alicia looks better than most of the world.

"You doing okay?" she asked. "Ugly couple of days."

"Yeah. I could have done without the follow-up visit from the Lieutenant Gov."

She smiled. "I love the way you put things."

"If you don't keep your sense of humor . . ."

"They might as well nail the lid down. Yep."

We laughed together, and I took a sip of my coffee.

"The Lieutenant Gov is a piece of work," Alicia said. "Lives in the next town over, and drives 'em nuts."

"Oh, yeah?"

"Yeah. Alma Perkins is the chief in Chester, and she's told George that Slater expects to have an officer whenever she leaves her house, and treats them like an assistant, making them carry her stuff and things like that."

"Jeez. The *governor* doesn't do that."

"The governor is a pretty low-key guy, far as I can tell."

I just nodded and took a sip of coffee. I didn't want to give anything away and distract her from Charity Slater. "Seems like it."

"Heard he stopped by after the pipe bomb Monday."

Ratted by my officer. "Yeah. I covered him back in the day . . . we're sort of old friends. Just making sure I was okay."

"Nice."

"Yeah. Good guy."

Alicia started to say something, but left it. "So anyway, Charity Slater is bad news. Thinks she's more important than she is, plus being mean and clueless."

"Ugh. Bad combination."

"Worse than you think. She's trying to undercut your pal."

"How so?"

Alicia drank her coffee and thought for a moment, deciding how to express it, or how much to tell. "I'm on a county development council, and she's been pushing us toward a couple of projects that don't really make sense for the area."

"Don't make sense how?"

"Environmentally bad—like trying to revive that stupid brewery project on Quarry Hill—or just wrong. She actually took a meeting with HyperMart."

"That big French-Canadian chain?"

"Yup. We sure don't need big boxes around here. Gurney's Hardware and the other local stores are just hanging on as it is."

"No kidding. And it's practically political orthodoxy here that Vermont doesn't like that kind of stuff."

"It was, Jaye." Alicia shook her head. "Not so much now. Some of these new retrograde types don't care what they destroy as long as their people get theirs."

"That fell apart pretty bad at the national level."

"Yeah, but you know deadenders."

"Ah. She's not just running with Harold and Howard for fun. She actually believes that crap."

"Oh, yeah. It's not an act." She tapped her coral nails on her mug, making me admire, and envy a teeny bit, her manicure. "Want to get sick, see girlfriend's social media feed. All that nonsense about how there's no real racism anymore and the poor conservatives are the real victims."

"So that's why I got a pipe bomb." I managed a wry smile as I drank the last of my coffee.

"George doesn't know if it was a real one yet. Takes the feds a few days."

"Either way,"

"Yep." Her bright, deep brown eyes narrowed. "They'll get whoever it is. I don't know how the New York feds are these days, but ours are good."

"I'm sure they are. I got the occasional threat and all when I was in the city." I shrugged. "But I never got anything like a bomb."

"You have to come up here to have the full experience." Her voice was teasing, but her face was concerned. "Sucks. A lot of people in town don't like it either."

"Well, there's that. Hopefully, they'll listen."

"We've got it on in the bank."

"Thanks."

We exchanged smiles.

"Just keep walking, Jaye. Most of the time, all it takes to win is staying on the field until the other guys give up."

"I like that. I might use it—with credit, of course."

"Well, yeah."

The universe must have known I needed some extra support from my friends that night, because Maeve turned up after eleven, with a shiny rose-gold makeup bag and a big smile.

"Care package!"

"Cool! The coffee's fresh."

Maeve put the bag in the studio and let me pour her a cup, the two of us bouncing like little kids at a birthday party. Her sister Liz is a beauty editor in the city, and considers it her religious obligation to keep her holy sib in the good stuff. For years, Maeve enjoyed her loot alone, until I came back and admitted that I'm totally into it too.

Now, whenever Liz cleans out the beauty closet, Maeve shares the swag with me, and sometimes Ryan. At least one Sunday afternoon a month, we three end up in my tiny living room with the latest organic face masks, new nail polish, and bad sitcom reruns.

"Liz says shimmer and face oils are big again," Maeve said, sitting down in the guest spot.

"Let me rack up a couple of songs and we'll see."

While Lisa Lisa and Cult Jam got "All Cried Out," we sifted through Liz's latest offerings. Shimmer was indeed big, in several blinding forms that I did not think would be suitable for either a minister or a deejay. The face oils were a better bet, especially since we'd reached the point in winter where no moisturizer was enough.

Still, Maeve decided she'd try the "Soft-Gold Goddess Glow Stick" as a highlighter on her next date night with Niall, and insisted I take the little compact of "Pink Diamond Cream" for Saturday. I ended up with the "Lavender Soothing Face Oil" too, because she's over aromatherapy, while she decided to try a new almond and coconut oil treatment, which sounded more like food to me.

Oiled and highlighted and coffee'd, we relaxed in the studio as I kept the show going.

"Looks like you're handling it," she observed after I finished a break.

"I don't have any choice, but I'm okay."

"Good. A lot of people are bothered by that pipe bomb thing. It'll ultimately work in your favor, I think."

I drank a little coffee. "I'm just glad to know people are bothered by something."

"Right?" She sipped hers. "What did you think of Charity?"

"What the hell *is* she?"

Maeve gave a humorless chuckle. "I'd like to say she's from Mars, but she's from a local family. Her aunt, who's got to be in her nineties, is one of my parishioners. And nothing like her."

"I doubt anyone's like her."

"True. It takes a lot to be that mean and that clueless at once. Who comes after somebody who just got a pipe bomb? And brings her kid?"

"Kid?"

"Yeah. The guy with her, he was her son."

"I thought he was staff."

"No, he's stuck with her for life."

"Damn. Mommie Dearest for sure."

"Don't insult Joan Crawford." Maeve looked down at her coffee. "I shouldn't have more, but . . ."

I topped us both off with the last of the pot.

"He's a grownup and he's working for his mom?" I asked as I sat down and seg'd into the next song.

"Not just working for her. He's like her assistant or her minion or something."

"Does he have a life?"

"Not that I've heard. Looks like one of those angry guys who's blaming the world for not getting any play."

"Like Spence Lyle."

Our eyes held for a moment.

"Just like Spence Lyle."

Suddenly, the lavender soothing oil wasn't nearly so calming anymore.

# Chapter Seventeen
## Things Could Always Be Worse

"Man, we have been so lucky this week," Rob said as he walked out after finishing the voice-tracking, maybe half an hour before pickup time Thursday.

As soon as it was out of his mouth, he blushed and shook his head.

"Oh, hell, Jaye, I just meant with the weather. I didn't mean—"

I laughed. I couldn't help it. "It's you. I know."

He gave me a relieved little smile. "It was just so awful at the end of January."

"I know. What, three storms in MLK week?"

"Not often that there's too much snow for the resorts."

"Yep. Something to think about for next winter—maybe you do a Storm Center."

"Sponsorship?"

"Yeah, I seem to remember it was a good moneymaker, but it's been a long time."

"We didn't have to worry about the money then."

We shared a rueful smile.

"God, wasn't that nice? All we had to do was show up and do the thing." He shook his head.

"We didn't know anything." I shrugged. "But we didn't *have* anything either."

"Got that. I didn't even know until I was a parent how much I wanted to be one."

"Bet you didn't even let yourself think about it. I know I didn't."

"Yep. Just being able to say 'my son' is enough of a gift."

"I cried all over the forms at the hospital when I listed myself as Ryan's mother for the first time."

"I did the same thing at the foster office, and I can't even blame hormones."

We laughed together.

"Much as I love Tim, and he loves me, Xavi is the best thing that ever happened to us."

"He's a great little guy."

"Yours is no slouch. I'm glad they're friends."

"Me too. I'm not always sure about that when they're studying the schematics for the station . . ."

"I thought Xavi was kidding about that."

"Nope. You know they pooled their Snap Circuits kits . . ."

"Yeah."

"Well, they're talking about wiring something into the production studio, or just—improving—the board setup."

Rob's eyes widened. "I keep telling myself I'll be grateful when they invent the thing that will support us in a luxurious old age."

"Me too." I grinned. "I also keep telling myself that I don't mind having a kid who knows more about keeping the station on the air than I do."

He smiled. "That might come in handy someday."

"Sure hope not."

A little after five, shift change for the fire department, Chief Frank Saint Bernard dropped by.

Chief Frank, who unfortunately looks a bit like his namesake, is a normally a taciturn, but very kind and professional guy. I'd always enjoyed working with him during my first hitch, and I was very glad to know that he was Sadie's man, not that I could acknowledge that.

He patted Ryan on the head, praised her choice of book (Mae Jemison had been succeeded by Jackie Robinson, a personal hero of the chief's) and nodded to my office, meaning he had something serious to share.

I poured him a coffee and motioned to the worn-in leather couch as he closed the door.

"It was a dud," Chief Frank said. "You'll get the official word tomorrow, but I have an old friend in the ATF office."

"Thanks." I let out a long breath.

"Don't be too relieved. It wasn't a fake."

"Oh."

"Whoever it was didn't just want to scare you. They did in fact want to kill you, and anyone happened to be around you."

I put down my coffee as my stomach twisted, but hung onto some pretense of cool. "Not to mention anyone who came to help."

"That too." Grim nod. "My pal tells me the guy had the bomb part right, but screwed up the detonator. Looks amateur, and quite possibly the first time they've tried it."

"Oh, yay. I'm their first."

The chief bit back a snicker at the unexpectedly inappropriate subtext. "Hopefully last too. There were some weird things about this . . . and a fingerprint in the duct tape."

"No."

"Yep. Nothing turned up locally, so they're letting it cook in the national database."

"What was weird?"

"A couple of short white hairs in the package, and some mistakes in the assembly that suggested the person didn't have entirely steady hands."

"An elderly bomber?" I asked, as I added it up.

"That's what I'd start thinking." Chief Frank nodded. "That's why I'm not too worried, and I don't think you should be either."

"Why? Grandpa or Grandma would have made me just as dead . . ."

"I know a little about being old, Jaye," the chief said, holding my gaze carefully. "Takes a lot to change your ways or get you to do something unusual."

"Okay."

"And most of us oldsters were raised right, with good values and parents who'd kill us if we didn't follow them." He shifted in his chair. "Your bomber is probably feeling pretty bad about it by now, especially since at least some of the reports mentioned that a child lives at the radio station."

"They should feel bad."

"No argument. But here's what I think happened. That Edwin Anger guy had his people so scared and upset about the world, and then he turns up dead, and that scrawny weasel Lyle pops in and riles 'em up some more. You're scared, you're slipping a little, you don't have much else to do because you're old . . ."

It was the most I'd ever heard him say at one time, except for the annual fire department budget presentation. I nodded. "So you think maybe you can do something to stop it."

"Yep. It's sick and scary all right, Jaye, but it shouldn't be too hard to catch them."

I nodded again. I hoped I looked reassured, because I wasn't sure I felt it.

"And of course there's the fingerprint."

I managed a small smile. "That doesn't hurt."

"Nope. Now you know we're all keeping a good careful eye on you and your girl, so try not to worry too much."

"Thanks."

He stood, and so did I.

The chief gave me an awkward pat on the shoulder. "It's going to be okay, Jaye. Really."

"Thanks."

I walked him to the door and Ryan and I watched him go, exchanging knowing smiles when he reached the bottom of the stairs, where Sadie *just happened* to be walking to her car.

"They're together, aren't they?" Ryan asked.

"Don't say anything to them, but yeah."

"Pretty cool. Like Pop and Grands."

"I hope exactly like that. Your grandparents are a great couple."

My girl was watching me very closely.

"That's how a marriage is supposed to be, if you love each other and you're really lucky. Tim and Rob are like that too."

"Yeah. Xavi says they even argue sometimes, and make sure he sees them make up."

"That's how you do it if you have a good marriage," I assured her. "Not just love each other, but teach your child how to make love work every day."

"You and Dad loved each other."

"But we weren't lucky and we couldn't make it work. Or not the right kind of lucky, anyhow." I put my arm around Ryan. "We were the luckiest people in the world to have you, and that doesn't change."

She nodded and put her head on my shoulder, burrowing in a little, the way she had when she was younger.

"But people go through what your dad did, and—"

"And what you did too, Ma."

"What we all did, honey." I stroked her hair, the way I had when she was tiny. It was still soft and silky like a baby's, even though she was taller, stronger, and more mature every day. "Dad and I just couldn't find our way back."

"I know. It's okay. We're okay."

"As okay as we need to be," I agreed, kissing the top of her head.

Ryan grinned up at me. "And it's okay if you want the governor around."

"What?"

"I never see them, but I know Dad has friends. And when you told me you were having dinner with the governor, you said old friends the same way. So?"

"So, yes, I guess the best way to put it is, we're seeing each other."

"When you say old friend, did you see him before Dad?"

I burst out laughing. Ryan stared at me for a second, puzzled, then started laughing too, just because I was.

"Ma," she said finally, "what's so funny?"

"I was a fat, awkward, immature twenty-one-year-old when I was up here the first time. He was happily married to a beautiful adult woman and had a couple of kids. Yes, I had a crush. No, nothing ever happened."

"You had crushes?"

"Oh, yeah. Still do."

"Good to know."

I got the feeling my girl was starting to think about all the partner stuff, and had the sense to leave it, pulling her into a hug and kissing her on the top of her head again, getting a wince this time.

"You're pretty great, Ryan Metz."

"Who's better than us?" She started the little family affirmation we'd always done in the parking lot before we went into the infusion suite.

"Nobody."

# Chapter Eighteen

## The Yogis and the Moose

That Saturday, after yoga class, we all walked out into some unexpected sunshine. It had to be in the mid-forties, which felt almost like a heat wave.

"I'm going up to check the transmitter," I said, rummaging for my keys. "Want to come see Charlemagne?"

"I'm in." Alicia grinned. "I can't help it. I love the big guy."

"Me too," Maeve agreed.

"I'll drive," offered Sadie, as we all winced. "Oh, stop looking like that. We'll fit better in the Hummer and you know it."

Sadie somehow got her hands on an actual military surplus Humvee, which she drives with absolutely wicked relish. It's not as awful as it sounds, because she had it fitted out with a heater and stereo, but you're still riding in a combat vehicle.

After I dropped off my mat and grabbed a couple of hard candies for Charlemagne, we dutifully piled into the Hummer and Sadie blasted up Quarry Hill. Maeve drew shotgun, and Alicia and I ended up in the back, all of us hanging on for dear life and wishing Sadie would slow down a little. She knows the PD doesn't have the resources to stop speeders unless it's egregious, and more, that Chief George really wouldn't want to write that ticket.

Even though I couldn't see the speedometer, I guessed she wasn't really going that fast; it just felt that way because it was the Humvee, and because of her driving style, which she probably learned during her flirtation with demolition derby a few decades ago. That's not a joke.

Anyway, we all survived the trip, and I slipped inside the shack for a quick look at everything, finding no cause for concern. The others peeked in, as usual mystified by all of the equipment.

"Do you really know what all of this is for?" Alicia asked.

"Nah." I pointed to the control panels. "As long as these are moving and in the green range, and those two red lights are on and steady, we're fine. That's all I need to know—and all I know anyway."

Maeve laughed. "Bet Ryan knows a lot more."

"She and Xavier have been reading the schematic diagrams for the old production studio. They're thinking about wiring in my old DVD player just to see if they can."

Sadie shook her head. "Rob was the same way when he was a kid. Always taking things apart and building it into something new."

"Ryan's done that all along," I agreed, "and now that she has a partner in crime . . ."

The others chuckled as we walked out of the shack.

"Ready?" I locked the door and we walked a few steps away from the building as they nodded. I opened my candy and put it on my palm. Within seconds, we heard the rustling, which quickly became a crashing sound, and Charlemagne appeared at the edge of the clearing.

We all caught our breath, and somebody, I wasn't sure who, whispered a "Wow."

The moose walked out and daintily licked his treat from my hand, as I stifled a giggle from the tickling hair around his mouth.

He crunched for a few moments, just watching us. When the candy was gone, he just stood there.

"Want another?"

He didn't move. I slipped a candy to Alicia, as I'd done several times before, and Charlemagne waited patiently while she unwrapped it and put it on her palm. Like me, she held back a giggle while he took the treat from her.

This time, the moose took a little longer to finish the candy, just chewing slowly and regarding us with his giant, gentle brown eyes. Finally, he let out a little ruffly noise, and turned, slowly starting to walk away. He was probably a couple yards away when we heard it.

The sound was loud and unmistakable, and if we'd had any doubt, the eye-watering stench would have removed it.

We collapsed, not from the methane reek, but in gales of laughter.

"Some thanks we get!" Alicia choked out.

"Moose fart!" Sadie howled. "I never."

"I didn't know moose farted," Maeve said.

"I was never sure about that cow flatulence killing the environment thing," I began when I was able to talk again, "but if it's anything like that . . ."

"It's worse." Sadie's dry pronouncement just sent us back to howling.

It took a couple of minutes for us to get our breath, between coughing and laughing.

Finally, Maeve looked at her fitness watch. "I can't do lunch today. I have to get back and put my clericals on for a premarital counseling session."

Sadie shook her head. "And good luck to you—and them."

"I have to get back to the station," I admitted. "Some work to do for the weekend shows."

"And your date?" Alicia asked, cutting her eyes to Maeve.

"Um, yeah."

Sadie smiled. "He's a good one."

"What?" Even though this evening would almost certainly serve as a very public announcement, I had told no one but Maeve who I was seeing.

"Saw the Gov's SUV outside the station Monday after the pipe bomb thing." Sadie shook her head. "Small town, remember? Don't do anything you don't want everyone else to know about."

"Right." I shook my head as we walked toward the Hummer.

"But I like him," Sadie continued. "Smart, nice manners, and we wouldn't have had that stupid fight over the brewery up here if he'd been running the state then."

"Really?"

"Yeah. It's not a great site, because there's no easy way to deal with the runoff, even if that big aquifer is under there. Not to mention ruining the moose habitat."

"Rob told me a little about that."

Alicia jumped in: "They lost their financing because of the recession."

"Someone's looking again," Sadie said. "I don't know if it's a brewery or what, but your guy's big on environmentally safe business, so we don't have to worry."

"Yeah?" I just ignored the "your guy," a little amused that she knew more about Will's views on this topic than I did. Well, it wasn't like we'd had a lot of time to sit around and talk about development strategies.

"Oh, yeah." Maeve smiled. "Had a big conference last year in Burlington."

"So anything that comes in here will have to be decent, no matter who's trying." Sadie nodded definitively. "The governor gets a say on this one because of the land-use laws."

Alicia smiled. She'd caught the "your guy" reference back there, and added it to what she'd heard earlier in the week, putting her now firmly in the game. "So you *are* seeing the governor."

I sighed. "I'm not sure what I'm doing with the governor."

Maeve just *looked* at me.

"Well, he is pretty cute for a short white guy." Alicia had caught the look from Maeve, but thankfully Sadie had not. "Definitely the good end of the local talent pool."

We all laughed.

"Come on, girls," Sadie said, nodding to the Hummer. "I'll get us back to town."

We piled into the Hummer again, and Sadie glanced at me in the rearview.

"We will expect a full report next week."

Once back on solid ground, I moved into full-tilt date prep.

Work came first. I tracked the show, recording breaks and setting up songs the same way Rob did on a weekday, using requests I'd saved over the last couple of days so it would sound fresh, exactly as if I were in the studio instead of out misbehaving. That took about an hour, and then it was playtime.

It had been long enough since I had a real date that all of the girly stuff was part of the treat. I took a long hot shower, deep-conditioned my hair, and dug out some swag from some of Sister Liz's earlier care packages. The Rose Hydration Surge mask was soaking in when my cell rang.

"Hayman Stadler, age seventy-three, of Varina, Mississippi."

"What?"

"Alicia told me I should leave you alone till tomorrow, but I thought you'd want to know." Chief George chuckled, his tone giving no doubt that he knew I was up to something tonight.

"Know . . ." I probably couldn't strangle Alicia.

"Our pipe bomb suspect. Took them until now because he was in some old military database that had been down for maintenance. Washed out of the Coasties, no pun, worked in a factory most of his life, and hasn't accomplished a hell of a lot. No record, though, and a couple of kids who turned out okay."

"What now?"

"Oh, he's going to be a very busy fella. Federal bomb-making charge because it was real, even if it was a dud. No bail because it's such a serious offense. Gonna be a long spring for Mr. Stadler."

"Do they think he acted alone?"

"They know he did." There was a real, honest smile in his voice. "Dude confessed as soon as the feds showed up at his house. Said he just wanted to make sure Edwin Anger's mission continued, and he didn't want to hurt a kid."

"Didn't mind hurting a woman."

"Remember, guys that age think there are good women and bad women. And bad women get what they deserve. All due respect, Jaye, you, standing in the way of his *Edwin Anger Show*, are definitely a bad woman."

I burst out laughing at that. "Wow. I've always wanted to be a bad girl."

Chief George laughed too. "Don't let it go to your head."

# Chapter Nineteen

## Date Night

Not long after that, I got a chance to get down with my apparently very bad self.

The Old Grist Mill Tavern in White River Junction, besides being halfway between Simpson and Montpelier, is also the nicest place to eat in the state outside Burlington, which is a real city with all that entails. If you live in southern Vermont, you're planning a big night out, and you don't want to drive three hours to Burlington, or about the same to Boston, you go to the Grist Mill.

I knew all of this from my first hitch, though I'd never had the money or reason to go there at the time. David and I met when he was teaching in Connecticut, toward the end of my time there. It started when Orville, hoping to get his nevvy settled with a nice girl, suggested he look me up. We hit it off, as a couple of small-town kids working for better, with a shared fondness for classic New York, and collecting stupid grammar mistakes. And yeah, those sparkly green eyes of his.

Our big engagement night out was at the Stage Deli in the city.

I still love a good knish.

Knishes were not on offer at the Grist Mill. It was full-out fancy fine dining, and honestly, a little intimidating. I had no idea what dress-up was in Vermont these days, never mind what Will might expect, so I decided the hell with it, and just did me.

That meant the black wool tuxedo pants I'd scored on sale years ago, and my good dark red suede blazer, with a lacy black tee underneath. It was, I had discovered, the only lacy thing I still owned. At the bottom of a moving box, I found some underwear that at least didn't look orthopedic, but if this Will thing was going to continue, I needed to go online and buy some lingerie, pronto.

Too late for that now. At least I had the beauty part covered. In addition to the face mask and deep conditioner, I'd found a mini of some very high-end dark red lipstick and a perfume sample pack in the loot hidden in the back of my closet. The lipstick really was worth all the fuss, smooth and rich, making my mouth look absolutely delicious.

Perfume was less successful. I finally spritzed on something called "Dangerous Vanilla," which sounded like an oxymoron, but also didn't seem overpowering.

And of course the highlighter. Maeve would not expect a play-by-play of the naughty parts, but she would be very disappointed if I didn't tell her how the makeup worked out. I dabbed a little on my cheek and brow bones, and was surprised by how much of a difference it made.

I was almost not blue for a change.

I thought about even wearing cute shoes, but decided falling in the parking lot would ruin the moment and put on the Chelseas.

They, and I, would do. I made sure the voice-tracked show started properly, and hopped into the Jeep for the forty-five-minute drive. As I belted up, a familiar, lousy voice with worse delivery filled my Jeep.

"Keeping the Anger Alive. Join me, Spence Lyle, every afternoon as we annoy the liberals, disappoint the mainstream media, and stick it to the jackbooted feminist jocks . . ."

Him. On my freaking air.

My blood quite literally boiled for a few seconds. I took a couple of deep breaths while I figured out what happened. Of course. His crappy show was on the same sat service as my music, so promos would show up in the network spots. And under my music contract, I had to let them run.

I couldn't stop it.

But I *could* ignore it for tonight. Good thing the Wrangler is so old it has a CD player. I put in Britney's greatest hits (you got a problem with that?) and took off.

When I walked in, Will had already gotten a lovely table in a dark corner. He was busy perusing the wine list in the candlelight, wearing a pair of reading glasses that only made him cuter, the soft light turning his hair to spun gold and highlighting his strong features. If he hadn't already gotten me into bed, he wouldn't have needed much game tonight.

When he saw me, he stood. Damn, I love an old-school guy.

"Hey, Knickerbocker."

"Well, don't you look lovely."

"Thanks. I don't have a lot of going-out stuff—I did the best I could."

He took my hands and pulled me in for a very appropriate, yet very hot kiss on the cheek, before holding the chair for me. "You're perfect."

"Thanks. You're not bad yourself." I noted that it wasn't governor suit, but navy blazer and khakis—off-duty but dressy, the

French blue oxford finished with a tie that made me grin. Little red hearts with arrows. "Cute tie."

"Valentine joke from my chief of staff years ago. Everybody knows about me and the ties."

"Maybe I'll get you a radio themed one."

"Only if you want me to wear it." He grinned. "I have no boundaries when it comes to ties."

"Then I'm definitely getting you one."

We smiled together, and that's when I noticed Fortescue at the bar. He raised his club soda to me.

I raised my water to him.

"Yeah, I brought a chaperone. Too visible not to." Will shrugged. "He followed me here, and after dinner, he'll make sure I'm settled, um, we're . . ."

It was actually very sweet the way he trailed off. I hadn't been entirely sure of logistics either, but no matter what happened, I had to be back at the station to fire the first public affairs show at six. "You can come to the station if you want . . ."

"You can come to the Residence if you don't have to do something at the station."

"I have to play the public affairs shows."

"So private affairs . . ."

"Have to adjust a little."

"Okay for now." He watched me closely for a moment. "Is there some kind of technology that would play the shows for you?"

"I could probably program something to do it, or move the time."

"So maybe you could stay over with me some Saturday . . ."

"I think we can arrange that."

He took my hand, and we just sat there gazing at each other for maybe thirty seconds. A while. It felt like something, like the first corner in the relationship, maybe. Some sort of small commitment that implied there might be bigger ones in time.

A buzz from his blazer broke the moment. Will gave me a sheepish shrug. "I have to check—if it's Alex or Ari . . ."

I nodded. Parenting always wins for me too.

His face tightened when he saw the screen.

"Everything okay?"

"Not one of my kids. Charity Slater. She's called me three times in the last two days to push me about some land-use exemption. She's always nagging me to approve some insane project for a friend of hers. Always good for somebody's wallet and bad for the environment. I don't even listen anymore." He hit a button. "Decline."

Will had just taken my hand again when the server appeared.

"So, have you decided on wine?"

"I'd like a glass of the cab, and the lady?"

"Likes Shiraz," I said with a smile. Much safer to order by the glass, not to mention respecting my tastes. By the time dinner was over, even if we finished our glasses, big *if* for me, there was no issue with driving, a major concern considering how long we had to go.

"Hey," said the server, a slightly plump woman in her thirties who was probably at least a manager from her demeanor, "you're Jaye Jordan."

"Yep," I replied cautiously. Hopefully I hadn't just ruined Will's night.

"Joely Brett." She smiled and patted my arm. "Don't let those Gadfly idiots get you down, honey. There's way more of us than there are of them."

"Thanks." I gave her a relieved smile back. "I know."

"And you can always put some rock salt in that muzzleloader . . ."

"Don't think I haven't considered it."

Joely's amiable face tightened. "I'd help you. That Edwin Anger guy and his weaselly little producer were up here the Friday before he turned up in your snowman."

"Really?"

"Yup. Talking about the stupid locals and how they were going to teach that uppity woman a lesson. Of course, we were too stupid to hear any of it."

"People like that always think we're stupid," I agreed. "I'm probably the uppity woman."

"It's okay, we're all uppity up here. Goes with the territory."

"And your men like it that way." Will's eyes were much more serious than his comment. "Overhear anything else?"

"Not much. The Anger dude asked me where there was a bar that he could meet people."

Will and I blinked at her.

"Oh, come on. Guy like that absolutely figured he'd get himself some woodchuck action. I told him about the sports bar on Route 11 and sent him on his way."

We all laughed together. The entire state knew about the sports bar on Route 11 and the occasional brawls there during hockey season. Also football and baseball seasons.

"Sounds about right to me," Will said.

"He just said he wanted to meet people, after all," I agreed. "People are people."

"That they are." Joely grinned at Will. "She's a good one, Gov. Keep her if you can."

"Do my best."

"Yeah." She cut her eyes to me, then gave Will a mock-stern look. "Good to see you here with a real date for a change."

I froze for a second. What the hell did that mean?

Will, though, just laughed. "I'll bring the warrior queen in again once her semester is over."

Of course. His daughter.

"Yeah, but tonight you might get something for the fancy dinner." Joely gave us both one more grin. "I'll get the wine."

Will was laughing, but blushing like he was me as she walked off. "Fine dining experience it may be, but we're still in Vermont."

"Good thing too." I watched him for a second.

"I think so. I suppose I should've found another place, but there's nothing this nice closer to you." He toyed with his fork. "Alex prefers the diner in Barre, but even though she is defiantly not a princess, Ari has rather high-end taste in father–daughter dinners."

"Ah. I know this one." I returned the smile. David and Ryan went to a Chinese restaurant in Charlestown most Saturdays. "You don't mess with the daddy–daughter tradition."

"True. And I like the idea that she's comfortable with a fancy night out so some slick guy can't turn her head with a nice dinner."

"That's pretty smart."

"Probably not respecting her agency as a woman in the modern world, but I'm a man in the modern world and I know what's out there."

"You've got the talk down."

"She'd kill me if I didn't." He shook his head. "I don't buy every creep who says he's the father of a daughter so he can't possibly mistreat women . . . but there's no doubt that it changes everything."

"Being a parent changes everything." I smiled. "You think you're one person until they hand you that baby, and then you discover you're someone else entirely."

He took my hand. "Yeah?"

"Yeah. You were pretty much who you are when I was here last time. I wasn't even close."

"Well," he said, lacing fingers with mine, "you're pretty cool now."

"Thanks."

"And I'm really glad you're here . . . even if the snowmen will never feel safe again."

We shared a smile, the kind of happy, goofy thing you can do at a semi-dark, very romantic restaurant on a Saturday night. I'd forgotten how good that feels.

"Excuse me folks, wine?" Joely set down the glasses. "And what are you eating?"

With apologies to Rob, dinner (butternut squash ravioli for me, roasted free-range chicken for Will) was the best meal I'd had since my last wedding anniversary dinner. David and I had splashed out on some fancy waterfront place in hopes that a romantic evening would bring it back. But you can't resuscitate something that's dead, and within a few weeks, we were talking to a lawyer.

I only remembered that last dinner as Will and I were splitting a chocolate mousse, and I noticed that he was a much more considerate sharer of dessert than David had been. David had an unerring aim for the best bite and no qualms about taking it, but Will actually left the last bite of whipped cream for me.

"Nice. You're very good at sharing."

"Dessert yes, other things no."

"Really?"

His eyes were suddenly sharp and serious on mine. "You don't have to worry about me and the girl of the week."

"Well, you don't have to worry about the guy of the week, either."

"It's not the guy of the week who worries me. It's the home team."

I shook my head. "He's not the home team anymore."

He let out a breath I hadn't realized he was holding. "He's your daughter's father, and you're on good terms. I had to ask."

I managed to avoid a spit-take and just smiled. "There is no circumstance under which David Metz and I will ever share a bed again. I know where he's been."

Will *did* spit-take his coffee at that. "Okay, I deserved that."

"Yeah, you did. People vote with their feet. We are where we want to be."

"I sure am." He reached across the table and took my hand, lacing fingers with mine again. "Well, almost. I can think of one place I'd rather be right about now."

"Hmmm. The legislative office building?"

He laughed, but there was enough heat in his eyes to keep the whole Connecticut River from freezing over.

Out in the parking lot, Will bid Fortescue a friendly good night and clicked the locks on a surprisingly low-key little American-made sedan. It didn't even have a special tag, just a vanity plate reading "CHAMP."

I smiled at that. "Either you're really good at something, or you believe in the lake monster."

"I am really good at many things, Jacqueline," he said, with a smile that reminded me of some of them. "But the tag is a monster reference."

"Nice."

He shrugged. "I don't know that I actually believe in it, but I don't not believe in it, either."

"Yeah?"

"I like the idea of something I can't be sure of and can't explain out there, happily swimming around the lake. I know it's weird, but . . ."

He trailed off awkwardly.

"I like bumblebees."

Will looked puzzled. "Bumblebees?"

"Scientifically, there is no way they can fly. And yet they do." I was giving away a lot here too. "It speaks to me. By all odds, I should be in a trailer park in some corner of western P-A. I shouldn't have been able to become much of anything."

"And yet you did."

"Yep."

He put a hand on my arm, and nodded to my Jeep. "C'mon, tell me the rest back at the station where it's warm. And maybe I'll tell you more about Champ."

"Come back to my place and tell me about your lake monster."

"I've always dreamed of hearing a woman say that."

I hopped in the Jeep, and Will started his car. Fortescue flashed the lights on his SUV and waited as Will drove out of the lot first, the trooper following him, and me last, so I had a perfect view of it as it happened.

At first, everything seemed fine, as we turned out of the lot and into the drive. But when we reached the main road, it started downhill, a gentle grade at first, and soon sharper. On the slope, Will seemed to be going faster than he should, and picking up speed when he should have been slowing down. I was surprised and concerned to see he was such a reckless driver.

Soon, though, I realized he wasn't reckless at all.

At the bottom of the hill, the small state highway widened out and flattened. As soon as he hit the straightaway, Will drove off the left side into a hay field, the car still moving fast, plowing through old snow and dead grass for a few hundred yards as it finally slowed.

As Will drove off the road, Fortescue pulled over. Doing my best not to think about what might happen in the next few minutes, I parked behind him. We were both out on the shoulder in time to hear the last of the crunching as Will's car rolled to a stop in the frozen grass ends.

The car stopped and just sat there for a moment, lights still on, no sign of Will.

Fortescue and I both started running. Even in my cute Chelsea boots, I was faster, but he had a flashlight.

By the time we got there, Will was out of the car, shaking his head. When I ran up, he grabbed my hand and pulled me to him, just holding me tight for a second.

"You okay?"

"Yeah. Fine." He buried his face in my hair, and I could hear his breathing, still harsh.

"What the hell, Boss?" Fortescue panted. Sprinting across frozen fields wasn't exactly in the security detail job description.

"Brakes died."

In the weak reflection of the headlights, I saw the trooper's eyes narrow. "Did they now?"

"I haven't driven it in a couple of days, and it's been really cold. It could be a broken line."

"Could be." Fortescue shook his head. "I'll have it towed in the morning and someone at the state police garage will take a look."

Will nodded.

He hadn't let go of me, and I didn't want him to.

"You want a ride back to Montpelier, Boss?"

"Not tonight."

"Might want to make sure Ms. Jordan is still cool with that."

I managed a small laugh. "Very cool. Long as he doesn't back-seat drive."

"I'll be sitting shotgun, and I'll keep my mouth shut." He turned away long enough to pull a briefcase-ish carry-on bag from the front seat of his car.

"Good enough. Long as you have your phone set to dial me, Boss."

"I hear and obey." Will was trying for wry, and almost got there.

Fortescue gave him a trace of a smile. "I'll come get you in Simpson. When?"

"When do you get back from Mass?"

"I'll go to the early one. Ten okay?"

"If she can tolerate me that long."

"Better make yourself tolerable, then." I took his hand. "Let's all get warm and sort this out in the morning."

# Chapter Twenty

## You *Wish* the Morning After Was Just a Cheesy Song

Will was as good as his word, and made no comments on my driving. We didn't talk much at all, actually. Even assuming it was an accident, the whole thing was pretty scary, at least to me. I knew he was more unnerved than he was letting on, and it made sense to just put on my old U2 CD and leave him to deal with it his way.

I found out what his way was when we got to the station. I took a quick listen to make sure everything was running all right, and led him up the stairs to the apartment. He was right behind me when I locked the door, and when I turned back to him, he pulled me into his arms.

It wasn't desperate and nearly ferocious like it had been that first night, but it was clearly, and deliberately, all-consuming. A reminder that we're both still alive and together and sometimes you don't need to talk it out. Sometimes, there are other ways to handle things.

Fine by me. I'd spent much of the last two years trying to talk things back to okay, one way or another, and failing miserably. Whether we were just taking a break from the ugly reality, or processing it in our own way ultimately didn't matter much.

What did matter was that we were dealing with it together, instead of on opposite sides of a very cold bed.

It seemed like a long time later when we curled up under the covers, satisfied and spent and sleepy, aware that the balance between us was different, and equally aware that we didn't need to discuss it right then. When Neptune jumped on the foot of the bed, sniffed at Will, nested between us, and promptly fell asleep, it felt like the final seal of approval.

I wasn't sure where this was going, but I knew it was a whole lot more than resetting the dials, as Maeve would have said. Not that the dials weren't reset but good.

I woke before my alarm went off, a few minutes before six, and carefully untangled myself from a lightly snoring Will. Scrambling into an old WSV fleece and leggings, I headed downstairs to play the public affairs shows and set up the rest of the day. It took a couple of hours, running some local stuff recorded years ago, and a newer religious commentary provided by Maeve's church.

On a normal Sunday, I read a book or magazine and drank coffee while things ran. This week, I didn't have the concentration for it.

At eight, I got us back into the sat service, and headed back upstairs with two mugs of coffee. I didn't need to bother.

The apartment smelled like coffee and something heavenly. Will was in the galley kitchen fussing over a skillet, in a dark blue UVM fleece and jeans, looking very sexily disheveled.

"How do you feel about pancakes?"

"I don't usually even eat breakfast," I admitted.

He looked hard at me. "You've been skipping a lot more than breakfast lately."

"C'mon, I had dessert last night."

"What else did you eat yesterday?"

Coffee, not that it was any of his damn business.

Will just nodded. He either knew or suspected. "I know why, but you need to do better for yourself, okay?"

"Um, yeah." I put down the two mugs of coffee. The pancakes did smell awfully good. "I have burned off a few extra calories in the last day or so, and I do love pancakes."

He grinned, dropping the issue for now. "These, my dear, are not ordinary pancakes. These are Magical Maple Pancakes, beloved of generations of Ten Broeck females."

"Really?"

"They're also the only thing I can reliably cook from scratch." He handed me a plate, with a mock-stern glare. "I almost had to break up with you this morning."

"Why?" I knew it would be a mistake to acknowledge that we would require a breakup. But that twenty-year-old corner of me let out a little squeal. So okay, maybe I do want to be with somebody. If I can have the Knickerbocker, anyhow.

"You appear to have that liquid that cannot be called syrup in your cabinet."

"That's for Ryan."

"In certain parts of Vermont, that would merit a call to Children's Services."

"Probably. She won't eat anything else. So I keep the real stuff for myself."

"And dark amber at that." He picked up his plate and followed me into the living room.

"Well, of course. I learned from the best."

We sat down on the couch, and I took a bite. The pancakes may have looked like any other, but they surely didn't taste like it. I had no idea what he'd done with the limited ingredients in my pantry, but I didn't care. "Generations of Ten Broeck women can't be wrong."

"Just my mother, daughter, and ex, but still." He grinned and took a bite of his own. "I admit I'm showing off a little to impress the lady."

"It's working."

He watched me for a couple of bites. "I'm sure guys show off for you all the time."

"Not really." I shrugged. "David was my first serious relationship."

"And you married him." He shook his head.

"Western P-A good girl," I explained. "You love him, you marry him, you stay."

"So he left?"

"He left a trail." I put my plate down. "It wasn't even really cheating by that point. Things happen, especially after what he went through, I know that. That wasn't it."

I took a breath. Will waited.

"It was the meanness. He was sick and he was angry and I was the only one he could be mean to. So he was."

Will's jaw tightened but he said nothing, just let me talk.

"It's true that he saw the chemo suite when he looked at me, but it's also true that all I heard was the Mean Guy, even after he was better."

"You can't un-say things."

"Yeah." I shrugged. "And I expected the Mean Guy, so I was already cringing a little anytime things got tense. Not a good way to run a marriage."

Will nodded. "So you just couldn't find your way back."

"Yeah. We're better as friends and parents."

"Me and my ex, too." He smiled ruefully. "But we didn't have nearly as much to get over. There just wasn't anything left once we didn't have to take care of the kids."

"It happens."

"Yep." He shook his head. "And we were smart enough to end it while we could still be friends."

"So were David and I."

"Probably a lot harder for you two, young as Ryan is." Will's eyes held mine, deep blue and bottomless like that lake he loves. "You and Metz are pretty impressive."

"He lived. It's all that matters for Ryan, and everything else is editorial."

He put his own plate down, and pulled me into his arms. "I'm sorry you had all of that, but I'm not sorry you're here with me now."

"Me either."

For a second, I snuggled into his embrace, just enjoying the closeness.

Then he gave me a little shove. "Eat. The pancakes are terrible cold."

We'd only had a bite or two more when Fortescue called, telling Will that his car had been towed, and he'd be coming to get him at ten.

"I don't know enough about cars to know," I started carefully, between bites, "but was that just bad luck last night?"

He shook his head. "The state police mechanic will take a good look at it, but I can't imagine it being anything else. I hadn't driven since last weekend, and you know, it was really cold early in the week. It can happen."

"Okay."

Whatever I'd said, Will heard what I meant, and he held my gaze sharply and seriously. "You do not have to worry about me, all right?"

"All right."

"Want to worry about something, worry about me feeding you to Champ if you don't finish those pancakes."

We were both laughing as we returned to breakfast.

Once the pancakes were gone, it was still only about nine, so we had to think of something to do with that hour. Of course, we talked about good books we'd read and discussed the finer points of environmental policy.

We did actually manage a little talk about books. Later.

Despite our best efforts to burn off the sugar high, we were still pretty happy by the time Fortescue got there. I'd managed to get my hair pulled back so I didn't look like a PSA for sex, but it would not have taken Fortescue's detective skills to figure out how our date had gone.

Will and I were on my office couch, watching one of the Sunday news shows, when the doorbell rang. Fortescue was on the porch with a very troubled expression.

"Hey, it's okay," I teased, thinking he was reacting to my unmistakable morning-after look. "I'm not going to make him marry me."

"You should," he replied grimly. "You need some protection right about now."

"What?"

"Down there." He nodded to the bottom front of the porch, and I walked over and looked from the stairs, not wanting to step into the snow in my slippers.

When I saw what it was, I wasn't worried about wet feet anymore.

It was another "Edwin Is Angry and So Are We," but with something new.

A symbol. And not even drawn right.

A backward effing swastika.

# Chapter Twenty-One

## Not in Our House

People describe shocking things as a gut punch for a reason. It feels like you've been hit with something heavy, and your whole body reacts as if you're in a fight.

I'd had that feeling a couple of times before, but it never gets easy.

I took a breath, pulled my fleece closely around me, fought for cool, reminding myself I'd lived through worse.

"I'm calling hate crimes, Boss." Fortescue was dialing as he nodded calmly to Will, who walked down to the steps and stopped cold.

For maybe a full ten seconds, he was speechless. Stunned. Unable to find any words bad enough for it.

Then: "We are not having this in my state."

Upset as I was, I tried for downplay because there was something truly frightening in his eyes. "It's just the morons again-"

"Jacqueline, I don't care if it was the aliens from Saturn." Will stomped down to the graffiti. "Nobody gets to do this here. This is Vermont. We are better than this."

"Most of us are," I agreed.

"And," Will said, gently and deliberately taking the hand I hadn't even realized had moved to clutch my star necklace, "the ones who aren't are about to learn a very tough lesson."

I took a breath. "Please don't go too hard because it's me."

"I'd be just as angry if it was the mini-mart on Rockingham Road." He met my gaze very coolly. "Some things can't be brushed off. You have to know that."

"I do."

We stood there for a second. I knew he wanted to hold me, and I really wanted him to, but it was the wrong time and place.

Fortescue cleared his throat.

"Would you like some coffee, Trooper Fortescue?" When in doubt, be polite. The country manners I learned as a girl are always a good default setting.

He gave me a determined and friendly smile. "I reckon you'd best start calling me Len, and I'd definitely like some coffee."

"Only if you call me Jaye. Black?"

"There is any other way?"

By ten thirty, the state police hate crimes squad and forensic unit were rolling from Barre, and some of Maeve's parishioners were filtering over to Saint Michael's, stopping to look and shake their heads.

I saw most of that from my office window; Will had very calmly but firmly suggested I go inside and stay warm, which meant he was going to do some things he didn't want me to watch. I would have taken issue with that most days, but this time I let it slide. Two, maybe three reasons: he was going to do it anyway, there were things he could do that I couldn't . . . and a tiny, thoroughly old-fashioned part of me really enjoyed having my powerful macho man take up for me.

Yes, I felt a little feminist guilt about that. Not a lot, though.

"Rowr!" Neptune appeared behind me and nipped at my bare ankle. He was clearly upset about the upheaval, which was only going to get worse, so I scooped him up and penned him in the apartment with a mini-can of tuna for consolation.

My day was ruined, but his didn't have to be.

Rob and Tim blasted in just before eleven, easily as angry as I'd ever seen them.

"Who the hell?" Rob snapped.

"In this town?" Tim added.

Neither, despite Tim's service in Iraq, is exactly dangerous, but both had the same look as Will, ready to kill whoever had violated the sanctity of their town with that evil backward symbol.

"Thanks for checking on me, but the staties are on the way."

"Governor's already here." Rob had a tiny smile in his voice.

"Been here a while." I couldn't resist.

"He has, huh?" Rob's expression told me there would be teasing later.

Tim's eyes widened. Rob shot him a look, but he still said it. "It's like that?"

"I don't know what it's like," I admitted. "But I'm sure glad he's here."

They nodded. Tim patted my arm. "We'll be back after church."

Turned out the entire congregation was back after church. By that time, there were a couple of state police cars on the scene, and one very serious and very offended Sergeant Ava de l'Evesque, the head of the Hate Crimes Division, was taking pictures and chatting grimly with Will. As it happened, she'd been his security detail during his first hitch, while her kids were small, and once the evidence shots were taken, they caught up over coffee in my office.

De l'Evesque was a little older than I was, low-key elegant even in weekend khakis and navy parka, her red hair pulled back in a neat cop bun, emphasizing strong cheekbones and clear hazel eyes.

I gave her the memory stick from the surveillance cam, but she told me it probably wouldn't help much, since most of them get a good shot of anyone going inside a building, and not much else.

Despite that, she was cool and encouraging.

"We usually catch these idiots," she assured me, patting my arm with practiced calm. "And they're usually idiots."

"That's soothing, I think."

"Yeah. It's probably not the same person as the pipe bomb. Two separate MOs."

"You're still going to talk to the feds."

De l'Evesque gave Will a look that would have wilted most people. "Already called 'em. I'm sending Hardiman the evidence pics."

Will nodded, and shrugged a little. "Sorry. I shouldn't have tried to tell you your job."

"Understandable." She gave him an indulgent nod. "It's upsetting even if you don't have a personal interest."

"Ms. Jordan is an old friend."

De l'Evesque shook her head. "You can't even sell that one to me, Boss."

The discussion might have gone any number of ways, most uncomfortable for all concerned, if we hadn't heard a commotion outside.

Maeve—in full vestments—and what sure looked like all of Saint Michael's parishioners were standing at the base of the porch, many muttering things that would not have been appropriate in a sanctuary.

"How can we help?" she asked Fortescue, who was still running the scene.

"Ask her, she's hate crimes," he said, with a deferential nod to de l'Evesque.

"You can let us do our jobs for another hour or so," the Sergeant told her. "And then you can maybe help Ms. Jordan with the cleanup."

Maeve nodded. "Any problem if we stay around for support and solidarity?"

"As long as you don't touch the scene, you can hold a revival meeting on the Plaza."

They exchanged collegial smiles.

"We don't really do that, though we may offer a prayer for peace and goodwill."

"I won't argue with that, Reverend." De l'Evesque nodded to the Plaza. "I suspect you aren't the only people coming with good wishes."

Two pickups and a small SUV were pulling in, along with Chief George's Simpson Police Jeep and Chief Frank's bright red fire department SUV. And, of course, the Hummer.

"Oh, holy hell," I muttered.

Will, who had materialized like Neptune again, was the only one who heard it, and he pulled me back into the foyer, closing the door and taking my hands. "This is good, Jacqueline."

"Okay."

"They all want to make sure you understand this is not what we're about. Let them do it."

I nodded. My—old friend?—obviously knew this one.

He laced fingers with mine, pulling me a little closer. "I'm betting I won't get a word alone with you again for a while, so just let me apologize in advance."

"Why?"

"I'm probably going to offend you with my handling of this."

"How so?"

"I'm going to come down on it with everything I've got, and you're probably going to think it's because of what's happening between us. It's not."

"I know that." I met his worried gaze calmly. "You can't tolerate it in your state. This idiot just violated your house as much as mine. I understand."

"Damn, you *are* good."

"You've said that before."

He smiled ruefully at the deliberately smutty subtext, then shook his head. "I'm very serious about this, Jacqueline. Nobody gets to do this in my state."

"I respect that." I nodded.

"But that said," he continued, pulling me to him, "you are the woman in my life, and I am going to protect you as much as you will let me."

The woman in his life. We had moved a long way past old friends.

He bent and kissed the star necklace at my throat. It wasn't hot, but almost reverent.

"They come for you, they come for me, Jacqueline."

I leaned into his embrace and put my head on his shoulder for a moment. "It's probably retro and sexist, but I'm glad you're here."

"I won't rat you out to the local chapter of Badass Women of America."

We shared a little smile at that.

"Now, I have things to do, and I'm sure you do too." He stepped back and took a breath. "We'll talk later."

Will opened the door and strode over to de l'Evesque, his professional face firmly back in place.

The rest of the day is a blur. I know we had more people wanting to paint than there was graffiti to cover. So they just painted the whole front of the porch, which didn't need it—but that wasn't the point.

Some of Maeve's parishioners started bringing cookies and casseroles. A couple of TV trucks and the last print reporter standing, Marianne Manon, showed up at some point. She had seemed wryly amused by the whole Charity Slater cuchifrito, but this one hit hard.

After I gave her a couple of cool sentences on how grateful I was for my neighbors and their support, and my determination to just keep doing my job, she closed her notebook and patted me on the arm.

"You really okay?" Her blue eyes were sharp behind the retro cats-eye glasses.

"I'm going to be."

She nodded, her mouth a grim line. "There's support at Kunin if you need it."

"Thanks."

"Counselors jumped right in when some rotten little guy from a fundamentalist family was bullying Sophie because she has two moms. They don't mess around."

"Good to know."

Marianne's grim expression eased a bit. "This is a good town, Jaye. Good people."

"I sure think so."

"All right, off to another fun afternoon of informing and enlightening." She stuffed her notebook into a pocket of her serviceable dark purple parka and pulled the hood up, leaving a bunch of her curly wheat-colored hair trailing out, the same thing that happened to me when I didn't wear a clip. Major hair is a pain.

We smiled together. It was, I realized, entirely possible that we might become friends. I'd known her slightly back in the day, but even then, it was clear that she was staying and I wasn't. So neither of us had made much of an effort.

Different time, different world now.

Soon after I talked to Marianne, the staties, as well as Will and Fortescue, all cleared out at about the same time, Will at least probably for the sake of appearances. The TV reporters left too, after hitting Will up for a couple of fiery bites making clear prejudice was not welcome in his state, with no mention of the target of same.

They didn't ask why he was in Simpson on a Sunday morning, and he didn't volunteer anything. I wasn't fool enough to expect that to last.

By the time David drove up with Ryan, in what had originally been a very nice gesture toward giving me my naughty weekend, things were winding down, with the twins, the chiefs, and Sadie keeping me company in my office.

"What the hell happened?" David asked as Ryan started prospecting in the display of food in the old reception area. "It looks like somebody died."

"You'll hear it on the news soon enough," I said. "More graffiti."

"Yeah?"

"A swastika this time," Oliver spat.

"Backwards. Morons," Orville contributed.

"State police hate crimes is handling," Chief George assured him.

"Dammit, Jaye." David pulled me into a hug I didn't need or especially want by this point. "I'm sorry."

"It's not your fault. We've covered that." I backed away, but he kept a hand on my arm. I hadn't minded when Will did something similar earlier in the day, but I did now. It surprised me.

"I know. I just—"

"David," Orville said. Oliver just glared.

"This is not about you," Sadie told him quietly, words that he probably hadn't heard in years. "It may not even be about Jaye."

David nodded. "Sorry."

"The staties know what they're doing. Leave them to it," Chief George said.

"And the rest of us know what we're doing too," Chief Frank added. "Jaye here will probably have more protection than she wants for the next little while."

"But that's not really about me," I put in, with a nod to him.

"Exactly." Oliver's grim face softened a bit. "People want you to know that you're welcome and prejudice isn't."

"So you're probably going to see a lot of casseroles." Orville smiled, gazing at the spread in the reception area. "The wife is at a conference this week . . . I could probably take some of them off your hands . . ."

"Just leave me the green bean thing."

"Really?"

I wasn't sure who said it, but everyone was staring at me.

"Well, yeah. Western P-A Appalachian, remember? It's my comfort food."

Ryan went to bed with a tummy full of casserole and cookies, and a head full of reassurances from pretty much the entire cast on hand. That was good, because I didn't have much myself other than the usual hug and promise that anyone who wants her has to come through me. It was enough for the moment, if only because the incident had triggered all of the natural fighting instincts lurking within her half-Jewish, half-Scotch-Irish soul. Not in my house, you won't.

Once again, I had all the requests I could handle, playable and otherwise. Plus calls from media organizations from Boston to Halifax, all of whom got the same answer: I'm horrified that someone would resort to such a display of hate, and even more horrified that they have such a poor knowledge of history that they couldn't even get it right. And no, it won't change anything we do here.

Don't give the bastards an inch.

It was only when I hung up with the Boston station, which I remembered was a CNN affil, that I realized I'd better call Mom. I sure didn't want her finding out on the eleven o'clock, which she might well because she and Uncle Edgar return from their evening activities and complain about the news while comparing notes—and their local station tends to pick up stories like this because of the large Jewish community in the area.

With an anniversary request for Whitesnake (gotta wonder what *kind* of anniversary, don't you?) humming on my monitor, I dialed Mom's cell.

She picked up, sounding worried. "You all right? I'm at knitting club."

Sunday evening knitting club was more like the bad girls drinking and gossiping while purling a little, but we maintain the pretense. "You might see this on the news . . ."

Knitting club and the associated libation made it much easier to downplay and soothe her with the promise that everything was being handled. I didn't doubt I'd hear more about this later, but I'd checked the box for now, and it would do.

Probably the only time in my career I was glad to turn the monitor up and still hear Whitesnake.

At about ten, I had given in to sheer cheese and put on "The Glory of Love" for a milestone couple when my cell buzzed.

"That's about where I am right now," Will said.

"What? Drowning in Velveeta?"

He laughed and I joined in, my first real laugh since I saw it.

"Very funny, but not what I meant, Jacqueline."

"What did you mean?"

"Understand, I'm not going to do it, but I want to fight for you." His voice was gravelly, tired or emotional. "It's not just that nobody gets to do this in my state. Nobody gets to do this to *you*."

"I don't—" I had no idea what to say to that.

"You don't have to say anything. I just need you to know." He took a breath. "I respect your right to take on the world. But maybe you could let me reload your musket once in a while . . ."

"I can do that." My own throat was tightening a little. "Thank you for today."

"I didn't do much of anything."

"You were here, and you stood by me. It's all I needed."

"You and Ryan are okay for now?"

"Way better than okay, Knickerbocker."

# Chapter Twenty-Two

## It's What You Do Next

The next day started really well. Ryan was in full warrior queen mode, wearing a bright blue tee with a silver Star of David and the word "Chosen" under the black cardigan she favors for school, and the minute she and Xavier got out of the Jeep at Kunin, about a dozen kids, not all of whom I recognized as close friends, came up and greeted them with hugs.

Some of it was likely thanks to moms and dads who wanted to make sure that Ryan felt welcomed and protected, and told their children what to do; but I could tell that most of it was the kids taking care of their own. Stand-up guys come in all ages and genders, and thank G-d for them.

My red tee was a little more in-your-face than my girl's: *Hate Is Not a Family Value.*

When I got back to the station, I got a little encouragement too. An exec from the phone company whose name I just barely recognized from a parent meeting called, asking if we had a sponsor for our Storm Center coverage.

We didn't *have* Storm Center coverage yet. We had me, and Ryan if she had time to answer the phone, just scrambling cancellations as they came in—and reading them whenever I had a break.

But if the phone company wanted a naming sponsorship, we sure would have Storm Center coverage, and glad for it. My new friend and I quickly made a deal—very quickly, considering an ice storm was coming the next night—and she e-mailed the contract right over.

The check would come by the end of the week. We might actually make a go of this thing.

So I was feeling pretty good by around noon, as I sat in my office looking at the forecast for the ice storm and planning out how I would do the evening with Ryan fielding cancellations, take a sleep break in the wee hours, and come back live for morning drive. Maybe Rob could track some fairly generic breaks . . .

I wasn't the only one getting ready. When Will called, trying to sound casual but really making sure I was okay, he told me he'd just gotten off the phone with Emergency Management—and Public Works was next.

We might have managed a fun little talk anyway . . . except that the conversation ended with a surprisingly familiar shriek in the background: "You have to approve this one!"

Charity Slater. What now?

From the tone of his voice, I could tell he had ways to push her back that I could only dream of. I wished him joy—and wished I could watch.

Maybe half an hour before pickup time the phone rang again. Chief George. "Got an arrest. And it's worse than I thought."

"How's that?" My stomach lurched a little at the idea of what might be worse than our former NYPD lieu thought.

"It's just a local kid who says Spence Lyle paid him to do the graffiti. Fifty bucks extra for the swastika."

"Oh, hell."

"Oh, hell indeed. He's so dumb he had no idea what it meant."

"No." He was right. That was sickening on so many levels, I couldn't process it all.

"Schools aren't what they used to be, Jaye," the chief said wryly, not at all subtly pushing me toward an appropriate reaction.

"Guess not." I managed to get a dry note into my voice. "So much for the Common Core."

"It's okay. He'll have plenty of time to work on his education."

"Young enough for juvie?"

"Young and scared. We might be able to turn the little weasel in the right direction."

"That's something."

"Not nearly enough," growled the chief. "Now we have to figure out what to do about that creep Lyle."

"Hopefully something."

"Don't count on it, the way things are going. Sorry, Jaye."

"I know you're doing all you can. Love to Alicia."

"Thanks. She'll probably be over later in the week."

That night, I was just setting up the show when the phone lit up . . . business line, not the request line.

"Got any Perry Como?" asked a voice that sounded loud, and unbelievably old.

"What?"

"JJ, I'm making a request."

"Grandpa!" Holy hell, what was Seymour Metz doing with a radio and a phone?

"Yes. I just want you to know, I'm done with those blasted Gadflies. They talk like friends of Israel, and then they encourage people who attack Jews here. I may be old, but I'm not stupid."

"Not even a little."

"Damn right," he spat. "Sorry, JJ. They spent all that time talking about poor Edwin Anger ending up in the snowbank, practically saying you'd put him there—but not a word about the swastika, even though that's a real hate crime. And tonight they start this big thing on how that Hayman Stadler guy shouldn't go to jail for trying to bomb you and my little Rina."

"I'm not surprised. And he is old—he deserves some mercy."

"He deserves nothing," Grandpa Seymour growled. "I've got thirty years on the little snot, and I'm not out bombing people."

"True."

"We didn't fight a war to preserve democracy so those fools could run their hate machine."

"I'm not going to argue."

He gave me a rusty chuckle. "You've been trying for years—so have Alan and Sally. Honey, I had to see with my own eyes what bastards they are, sorry. I'm a stubborn fella."

"And a pretty great one." My throat was a little tight.

"Anyway, I'm done with those folks." He had an impish note in his voice. "I'm watching the Food Channel now. Alan and I can talk about things again."

"Pretty cool."

"Yep. You just take care now. Give little Rina a kiss for me. And play me some Perry if you've got it."

"For you, I will." I found "Impossible" buried on a Great Voices anthology CD, and put it on, dedicating it to A Stand-Up Guy in Charlestown.

My cell phone buzzed soon after, even as that silky, very nearly sedated, baritone was cruising to the end of the song. I picked up without even looking, figuring it would be one of the younger Metz men.

"Yes?"

"Why are you playing that for your ex?"

If Will had been angry or even a little possessive, he might well have earned himself a very nice set of walking papers right then. Instead, he sounded genuinely hurt. Not manipulatively, either.

"It's for his hundred-and-three-year-old grandfather, you big Dutch dodo bird."

"What?"

"Grandpa Seymour has decided he no longer loves the Gadflies, and he called to let me know. Of course, I played him a request."

Will laughed, happy and relieved. "Of course you did."

"A little green-eyed monster, Knickerbocker?" I could not let him just walk away from that.

"A lot of stupid, Jacqueline." Good answer, and better with an honest follow-up. "I suppose I'm afraid that you'll decide I'm part of your problem."

"What? This is my mess, not yours."

"It might be especially fun for them to come after the governor's girl."

"Is that—"

"How they'd think of it, right?"

"Right." I was really impressed by his care and caution. "This started long before we did, and it has nothing to do with you. You've been helpful and supportive the whole time . . . and I'm so glad you're here."

"I'm glad you're here."

"And," I went on, realizing it was easier to say without looking at him, "if you're starting to think of me as your girl, that's okay."

"It's probably sexist and old-fashioned. I'll try to come up with something better."

"Just make a request right now, and worry about that later."

"Good idea." He thought for a second, leaving nothing but the crackle of the cell line. "Do your U2 song, 'Pride in the Name of Love.' Seems like a good time to remind people of Dr. King."

"We can't kill our way out of it, we can only love our way out of it."

"That's the one."

Tim turned up an hour later, with the sweater Ryan had left in their living room, and something on his mind, I couldn't tell what. I poured him a cup of coffee, and motioned him to the still-significant selection of baked goods in the kitchenette.

"Hear they got an arrest in the vandalism." He had a couple of somebody's great-aunt's shortbread. Excellent choice.

"Yep. Stupid kid."

"Stupid kid paid by a very bad actor in Atlanta." Tim shook his head as he sat down in the guest spot. He looked like the end of a long day, still in his court suit, with his dark hair a little mussed and shadows under his brown eyes. "Hopefully this is the end of it."

"Your lips to God's ears."

"How are you doing?"

"Hanging in." I shrugged. "Just get up and do the job, you know."

"I do. Good thing." He smiled, but there was something a little rueful there, reminding me that he'd seen action in Iraq during what had started as a National Guard hitch to pay for law school. "Rob loves pitching in, you know."

"I love having him around."

"Good. Have him around more."

"Why?" I asked slowly.

Tim's smile widened. "I'm not trying to get rid of him. I'm trying to make him happy. He misses it, Jaye."

"Of course he does." I couldn't imagine what Rob had been through. A year after they married, the station went satellite and he had to figure out what else to do. Fortunately, he'd put himself through college cooking, and the restaurant owners were looking to retire. I always suspected they moved up their timetable and accepted a lower price because it was Rob, but I never asked. None of my business. I was just glad he ended up okay.

"Don't get me wrong, he loves the restaurant, loves raising Xavi, loves his life."

"But . . ."

"But since the station went under, there's always been this little gap, or missing spot . . . a look on his face sometimes when we listen to the radio in the car, just something."

"He was great, and he loved it. He *is* great."

"I think so too." Tim nodded. "So maybe you find reasons to need him more? Don't worry about the money-"

"I have to worry about the money. Pros do. But I did get a call from the phone company this morning asking to sponsor our Storm Center coverage."

"So . . ."

"So I can at least bring in some extra help in bad weather."

A grin from Tim. "Good start. I'll start praying for snow."

"Don't pray too hard, huh?"

# Chapter Twenty-Three
## Another Precinct Heard From

When there's a storm coming at night, everyone spends the day getting ready in their own way. That means the locusts sweeping up every scrap of bread and milk at the Grand Union, the town road crew loading up salt and sand, the fire department putting the chains on the truck tires, and the whole town giving off a crackly excited vibe I could feel in the drop-off line at Kunin.

Of course, one of those damn promos for Spence Lyle's show popped up as I was driving home. I muttered something that would not have made my grandmother proud and punched off the radio. This jackbooted feminist jock had no time for his garbage. Too much work to do.

I'd been smart enough to stock up on all of the basics earlier in the week, so I didn't need to dive into grocery store madness, but I still had plenty to do, especially with the new sponsorship. The cancellation spreadsheet was set up and the Storm Center format sheets were printing out when my phone rang.

Mom. Uh-oh.

"Jacqueline, why didn't you tell me it was so bad?"

I sat down at my desk. This was going to take a while. "It's not really that bad."

"Bad enough that it made the news here. Edgar's ready to come up there and—"

Of course he was. Uncle Edgar put in thirty years at the Mineral County sheriff's office, and though he had never drawn his weapon outside the firing range, he sometimes thought he was Kojak. "Talk him down, Mom. Talk yourself down. The cops have this."

"A couple of the girls at the community center watch the Gadfly Network. I know you didn't bury that talk show host in the snowman, but what's this about a pipe bomb?"

"The feds caught the guy." I do not need this right now.

"Honey, I'm worried about you and Ryan. I know you had to do this for David, but—"

"We're safe. Really. There's been an arrest, so it's just about over."

She was silent for a moment. I knew she was weighing her concern for me with her desire to continue enjoying the delayed teenage rebellion with Uncle Edgar and their crew in Palm Fountains.

"Aren't you getting ready for the Sadie Hawkins Dance?" I asked, hoping to give her a shove. She and her three best girlfriends, fellow retired teachers, had been wrangling for weeks about which of the gentlemen they were going to take—and two of the girlfriends were fighting over Uncle Edgar.

Mom let out a long breath. "I hear you."

"Yeah. Everything is really fine—practically the whole state is trying to protect us."

"The governor seemed to be pretty concerned."

"What?"

"He was in the piece on the news—looked really upset."

"He, uh, probably is."

She is not my mother for nothing. Of course, she knew about my old crush, but that was all she had known, until this exact moment. "You're seeing him."

"Um . . ."

Mom laughed. "Well, I'm not worried at all now." She turned away from the phone for a second. "Edgar, you can stop worrying about Jaye—she's dating the governor!"

I heard some kind of roar, probably a laugh, from across the room, and I knew I'd only have about ten more seconds with Mom.

"Thanks," I said irritably. "Please don't spread that around."

"Don't worry." She actually giggled. "I can keep a secret."

I was not optimistic.

"Jacks!" Uncle Edgar had grabbed the phone away. He is, you will know, the only human on earth permitted to call me Jacks. "You're going out with that Ten Bucks guy?"

"Ten Broeck. Yes."

"Good. He treating you right?"

"Very much so."

"Is he keeping you safe, or do I have to talk to him?"

Oh, hell no. Please not that. "No, no. He's talked to some of his friends in the feds, and everyone is taking a very good interest in watching out for Ryan and me."

I didn't have to see Uncle Edgar to know his tense scowl was easing into a smile. "Good. Ryan's all right?"

Uncle Edgar had two sons with Aunt Mellie, a nurse who had left him for a urologist shortly before he retired—just keep walking past that!—but I was the closest he had to a daughter, and Ryan to a granddaughter.

"She's doing great. Warrior queen all the way."

"Why don't we videophone Sunday night?" he asked. Uncle Edgar is also almost as tech-savvy as Ryan, which always amuses and amazes me.

"Sounds great." The tech-savvy reminded me of another area of his expertise. "Hey, do you know much about brake lines?"

He chuckled. "I've only replaced dozens of them in my hot rods over the years."

"Thought so."

"Why?"

"A friend's brakes failed the other night. He thought maybe it was because something broke in the cold."

Uncle Edgar made the growly little noise that meant he was thinking. "What kind of car?"

"Smallish American-made sedan."

"So not a heavy-duty vehicle . . . and not a sports car, either."

"No."

"Car wasn't driven for a few days in very cold weather?"

"Yep."

"It can happen. But his mechanic should take a good look at it."

"They are."

Uncle Edgar was silent for a moment, and then: "This your governor guy?"

"Um, yeah."

"His mechanic should take a *really* good look at it, Jacks."

"I'll tell him."

"Good. He seems like a good guy. Is he?"

"Really good. Not sure where this is going yet, though," I added quickly.

"You don't have to be. It's okay to have a little fun."

"Speaking of fun—are Mom's friends still fighting over you?"

He laughed, the full-out big guffaw that I love. "Oh, yes. I'm probably going to go stag to the Sadie Hawkins to avoid all the drama."

"Edgar!" I heard my mother snap in the background.

"Judy wants you back. Don't kill any more talk show hosts, huh?"

I managed a laugh.

"Seriously, be careful, Jacks. Love you."

"Love you."

"He's enjoying this way too much," Mom said irritably.

"You'd rather he were getting serious about one of them?" Not that he would; Uncle Edgar was having a blast being one of the relatively few single, healthy, and fun men in town.

"Oh, hell no."

"So chill." It was a relief to be talking her down about the latest little donnybrook at Palm Fountains. "I've got to get ready for an ice storm. See you on videophone Sunday."

"Okay."

We paused for a long second.

"Be careful, Jacqueline. I love you."

"I love you, Mom."

I put down the phone feeling much better about them, at least. Lord knows they deserved some fun.

Mom had raised me on her own after my father left for a woman in the next town over and promptly died in a car crash. I was six. She wasn't thirty. It hadn't been easy, even on the relatively good and reliable income of a middle school teacher.

And I wasn't an easy kid, completely uninterested in most of the conventional little-girl things, determined to be something different and better than what was available in Punxsy. Even when

I was growing up, most girls still became teachers or nurses, or took some nebulous business job with the idea that their real vocation was marriage and family. That wasn't me, and I knew it.

I needed to be someone before I was someone's wife, and damn sure before I was someone's mother. Not a common attitude; feminism—second-wave, third-wave, wave at Momma as she marches—never made a big dent in Appalachia. And make no mistake: western Pennsylvania is still Appalachia, just slightly better upholstered.

But Mom backed me up when I took the partial scholarship at Pitt instead of the full ride at community college, and even when I turned down a spot in a graduate writing program to stay in radio. That one hurt, though—she still doesn't understand why I gave up the chance to get an advanced degree.

Still, she knew I was where I belonged, and that was enough for her. And when, a couple of months before David was diagnosed, she and Uncle Edgar moved to Palm Fountains, I knew they were where they belonged. She came up a couple of times to support us during the chemo, and I appreciated it . . . but it was almost as good for me to know she was happy and safe in her own life.

I'd been her little protector from the time my father left, after all, and knowing she was okay meant one less thing for me to worry about. I also didn't need to deal with anyone else trying to help, which, honestly, would have just made it harder.

The doorbell rang.

Jerusha was standing there with a box and a rueful smile.

"What?"

"I think somebody tried to send you something nice—but thanks to the feds, it may not be very nice now."

"Okay." I took the medium-sized box. "Still way better than the last package I got."

"I'm just glad I get to hand it off and keep going this time."

We shared a wry laugh and I carried it inside. The box had been opened and resealed, marked "SAFE" in Sharpie.

It was from Wicked Maple Farms in Barre, a little shipping cooler with two pints of ice cream. Or what had been ice cream before it sat out long enough for some fed to make sure it was safe.

Maple Vanilla and Triple Chocolate Nirvana, with a card:

*"Thought you and Ryan might need this. Will."*

Better than flowers. I grabbed my phone and sent a quick text.

*"Thank you note to come, but the ice cream just arrived."*

*"It was supposed to be there yesterday. Melted?"*

*"Melted and curdled. Feds checked it out. No bomb, but we can't eat it."*

*"I'll owe you."*

*"Still really sweet. Literally."*

*"Easy to be sweet to you. Talk later. Busy with the storm here."*

*"Good luck."*

We were all going to need that.

# Chapter Twenty-Four

## Sleepless in Simpson—and Montpelier

Sharon Snow, yes, really the name with which she was born, runs a small Burlington-based weather service. We, and the other remaining local stations, use her for the same reason she gives us way more than we pay for: we're all dinosaurs hoping that this asteroid isn't the Big One. In addition to being a duly certified meteorologist with a lovely warm vocal quality, she also possesses an eerie skill for calling storms.

The Burlington and northern Massachusetts TV stations were going moderately nuts about this one, but Sharon just laughed when I talked to her during the afternoon weather feed. "It's going to be nasty for the night, but by midday tomorrow, everyone will be back to work."

"Think so?"

"I call it the perfect storm. Everyone's got enough warning to get out of the way, it messes up a boring weeknight, and it melts before it becomes a big issue in the morning. Oh, and we all get to sleep late."

"Not all of us."

She laughed again, and the silky tone reminded me that she had a nice little voice work operation too. "Me neither. We'll get ours later."

"Right we will."

"Well, at least the kids will be at school tomorrow." Sharon has twin sons, seniors in South Burlington.

"Yay for mommy nap time."

We were both laughing again as I hung up.

Just as Sharon had called it, about an hour after pickup, the rain started, and before the temperatures started dropping, I sent Ryan over to tell the guys that they were welcome to come over and stay for the storm, since we had a generator.

Everyone trooped into the little reception area a few minutes later, Tim with a box of candles, just in case, and Rob with blankets and quilts.

"You'd think the hearth room would be warm, but when there aren't a lot of people, it can actually get pretty cold unless I want to start a really big fire."

"And we still have plenty of casseroles and baked goods," I reminded him. "Most of it's in the kitchenette downstairs."

"Party!" Xavier and Ryan cheered.

"No TV or video games if we lose power," I warned them. "But you can prospect around the station and as long as you don't mess with the air product, you can play with anything you find."

"Cool!"

"Great!"

Rob and I laughed, watching our kids run off to sift through our collective past.

Tim shook his head. "Hope you don't live to regret that when they build a car out of the old reel-to-reel decks."

The phone rang again then, and Tim picked up.

"You doing cancellations now?" he asked, covering the receiver.

"Yep, going on early—"

"Hey, since we'll all be here in the morning," Rob said, "let's do the show live."

"Live and local is always better." I winked at Tim.

"Always." Rob didn't notice the wink.

"I can even pay you a little since the phone company is sponsoring cancellations."

Rob nodded, understanding how important that was to me. Really, to us, because we're both pros. "I'm in, then."

And the rest, as they say, is history.

Rob took the evening shift while I got the kids fed and settled. I took the night, and we got back together at five AM to take it through to the end.

Tim and the kids became the Storm Center desk, fielding calls and entering listings in the computer. It was busy through the late afternoon as the church and community events were canceled, and again between eight and nine as the first batch of school calls came in.

As the night wore on, the weather got worse, and things got quieter and eerier. Real ice storms, even in Vermont, are rare, but they're extremely dangerous when they do happen. Most civilians are smart enough to get off the roads and stay put, but then come the power outages, and the emergencies, and it gets really bad and scary as the storm wears on. And quiet. Way too quiet.

In that silence, people need their radios more than ever. Sometimes, the battery-powered radio is the only friendly and safe voice they will hear until the lights come back. I'm pretty proud to be somebody's lifeline, even if that lifeline comes with bad '80s ballads.

That fact takes the edge off. So does knowing that my child is safely asleep right upstairs. When I got trapped in the city, even though I knew Ryan was just fine in the suburbs with David, I missed her horrifically.

Well past one, the calls had tapered off to nothing, and I was seriously considering putting on the satellite and letting it roll so I could sleep for an hour or two, when my phone buzzed.

"Jacqueline."

"Hey, Knickerbocker." I couldn't help smiling at the sound of his voice, even if he didn't sound especially happy.

"Heard your last break. Staying up for the storm?"

"Some people don't have power. I might bag it for a couple of hours in the really dead time, but I don't feel right leaving people alone in the dark."

"Good for you."

"Iced in tonight?" I thought about asking for a couple of sound-bites for morning, but there was something off in his tone.

"Pretty much. Left the storm command center to get some sleep—and get away from Charity Slater's fake concern act . . . only to bug out of the Residence because of a carbon monoxide scare."

"Uh-oh."

"Yeah." He cleared his throat, kept his voice cool and wry. "Closer call than I like. If Fortescue hadn't insisted on installing a separate detector that isn't connected to the main power line, I wouldn't have known about it."

"Scary." Understatement of the year. In a bad winter, we probably lost a dozen people that way. The idea that one of them might have been Will—I could not let myself go there.

"Well, at least I can speak with authority at the next CO safety newser."

"There's that." I tried for dry too. I wasn't a hundred percent sure what to say, but since he'd called me with that off-balance note in his voice, I decided he needed a little tending, whether he wanted it or not. "You okay?"

"Okay enough." He let out a long breath. "Hate being alone in hotel rooms."

"Me too." It had happened maybe once every winter when I was jocking in the city, and I'd always had a hard time sleeping away from Ryan and David. The quiet was just too weird. "I always missed my daughter when I was snowed in."

Will gave a tiny laugh. "Called both my kids. Just a little rain where they are and neither understands why their boring father is unhappy about a hotel night."

"It's still fun for them."

"Yeah. They're right, too. If you're gonna be in a hotel, it should be for fun. Nothing worse than being alone in a big white room."

"Especially tonight, probably."

"Something like that. Talk to me, Jacqueline."

"I know the voice and all," I started, a little embarrassed at what I thought he was looking for, "but I'm really not good at dirty talk—it always comes out silly."

"I don't want dirty talk when we can't do anything about it." He tried for a wry chuckle, but when he spoke again, his voice was surprisingly small and vulnerable. "Tell me a story. About you. How you got to be you, what it was like growing up, anything you want to tell me."

"Okay." I thought for a moment, and decided this poor guy needed a laugh. "So you know I'm a western Pennsylvania Appalachian."

"You keep telling me that. I'm not sure I believe it."

"Go ahead and check my background. I really did grow up in Punxsutawney."

"Groundhogs. So that's why you like woodchucks."

"Well played."

"Gotta keep up." He sounded a little better.

"Anyway, so I did a lot of musicals in school."

"You sing?"

"Not anymore."

"Too bad. Okay."

"And one year I was in *Man of La Mancha*, which, you will know, is about the Cervantes hero . . ."

"Don Quixote?"

"That's the one. Unless you're in Punxsy, where the pronunciation is a little different. One of my castmates had exactly one line, and most nights, despite the director chanting 'Don Quixote' at us all day, it came out . . ."

"Yeah?"

"Behold, Donkey Hotey!"

Will laughed, an unexpected and wonderful howl. "You don't have an accent."

"Had to lose it for the job. Nobody wants a Queen of the Night who says Donkey Hotey."

"I guess."

"And nobody wants to hear a jock who pronounces the number four as a two-syllable word: fo-wer."

He didn't laugh this time.

"I still do that sometimes," I admitted. "And announce the Pittsburgh football score as the Stillers."

"Jacqueline," he said slowly, "I'll take you any day and twice on Sunday, accent or no."

"Thanks, Knickerbocker. Gotta watch out for Donkey Hotey."

He chuckled. "Thank you for taking the edge off."

"Glad to."

Will started to speak and broke off in a yawn. "I might actually be able to sleep now."

"Good thing."

"Still rather be with you."

"So maybe we do a nice grownup getaway some Saturday."

"Sold. I'll check my calendar and you check yours."

I smiled at that. "You already know where I'll be."

"Live and local. The Queen of the Night."

"That's me, babe."

"Good night, Jacqueline."

"Sleep well, Knickerbocker."

# Chapter Twenty-Five

## What Ice Storm?

People can make fun of Sharon Snow for being gauche enough to use her real, perhaps overly appropriate, name on the air, but they can't make fun of her predictions. She absolutely called this one.

Ruined a bunch of evening events, but everybody was back to work by midmorning.

It was above freezing by seven thirty, so we knew it was going to be quick. Rob and I went live together until nine thirty, reading school delays and whatever else was left. After a quick nine thirty news update, I piled the kids into the Wrangler (which the helpful little darlings had cleaned and scraped with expectations of treats later) and took them up to Kunin on schedule for their own two-hour delay.

By the time I got back, Rob had turned it back to the satellite, neatened up the studio, and left the board in apple-pie order for my show, with the commercial log neatly folded to my first page, and the pen lined up beside it. Exactly what every pro does for the next guy; no matter how much of a slob you may be in real life (and I'm a mess!) you show that respect to your colleagues.

It was really nice to *have* a colleague again.

We crossed as he walked out of the studio, looking like I felt: exhausted, proud, and happy, and just stood there smiling at each other for a second.

"Good job," I said.

"You too."

When you're doing it in a big fancy studio with a set schedule and a company format, plus a program director, three consultants, and a sales department telling you what they want to hear, it's easy to forget how wonderful it is to just spin some songs for people who need them.

It hadn't hit me until just then that I really, really liked putting on a show without the desk jockeys. Nobody had told me what exact words my target audience wanted to hear, or which songs tested best, or why it was a very bad idea to make cultural references that millennials might not get, in most of a year.

Maybe there was something to be said for being out here in East Hell.

Rob grinned at me. "It was pretty great. Call me for the next storm."

"Oh, I will."

Another silly, sleepy shared smile. The most wonderful thing about this business has always been the people we work with, and Rob was one of the best ever. Now, *is* one of the best ever.

Only another jock can understand what it's like to walk out there on the wire every day and charm their socks off, hoping you hit the marks and sure that there's some freak out there hating you. Not to mention that only another jock will understand how proud you are when you have a weather alert and still manage to get in all the spots and finish the hour on the second.

Usually, that's when the desk jockey shows up and tells you that he didn't hear you mention the website.

No more desk jockeys here.

"I think I'm glad I'm back," I said, realizing how silly and blurry it sounded.

"I know I am."

As we nodded at each other, we were both very well aware that the walls were holding us up.

"I'm going to go nap now," Rob said finally. "Want me to pick up the kids?"

"Nah. I'll set an alarm. I can sleep later than you because I don't have to do dinner prep."

His eyes as widened as much as they were capable of doing. "Dinner. Yeah."

"Watch out, jackbooted feminist jocks, media liberals, and woke whiners—I'm coming for you!"

Rob jolted awake. So did I.

"What is THAT?" he asked.

"Spence Lyle. His show's on my sat service, so his stupid promos show up sometimes." I sighed. "He really is that bad."

"Terrible. Bet he killed Anger to get his spot. Only way anybody would put that on the air."

"No kidding."

"Let me guess. You're the jackbooted feminist jock."

"Oh, yeah."

"Ugh. If you just ignore him, he'll get bored and give up."

"I hope you're right."

Rob managed a little smile. "I'm always right."

"Modest, too."

We headed off to our respective naps, and I really did feel better by the time my alarm went off. Better still when I checked the station e-mail and found about ten notes praising our storm work.

The ones that really counted were from a dad at Kunin who told me they'd lost power last night, and his family had stayed by the woodstove listening to the radio—and a clearly older listener who said we kept her from being alone in the dark.

The phone company was happy too, and wanted to talk about a more expansive sponsorship plan next winter.

Yeah, Rob likes to say "No Bucks, No Buck Rodgers," but at that exact moment, the money wasn't my main motivator.

My phone also had a text from Will, sent a few hours before: *"Thanks for making time for me in the middle of the storm last night. Wish you were here."*

I texted back:

*"Just woke up and got this. Miss you, Knickerbocker."*
*"I'd like to wake you up right about now. Miss you, Jacqueline."*

I was smiling and humming whatever nebulous power ballad the satellite was playing as I walked out the door for pickup. The kids were bouncing like popcorn the way they do on the day after a storm.

Sharon Snow would probably tell me there is no atmospheric reason for it, but the fact is that changes in the weather make kids just *wired*. They'd been crackling with energy in the morning, and were every bit as jacked up when I got them.

That was fine, because Rob and I had planned for this.

In the wake of the storm, I had one other important thing to do, and I'd waited until the kids were with me because they deserved a treat too. Rob would have tagged along if he hadn't been so exhausted and behind in dinner prep.

They knew as soon as I turned right instead of left out of the traffic circle at Kunin.

"Charlemagne?" Ryan asked.

"Can I give him the candy this time, RyansMom?"

"Not yet." I shook my head at Xavier. "He's still a huge wild animal even if he's a really nice guy. But we'll go see how he and the transmitter are doing."

Ryan and Xavier were happy to point out that the transmitter had come through the storm just fine, and to attempt once again to explain to me the finer points of how it was wired. I had less than no interest in this, but I listened attentively. They had clearly been studying the schematics for the station, as well as their Snap Circuit toys, and it was clear to me that they could rewire the place from scratch if necessary.

I swallowed a smile as I locked the shack. One of the first places that big radio operations looked to cut in consolidations was engineering. It wasn't unusual for a cluster of five or so large city radio stations to share one engineer. But WSV had two!

Out in the clearing with my crew, I took the candy out of my pocket and unwrapped it, holding out my hand. The sound started immediately, and became louder, light crashing and crunching resolving into the heavy clomp and smash of a huge animal's approach.

Charlemagne stood there for a second. He knew the kids, but because they were smaller than the other two-legged creatures he's used to, different, and therefore unpredictable, he always paused for a second to be sure they were okay. They knew, and they just stood a few feet behind me as always, watching in awe.

Soon enough, he walked slowly over to me and took the candy, watching us as he chomped.

He never stayed for a second piece when Ryan and Xavier were there, which was fine. It was enough for us all that he came.

For a few moments, he stood there studying us all, huge and majestic. Then he turned and started away.

This time, he was far enough out of range that there was at least a little question about what happened. Not enough for Ryan and Xavier, though, who heard the rumble and squeal and started giggling.

I'm going to assume that Charlemagne was just startled a little by the kids' reaction, not embarrassed, because he suddenly just ran off, faster than you think something that big can move. But who knows with moose?

"Ma, the moose farted!"

"You don't know that—" I started sternly if hopelessly.

Xavier gave me the standard tween look of disdain. "Ryans-Mom, trust me, that was flatulence."

What do you do with that, except start laughing?

We were still howling as I herded them into the back.

"Now when you tell this story at school tomorrow," I said in my best professional voice, making significant eye contact in the rearview mirror.

They both tried to look innocent.

"I was ten once, remember? I'd tell the story for sure."

"Okay." Unplanned but undeniable unison.

"Just tell Ms. Featherstone the moose passed gas."

Ryan sighed. "Fart is a playground word."

I was pretty sure that was a direct quote. Me or Ms. Featherstone, though, it was hard to say.

Xavier snickered. "We *know* that. It's not like we're six, RyansMom."

I nodded gravely, well aware of the risks of offending the dignity of the tween. The giggling replays of the incident continued from the back seat until I got us back to the Plaza. Rob was writing out the specials board when we walked up, and Xavier ran up to his dad.

"The moose farted!"

Rob, his eyes still shadowy and a little unfocused, looked up at his small adorable son, then to me and my small adorable daughter, and shrugged. "Just another fun day here in the Green Mountain State."

"Don't tell Travel and Tourism."

# Chapter Twenty-Six

## We All Hang Together

Thursday started pretty normal. Kunin was open—and on time yet, so I dropped the kids off and came back to the office to get to work on all the things that got lost in the storm and the chaos and exhaustion afterward.

Midmorning, Chief George showed up with two fancy pretend cappuccinos from the mini-mart, a bizarre choice that I quickly realized was intended as some kind of sympathy offering.

"Jaye, I'm sorry." He shook his head. "The DA says there's nothing she can do." He opened the little flap on the top of his cup and took a sniff. "It's toffee mocha flip. Not a damn thing real or natural in it, and insanely tasty."

The little-boy pleasure in his face deterred me from screaming or throwing things like I wanted to do. "Yeah?"

"Yeah. I used to get these damn things at a bodega in Bed-Stuy when I was working the projects. Once in a while, you need something that is absolutely fake, loaded with sugar and caffeine, and basically total crap."

I laughed. I couldn't help myself, and I took up the cup. "Thanks."

"You're going to need it today." He took a sip of his and shook his head. "Here's what we've got. Anger was dead from a hemorrhagic stroke before he went in that snowman. And there's nothing in the tox but a bunch of fancy prescription drugs. He had a way better prescription plan than most of us do."

"So that little creep Lyle just takes over his show and walks away scot-free to spew . . ."

"She's not going to have him extradited from Georgia for abuse of a corpse, harassment, and vandalism."

"Even with the hate-crime enhancement?"

The chief shook his head slowly. "She's got a limited budget and a terrible opioid problem up in White River. She can put away a bunch of drug dealers for the price of pursuing this, so yeah, it's over."

"It's not over at all. He's got every crazy moron within the sound of his voice sending me postcards . . . and worse."

"I know. And the feds are taking a good strong interest in that, even if the Gadfly Network is trying to make it about one crackpot little old man." He took another sip of his drink and a smile tugged at the corners of his mouth. "I hear a few calls have been made behind the scenes."

"It wouldn't surprise me. But I know enough about all of this to know that until one of them hurts someone, probably—hopefully!—me, nobody's going to get charged. And even then, it's usually not a heavy case unless they succeed in killing someone."

The chief's eyes narrowed as he turned his cup in his hands. "You also know enough to know that pretty soon people get bored and move on to the next target. You're playing it just right, low-key, not giving them anything to react to, so it will calm down soon."

"I hope so." I opened the flap on my toffee mocha flip and sniffed it. It did smell awfully good, even though I knew it was a slurry of calories, chemicals, and heaven only knew what.

"And we're doing what we can. You know the school resource officer at Kunin is going out at recess with Ryan's class."

"I didn't."

"She is. I don't think most of these mopes would really take it beyond the comment section, never mind find the energy to come here, but Marge needs a little fresh air anyway."

"Thanks."

"Haters are everywhere, Jaye. You were a New Yorker long enough to know. We don't give in to it. We just keep doing what we do."

"Yeah." I took a breath and reached for the plastic container of cookies. Goodwill offering. I wasn't mad at *him*, after all. "Ryan's grandpa baked another batch of hamentaschen."

"The little hat ones?"

"Yep. Raspberry jam this time."

"Yum." He took one with a teasing smile. "Only Jews would celebrate vanquishing someone who tried to exterminate them with a cookie."

"They tried to kill us, they failed, let's eat."

We laughed together, and I thought of Alan Metz grinning as he quoted that very maxim to me at Passover two years ago. When David and I had been trying to pretend everything was okay through the holiday because Alan had just had an angioplasty—

"Chief, you said Anger was on a bunch of expensive prescriptions?"

"Yeah. The blue pill, some fancy blood thinner, the high-end acid reflux thing . . ."

"Fancy blood thinner?"

"Yeah, you've seen the ads—people jogging by the sea with a big orange and yellow swoosh and a '60s Motown riff on the name."

"That's the one David's dad took for the first six months after his angio. Even with his state retiree plan, they wouldn't pay for any longer than that."

Chief George looked at me. "What are you thinking?"

"I don't know. I just know that while Alan was on it, he didn't even want to hug anyone for fear of getting horrible bruises."

"Because his blood was so thin."

"Yeah, and he kept counting his pills every time he took them, because one extra dose would kill him."

The chief put down his hamentaschen. I put down my pretend cappuccino.

"How?" he asked.

"I'm guessing a brain bleed . . . a stroke."

"So if, say, someone wanted to make Edwin Anger a martyr . . ."

"One expensive pill."

"I don't know if the ME counted the pills they found in Anger's room," he said with a thoughtful expression.

"I wonder if they fingerprinted the bottles."

"Probably wouldn't take much for Lyle to sneak one from it when Anger was busy."

"Or that little travel box," I suggested. "If you figure they'll be dead by nighttime, there's no problem in stealing the evening pill."

"Looks like I need to talk to the DA again."

"Maybe. I suppose she and the ME won't be happy-"

Chief George shook his head. "Actually, they'll both be thrilled. DA told me there was something she didn't like about all of this. And Dr. Derevenko said she just couldn't land it, and so she couldn't rule it homicide. That's why it was undetermined."

"Glad to make their day." I took a sip of the drink, and holy hell, it was astonishingly good, even though I knew it was full of all manner of food chemistry fakery.

"See? It is that good." The chief grinned and raised his cup to me. "Hopefully, we'll have something a little better to celebrate soon.

The authorities didn't give me anything to celebrate that day, but my old partner did a pretty good job. About half an hour before pickup, Rob walked in with a plate of cinnamon rolls and set them on my desk. "I have a proposition."

"We already know what team you're on, sweetheart." I grinned. "And Tim would kill me."

He grinned right back. "Will Ten Broeck would kill me."

"At least dent you a little."

"Uh-huh." Rob took a roll and sat down in the side chair. "So Tim isn't good for much in the restaurant, but he can *mise en place* like a maniac."

"Yeah?" It did not surprise me that the very precise Tim would be a master of setting up a kitchen, even if I wasn't sure why this was important.

"And I really, really want to do a morning show again."

"It was pretty fun the other day, wasn't it?"

Rob smiled wistfully around his roll. "Hell, yeah."

"I even got the kids to school on time."

"You could skip out after the seven thirty and be back for the eight the way the schedule is at Kunin."

"True." I sighed. I hated having to tell him this, but he had to know it was true. "I still can't afford to pay you a real salary. The phone company Storm Center sponsorship gets us live coverage when the weather's bad, but—"

"Hence the proposition."

"Okay . . ."

"Take me on as a partner. I'll run the morning show and handle spots and production. You do news, the night show, and the executive stuff. We both handle sales as we can. Fifty-fifty split after breakeven."

For a long second, I couldn't speak, my throat thick with emotion. But finally I found my voice. "I love it."

"Yeah?" His eyes lit up.

"Yeah." I smiled, even though my own eyes were damp. "You know we're not going to get rich."

"Who cares? I've got the restaurant, you've got the voice work, and we'll make enough to take care of our families while we still play radio."

"All that counts."

"Yep. We can do this. It'll be fun."

"Way better than going it alone."

"Way better than listening to you every night and wishing I was on."

"Yep. And Ben Franklin was right."

Rob knew the quote too. "If we do not hang together, we will surely hang separately."

"That's the one." I held out my hand. "Deal."

"Deal."

We shook.

Rob nodded to the plate. "You haven't even eaten any of the cinni rolls yet."

"You didn't have to bribe me."

"No, but as your partner, I'm going to insist you take a little better care of yourself."

I hadn't intended to have one after that awful cappuccino thing, but everyone was right. I was too damn thin. I pulled off a roll and clinked with Rob's. "To our new partnership."

"Good health and good luck."

"What else is there?"

We smiled together.

After a couple of bites, he nodded to my desk. "Have Orville do the papers, and we'll do some kind of woo-hoo remote to start the morning show."

"Sugaring week starts Monday," I reminded him. "School vacation week too."

"Sweet start." He thought about it. "Probably take a little time to work out the engineering."

"Yup."

"Tuesday? That's dark night at the restaurant, so I don't have to rush as much."

"Yeah. We can post on social media and the website now, and start getting the word out."

Rob laughed. "I know you like to be savvy and all, but remember where we are."

"Okay. You tell Sadie, I'll tell Orville, and everyone will find out."

"That's more like it."

# Chapter Twenty-Seven

## Shabbat Shalom, Simpson

And then it was Friday night again. I was walking David and Ryan out the door, when the crowd came.

This crew didn't have muskets or a beef.

It was a good two dozen people, walking over from Saint Michael's with Maeve in the lead, flanked by Sadie and Oliver, with Orville and the chiefs a step behind. Marianne was toward the back, with her wife, and also a notebook. There were other familiar faces, but I couldn't really process how many.

"We're hoping to join you in celebrating Shabbat," Maeve said, holding out two hand-painted ceramic candlesticks with dark blue candles. "The Sunday school kids made these for you."

I accepted them with shaky hands, and just stared at her. For the second time in two days, I was too choked up to speak.

It took me at least a full fifteen seconds to find words as I stood there, just smiling and silenced by the huge ball of emotion and unshed tears in my throat.

I never imagined anything like this. However much I reminded myself it wasn't really about me, I was still the one standing there on the porch with all of this love and support focused on me and my family. It was overwhelming.

Then Xavier, who had been in the back of the group with Tim, dashed up the porch to meet Ryan and exchange hugs and high-fives, and I took a breath. It was enough to get my vocal cords working again, and I didn't figure anyone would be offended that my eyes were a little wet.

"Good heavens. Thank you so much. Please, come in."

Our family candles were burning in the kitchenette downstairs, so nobody needed to worry about duplicating efforts. Everyone packed into the reception and office area, probably the most people the station had ever held at one time, and I set up the new holders, small beautiful pottery stands painted in swooshes of blue, with wobbly and perfect silver Stars of David on them, then turned to hug Maeve.

"This is—" I started.

"We wanted to make it very, very clear to you that hate is not welcome in Simpson—and you are." She was all lit up, in full minister mode.

"I really don't know what to say."

"Just smile and say thank you, dear," Sadie advised, coming up and enfolding me in a hug. "Sometimes it's not all about you, or even mostly about you."

"Exactly." Orville and Oliver spoke in unison, and glared at each other. I hugged them too, and they moved on to shake hands with David, who looked like I felt.

"And this is why I love this place," Alicia said as she worked her way over to me. "Vermonters may dress like rednecks, but they're the first ones to call out prejudice in any form."

"Got that," I agreed as we hugged. "I'm starting to love plaid and fleece."

She laughed. "Let's not take it too far."

Between more hugs and handshakes, with people I knew well and some I didn't, I rummaged a packet of matches out of the old receptionist's desk. As I turned toward the candles, I was stunned to see who was standing in front of me.

Howard and Harold. No weapons, and no greatcoats. Just a couple of older guys in ancient parkas and gimme hats.

"We're not happy Edwin's gone," Harold said slowly. "But we don't hold with prejudice."

"My grand-daddy didn't die fighting the Nazis to have some fool paint swastikas over here."

I stared. I hadn't even been sure Howard could speak, never mind share something like that. All I could manage was a hand-shake and a "Thank you."

Harold, who was at least as stunned as I was by Howard, shook my hand too, and patted my arm. "You're all right for a liberal, Mrs. Jordan."

After that, there was nothing to do but light candles. I struck the match, and Maeve and I shielded our eyes as Jewish women traditionally do. Alicia, Sadie, and the other women in the room joined us as the men followed David and bowed their heads.

I'd have to explain later that we don't look at the candles until after the prayer because it's a work-around: you aren't supposed to enjoy the blessing of candlelight before the prayers, but you're not supposed to do any work—even light candles—on the Sabbath. So we light them before the Shabbat prayer. Way more than any-one needs to know right now.

I nodded to Ryan, and she began the prayer in her perfect Hebrew. Her clear voice filled the room, the ancient blessing call-ing G-d in, and bringing us into the warmth of Shabbat. It's not just a religious thing; it's a community and culture thing. We're here and we're together. United.

When she finished, I turned to the crowd. "Thank you all for coming here. It means more than you know. I am so glad you came to share our tradition with us. You have made us feel welcome in a way that I could not have imagined."

"It's a *mitzvah*," David added, sounding very choked up, and without my skills to get past it. "A true blessing."

"It is for us too." Maeve beamed at her crew. "And now, let's leave the lady to her show and go have a nice Sabbath drink at Janet's!"

"Hear, hear!" the twins cheered, and the crowd proceeded out. Looked like Rob was going to have a very good night too.

Ryan and David were last to the door.

"Feeling better about everything, kiddo?" I asked her.

"A lot. Xavi told me something good was up, but he didn't say what."

"Been a while since we had a good surprise," David said, making significant eye contact over her head.

"Something like that."

We hugged, and it wasn't weird or awkward as it had been for most of the last year and a half. It was just comfortable. Guess we were finding our balance too.

"Have a terrific weekend," I told him as I pulled back—and meant it.

David grinned. "You too."

"I suspect I just might."

"Plans again?"

"No big drama, just dinner at Janet's."

"But dinner at Janet's with . . ."

"Her man, Dad," Ryan put in with a laugh, flouncing off toward the car.

"I don't know if he's my man," I admitted.

David gave me a warm and rueful smile. "He's damn lucky if he is, Jaye."

Make that three times I couldn't figure out what to say.

"We made the right decision," he said quickly. "But I'm really glad you're happy. He might even deserve you."

"I don't know where it's going, but it's good. I'll take it."

"Dad! Time to go!"

We parental units laughed, and David patted my arm before running down the stairs to his girl.

My phone buzzed as I turned back inside. Will.

*"Shabbat Shalom, Jacqueline."*

*"Thanks."*

*"All okay there?"*

*"Better than okay. Most of town just came to light candles."*

*"Good town. Good people."*

*"Hell, yeah."*

*"Tell me more tomorrow. I have to schmooze the Environmental Committee tonight. At least Charity doesn't come to anything green."*

*"You can schmooze me tomorrow."*

*"Schmooze is not the verb I had in mind."*

*"So come up with a better one."*

*"Don't worry. I will."*

Of course, I was smiling a little as I set up the studio. But I had some debts to pay before fun time tomorrow. I pulled out "Thank You," the Boyz II Men version, and "A Fifth of Beethoven."

I opened the show cold:

"You're all probably aware that it's been an interesting couple of weeks here at WSV. Some days more interesting than others. Well, tonight, the people of Simpson gave me the best moment of my career, and probably the second best of my life—sorry, but my daughter's birth wins all ties.

"You made me feel safe and welcome—and even loved—after a couple of weeks in which a few others did their best to make me feel anything but. And you showed me that Vermonters really do take care of their own, and that they have a very warm and open definition of their own.

"I'm honored that you've included me in the circle. I'm honored that you shared the Sabbath with me and my family tonight.

"*Shabbat Shalom*, Simpson."

Then I hit the song. Admittedly, it was a little R&B for this crowd, but it was the right message: absolute thanks for the love and support, delivered in perfect harmony, as so few things are in this world.

After that, I turned to the usual night full of requests, happy to give my listeners what they wanted for a while, even if it was "Afternoon Delight" for a couple marking the carefully unspecified anniversary of an event more than forty years ago.

I slipped the "Fifth of Beethoven" in between a couple of slow dance songs in the eight o'clock hour, figuring David and Ryan might be heading back from their dinner by then, giving it a simple little intro:

"For a stand-up guy in Charlestown who's never going to get me to Beethoven, and will always be a very, very good friend."

My phone buzzed about with a text about ten minutes later:

*"Nailed it as always, Jordan."*
*"You too, Metz."*

Just before eleven, the Marley Dude wished me a blessed Shabbat when I took his request for "One Love," what else, and I realized he had to be one of the parishioners. It was a surprise too, but a good one.

I had spent so much time over the last couple of years worrying about what was happening beyond my line of vision, afraid of all the risks and dangers I couldn't see. What I had completely forgotten is that some of the things you can't see are good. And some might even be on your side.

# Chapter Twenty-Eight

## Love Me, Love My Lake Monster

Even though the evening at the Grist Mill had ended spectacularly badly, Will was still very much into the idea of date night.

I wasn't sure if it was just because he liked to go out, or for the sake of a statement, and if so, what that statement might be. It might just have been a straight do-over. Really, I wasn't all that hung up on the motivation. The evening together was enough after the week we'd both had.

In the wake all of the stormy weather, literal and otherwise, we kept it simple that Saturday: dinner at Janet's, and then back to my place. Fortescue dropped him off with a grin and a teasing "Have a good night, Boss."

There was at least a small chance that he'd actually been calling *me* Boss.

Without even the tiniest snicker, but with a gleam in his eyes that promised the teasing would be stepping up significantly in coming days, Rob showed us to a nice dim and warm spot near the big hearth. It probably negated all the time I'd spent on makeup, but it also did a nice job of hiding the fact that my dark red silk blouse had seen better days. I guessed Will would be more interested in the lacy black thing just visible underneath (thank you, rush delivery!), but it was just as well he couldn't see the signs of wear on the collar.

Will had come straight from an event in Rutland, a regional high school science competition that Ryan and Xavier would probably enter one of these days, so he was still in governor kit: gray pinstripe suit, French blue oxford, and a tie that appeared to feature flamenco-dancing elephants.

"I like the tie."

"Back when we had a sense of humor about ourselves."

"You still do."

"I am not representative."

"But you are pretty cool," I said, taking up the menu.

We looked over the offerings in companionable silence for a few moments. I could almost get used to Saturday nights with Will.

"How are you doing on figuring out the tech for a Sunday morning?" he asked, after a rather star-struck Eddie the waiter had taken our orders for wine, mac and cheese (his with lobster, mine without), and big salads.

"I'll talk to my engineer Monday to make sure we're set for the remote Tuesday—I'll ask him."

"That's right." Will nodded; I'd given him the headline on my new partnership when we talked on the phone late Friday. "You're really going full-on live and local."

"A real morning show, anyway."

"Congratulations. That's a very big deal."

"Sure is. We're almost a real radio station again."

"It's not just good for you. We need all the local media we can get."

"Absolutely." I just gazed happily at him, basking in the praise and support.

After a few moments, though, something flickered in his eyes and he took my hands. "Now, how about bringing some live and local to my house one weekend soon?"

"Yeah?"

"My actual home, as you may or may not know, is a very nice little place on Lake Champlain."

"Do you look for Champ?"

"I have been known to sit on the deck and watch for the lake monster." Will smiled faintly as he laced fingers with mine. "Maybe you'd like to join me."

"I could manage that." It was going to be a hellacious amount of driving, but I'd done worse for less. "And I would love to see your lake monster."

Will's smile widened to a naughty grin at the undeniable filthy subtext. "Well, as far as we know, Champ is mythical."

"But you're not."

"True. And the sunset and sunrise are spectacular." He gazed at me for a second. "So are you, you know."

"You aren't bad, either," I grinned right back. "Throw in some of those pancakes and you've got a deal."

"Done."

Eddie appeared just then with the wine, and I jokingly raised my glass to Will. "To lake monsters."

"Mythical and otherwise."

I was taking my first sip when I heard a familiar voice from the door and tensed.

"What?"

I just nodded toward her.

Will put down his glass, and even in the low light, I could see his jaw tightening. "My esteemed second."

"Is that what you call her?"

"Oh, trust me, I had many better things to call her before she started causing trouble for you, and now, well, let's just say I don't use that kind of language around a lady."

I blinked a little at him.

"You, of course, are the lady. She . . . doesn't belong in the same sentence as you."

I'd seen him righteously furious after the graffiti of course, but most of that, I assumed, was about the offense to his state and his principles. This was straight out old-school defending his woman. By all rights, I should have found it presumptuous, sexist, and more than a little offensive.

Instead, I found it hotter than the proverbial hinges of hell. More so when he looked at me with a sheepish expression.

"I'm sorry, Jacqueline. I really, really try not to—"

"It's kind of cute," I said, taking his hand. "As long as you don't take it too far."

For a second, the tension eased in his face and he smiled at me. "You are just—"

"Why, Governor Ten Broeck, fancy seeing you here."

Charity Slater and the scruffy young guy from her little protest were standing by our table. "Eddie said you were here."

Eddie's tip just went down to the bare minimum.

"Lieutenant Governor Slater." Will let go of my hand and stood, moving seamlessly into polite politician mode. "And your son Chad. How nice to see you both."

The son, a slightly pudgy dishwater blond who looked about twenty-five, and about like he would have been happier anywhere else, just flicked his eyes in Will's general direction. It was weird, but I wasn't sure what kind of weird.

Charity actually shook hands, giving him one of those limp light shakes that some women do, I'm never sure why.

If you're going to shake hands, dammit, just do it.

"And I'm sure you know Ms. Jordan," Will continued, motioning to me.

I took my cue and stood too, immediately understanding why he'd wanted me to; I had a good eight inches on dear Charity, and she shrank back a bit, whether from sheer physical intimidation or the realization that the woman she'd been happily tormenting a few days ago obviously had a few connections.

"Why, I didn't know you were . . ." she began, preening her spun sugar hair with one bony ashen hand.

"Ms. Jordan and I are old friends." Will's matter-of-fact tone told me that's what we were going to call it, at least for now, but his narrowed eyes told Charity I was one old friend she'd better treat with care.

"Oh, of course. Ms. Jordan." She held out her hand for another of those limp greetings.

"Jaye. Nice to see you in happier circumstances." Not for nothing have I been a jock for a quarter century. My voice was as cool and smooth as the worn-in silk of my blouse as I gave her my usual firm shake.

The guy didn't offer a hand, and seemed surprised that I even made eye contact. Definitely weird.

"I'm sure you apologized to Ms. Jordan for that earlier misunderstanding . . . ," Will began, his eyes steely on Charity's.

Charity was silent for a full ten seconds while her son squirmed. I watched her, and Will, waiting to see how all of this would turn out. Badly for Charity, I suspected.

She finally trilled a laugh. "Oh, of course, just a misunderstanding."

"And the apology?" Will's voice was as cold as his eyes.

Charity moved a fraction closer to Chad, and I caught the glance between them. She was clearly expecting something from him, and he wasn't giving it. Really weird vibe.

"Understood, isn't it, Jaye?" Charity turned to me, with a caramelly sweet note in her voice. Might have worked if I didn't know the caramel came with a generous dose of strychnine.

"Oh, I think we understand each other." Better than you think we do. I smiled.

Will didn't. "Have a very good evening, Charity, Chad."

Chad twisted a bit, like an uncomfortable small boy. His mother put a hand on his arm and he winced. "Come along. Good night, Governor."

"Try the mac and cheese," I suggested brightly. "It's terrific."

Charity, whose mummified little body probably hadn't seen a full-fat dairy product in decades, shuddered slightly as she walked away.

"Well played, Jacqueline." Will picked up his wineglass as he sat.

"Can't give an inch." I took up my own. "She is some piece of work."

"Poison mean, and a lousy parent too."

It was the worst thing I could say about someone, and it sounded like he felt the same. "How so?"

"Treats her son like some kind of appendage. I'm not sure what's going on with him, but she uses him like a supporting player in her show."

"What about the dad?"

"Long gone. I don't know the story."

I wondered if I could guess.

"Bet he's her protector." I thought about the glance between them. "And he may be sick of it."

Will's eyes lingered on my face. "How's that?"

"Um, if you lose a parent early, one way or another, a lot of times you protect the one you still have. Sometimes the parent overplays the hand a little . . . or a lot."

"You know about this."

"Yeah." I shrugged. "I always protected my mom as much as I could after my father died. She still leans on me for a lot of emotional support, but she never tried to prevent me from having a career, or later, a marriage."

He nodded, and I was glad he didn't ask the questions he was probably thinking.

"But if I'd been less ambitious or Mom had been pathological . . . I don't know. It's very easy for a parent to take advantage of a kid."

"She's supposed to be protecting him, not the other way around." His voice was quiet, but hard.

"Got that." I took a breath. "I'm really careful not to lean on Ryan. She wanted to take care of David during the chemo, and me now, and I don't exactly push her away, but I make sure she's the kid."

Will smiled. "Good mom."

"Jacqueline Kennedy was right. If you screw up parenting . . ."

"It doesn't matter what else you get right." He nodded. "Terrible what that woman has done to her son."

"He'll get free one day. And she'll pay the price. Nothing worse than ending up with your child hating you. I'm not sure I wish that even on her."

Will nodded, and just silently held my gaze for a moment. Then something shifted in his eyes and he shook his head.

"I would like," he said, lacing fingers with mine, "to forget about that woman now, and focus my energies on this woman."

"And what would you like to do with those energies?"

"Well, after we enjoy your new partner's excellent cooking, you'll find out . . ."

# Chapter Twenty-Nine

## But What Does the Moose Think?

Once Charity Slater had gone on with her plans, our evening improved significantly. I don't have a lot of experience in relationships, but we seemed to be reaching a point where we had, if not exactly a routine, then a pattern for our time together, and it was starting to feel good and comfortable.

Still hot, though.

After a night I'm going to leave to your (hopefully good!) imagination, I woke up a few minutes before the alarm, leaving Will happily asleep, and ran the shows.

He appeared about halfway through the second one, carrying coffee. Today's fleece was Burlington Lake Monsters merch, and I did not think it was coincidental.

"Figured you might need a little caffeine."

"Thanks." I took the coffee and nodded to his fleece. "Champ's nice, but you really need a WSV one."

"Yeah?"

"Yeah. I have more than forty years of leftover swag in the promo closet. I bet you can find something you like."

He smiled like a little kid.

I couldn't stop a chuckle.

"What?"

"You're just cute." I grinned. "I know that's sexist as hell."

"On you it works." He gave me another smile, and nodded to the monitors as he sat. "What is this stuff, anyway?"

"FCC mandated public affairs time. Probably more than required under the current rules, but it doesn't hurt. Right now, I'm mostly recycling old shows. Eventually, I want to start taping more local programs. It's not like we don't have plenty of community groups that could use a little attention."

"From whoever's listening at eight AM on a Sunday."

"Church crowd." I shrugged. "I know we don't have a lot of listeners at this time, but we do what we can."

"I didn't mean to insult you."

"No offense taken. It *is* a tiny station in a tiny town."

"You had millions of listeners in New York."

"Different world. Different life."

For most of a minute, he just looked at me. "You miss it?"

"You miss D.C.?"

"We don't get to go back. And I like my life as it is now."

"Same here. I wouldn't want to go through the last two years again, but it's not bad on the other side."

We smiled together, knowing we'd just said a lot more.

"When is Fortescue coming for you?"

"He's going to a later Mass today—date night with his wife. So around noon."

"Cool." I faded up the instrumental that allowed me to rejoin the satellite service cleanly. "Want to meet someone special?"

"Who?"

"Just give me a few minutes to clean up and change up, and you'll find out."

"Okay."

About half an hour later, we were walking into the foyer when I heard it, right at the end of the network spot break.

". . . and the mainstream media, the cancel liberals, and the jackbooted feminist jocks won't stop me! Keep the Anger Alive!"

I dropped my keys, took a breath.

"What?" Will picked up the keys.

"You heard that, right?"

"Ad for some stupid talk show—I tune 'em out." His eyes widened a little. "Not just any stupid talk show."

"Nope."

"And not just any jackbooted feminist jock."

"Exactly. He's got three hours every day to say whatever awful thing he wants to about me. And since he's with the same satellite service as my music, the promos run on my air."

"Look, Jacqueline." Will reached for me, wrapped his arm around my shoulder. "You engage with people like that, it only makes it worse. Ignore him. Don't give him oxygen."

I leaned into him, rested my head on his shoulder.

"And," he said with a little grin, "I like jackbooted feminist jocks."

"There's that." I smiled back. "Want to drive?"

"Nah." He handed me the keys. "You're the one who knows where we're going."

"You can probably find Quarry Hill."

"Quarry Hill? The land that brewery was looking at a few years ago?"

"That's not all that's up there."

"Yeah?"

"So's my stick."

"Stick?" He gave me a small, naughty smile.

"Transmitter. A lot of small stations have studios in the same place as the stick, but we don't because the founders owned the townhouse."

"Makes sense." The naughty smile widened. "You're taking me out into the woods to show me your stick?"

"And so much more," I teased. "Anyway, the guy with the lake monster can't talk."

"Love me, love my lake monster."

We shared one of those delicious, wicked smiles couples do when things are good—and hot. I'd forgotten how great it was to just be happy with someone.

Once again, Will was a good passenger, riding in companionable silence, and watching as I parked in the little gravel area by the shack. He did give me a puzzled look when I took a couple of hard candies out of the glove box.

"What's that for?"

"You'll see."

He followed me to the shack, and watched as I checked the transmitter. Then I locked the door and guided him out into the clearing.

"Do exactly what I tell you, okay?" I whispered.

Will nodded.

I unwrapped one of the candies. The crunching started right up in the brush, so I took his hand, and pulled him into place, putting the candy in his palm.

"Now," I told him, "just stand there quietly and wait."

It took maybe ten very long seconds. Charlemagne walked out into the clearing, and sniffed. He smelled the candy, and he also smelled and saw something very different, namely Will. For what seemed like forever, the moose stared at him, assessing him.

Then, just as Neptune had done the night of the pipe bomb, Charlemagne decided Will was safe, and walked toward him. The moose seemed to nod at him, then took his candy. While he chomped the treat, he watched the two of us, relaxed and happy.

After the candy was gone, Charlemagne stood in front of us for a few more seconds, then turned and started for the woods, first slowly, then loping away at a good clip.

No extras this time.

"Damn." Will let out a long breath. "Thirty years up here and I've never been that close to a moose."

"Awesome, huh?"

"In every sense of the word." He took my hand. His palm was still a little sticky with moose spit and candy, but it didn't bother me. "Thank you."

"You're going to share your lake monster with me, the least I could do is introduce you to my moose."

"Yeah." He pulled me a little closer, and kissed me lightly. "C'mon. We can stay warm and watch the Sunday news shows till Fortescue shows up."

"Sounds good to me." As I rummaged the keys out of my pocket, I looked past the gravel patch, and saw something strange. Orange sticks in the ground at the edge of the clearing. "What's that?"

Will looked and his face tightened. "Survey sticks. And they look new. Is that the land the brewery was eyeing?"

"I think so. Rob's aunt the town clerk would know."

"Think you can ask her?"

"Sure. Why?"

"Tell you later. I'm not sure, but there may be something going on there."

He wasn't going to tell me anything else, and honestly, I was a lot more interested in staying warm and watching the news shows. We curled up in my office with Neptune, coffee, and the last of that box of hamentaschen from Alan Metz, and proceeded to tear apart the pols.

I stuck mostly to style points, because I didn't want to get into a political argument with him, but I realized pretty quickly that Will was noticeably to my left on some issues, especially climate change. New England Republican indeed.

"Oh, come on, that's a softball," he yelled at the upstate New York congressman who stumbled through what should have been a simple answer on improving public transportation.

I giggled.

"What?"

"You're more liberal than me."

"Why is that a surprise? You're the one who can fire a muzzleloader."

"I don't want to own one."

"That's soothing, anyway." He pulled me closer, chuckling. "You know, we've never actually talked politics. What are you?"

"Registered nonpartisan. Journalistic ethics never die."

"But?"

"I have political views in my own house, on my own time, of course," I said carefully. This might get weird, and I didn't want it to.

He toyed with a loose strand of my hair. "I'm not going to run out of here . . . unless you tell me Charity's too liberal for you."

"Nah." I chuckled. "I'm pretty easy. I'm strongly against mean and stupid . . . and strongly in favor of kind and sensible. Anybody who hits that gets my vote. Even if he's still a Republican."

Will gave a small laugh. "As you like to remind me, I'm a Knickerbocker. I'm not giving up a family tradition going back to

Lincoln and the abolitionists because of a few fools with bad hair and Gadsden flags."

"Stay, fight, and make it better."

"You got it."

"Maybe I'll reload your musket once in a while, too."

"Works for me." He rested his chin on the top of my head and I snuggled into him.

David had been so sick and sore during the chemo that we really couldn't cuddle, and not long after, of course, I didn't want him touching me, so all of this was a real treat. I had forgotten how much I liked just being in someone's arms. Hearing a trace of another heartbeat.

We were silent for a while, while Neptune purred and the pols sparred.

"I could get used to this, Jacqueline."

"Request lines are always open."

He kissed the top of my head, his arms tightening around me. "I know it's really early, but I'm not kidding."

"It is really early." I burrowed a little closer to him. "It's also really good."

"Yeah."

Before his ride came, Will found and appropriated a very retro navy sweatshirt with white block letters that had probably been in the promo closet longer than I'd been a DJ. I had coffee for the road ready for Fortescue, and the trooper just flashed a small knowing smile when Will gave me a very neutral kiss on the cheek after I walked them to the SUV.

"Have a good night with Ryan," Will said. "Maybe sometime soon . . ."

"I think that's a very good idea."

His face lit up. "Good."

Wrapping my old, but not that old, WSV fleece around myself, I stood on the porch and watched them go. This was starting to feel real and serious, and I wasn't sure if I should give in to it.

Look what happened the last time I did.

# Chapter Thirty

## Good News and Bad Moose

"Shouldn't you be inside, staying warm?"

Chief George was walking across from the cop shop, a CUNY sweatshirt and jeans under his usual leather raincoat.

"Shouldn't you be watching basketball with Alicia?"

He grinned. "I will be. But first some good news."

"Excellent. Come in—I have fresh coffee."

"See, that's why it's good to have a real radio station around here."

We laughed together.

Once we were settled in the office, he raised his mug to me with another big smile. "To overpriced blockbuster drugs."

"Yeah?"

"Oh, yeah. Edwin Anger did indeed have an extra dose of that fancy blood thinner. There was still residue in his stomach, so he got it in a meal within about six hours of death."

"Which is probably when he was eating dinner at the Grist Mill with Spence Lyle."

"Sure looks that way." The chief drank some coffee. "Entirely possible that being frozen in the snowman helped preserve it."

"Glad it was good for something."

"Good for plenty. If he'd been less hung up on making a statement, and just let Anger be found dead in his room, Lyle probably would have gotten away with it. Always a bad idea to get too cute."

"Keep your lies and alibis simple." I didn't remember whose proverb it was, but it was a good one.

"Got that." He smiled.

"But it wasn't just getting cute, Chief."

"What do you mean?"

"He wanted Anger to be missing for a while so he could fill in and become a fixture—give himself a better shot at the regular gig."

A canny smile. "Finally something that makes sense. Anger was supposed to be in the snowman till spring."

"And until Spence was well established as the host. Probably the only way someone as lousy as he was would get the job."

"Except that somebody lost her temper."

"Kept my aim, though."

"Always a good thing." He chuckled and took a sip of coffee. "There's more. Lyle's fingerprint was on that pill box you and Rob found."

"They had fingerprints?"

"Our little friend has a gun permit."

I winced. "Well, that will help me sleep."

"Better to find it out now than two weeks ago."

"There's that."

"It still wouldn't be a great case. Too easy to claim that he handled the pillbox as part of the job and it was an accidental OD."

"Maybe." I sipped my own coffee. "Except for the surveillance video showing him putting Anger in the snowman."

"Right. He'll claim it was a stunt to carry on Anger's work."

"I wouldn't want to be his defense lawyer."

We shook our heads together.

"Right about now," continued the chief, checking his watch, "the Atlanta cops are taking in Mr. Lyle, and he had better be packing a few of those stupid overpriced fleeces."

"So she's decided to charge and extradite him."

"Even as we speak. I'd expect an arraignment tomorrow."

I nodded. "White River court sends releases when it's a high-profile case."

"This will be high-profile enough."

"Sure will. Thanks, Chief."

He shrugged. "Glad to see the right thing happen once in a while."

"I'll drink to that."

A coffee toast, a little basketball trash talk, and he was on his way, taking my best to Alicia.

I was too wired to relax, and grabbed my keys to drive up Quarry Hill for the one thing that always calms me. A visit to Charlemagne. He wouldn't mind two candies in one day . . . and I needed the relaxation.

Too bad I didn't get it this time.

The first thing I saw was the big black SUV. The second thing I saw was antlers, just rising over the top of the vehicle.

What the hell?

I quickly parked behind the SUV and climbed out.

"Make it go away!" squawked a strangled little voice barely recognizable as Charity's. No exaggerated New England accent now.

"Tell it to stop," she choked.

"It's a moose, ma'am," a woman who had to be Murchison, her state trooper, replied in an almost bored tone. "They do what they do."

I took a couple of steps, and saw something I'd never imagined possible. Charity was cowering on the tin wall of the shack, and Charlemagne was sniffing at the top of her head.

Too bad moose aren't carnivores.

"Hi, folks."

Charity snapped her gaze over to me. Charlemagne made an unhappy noise.

"It's your moose—make it stop!" she hissed.

"Shut up." I hissed back. "Don't scare him."

She stifled.

There was still an extra candy in the pocket of my coat. I reached in and crinkled the wrapper. Charlemagne's huge head slowly turned my way, and he seemed to relax at the sight of me.

"Hey, fella." I said in my best soothing tone. "How 'bout a treat?"

The moose watched as I started to unwrap the candy. Charity started to scrabble away, and he tensed again.

"Stop it." I whispered with as much intensity as I could manage while keeping a soothing demeanor for the moose. "I said don't scare him."

"She's right, ma'am."

Charity pursed her lips into an even tighter line, but said nothing.

Charlemagne took his candy and gave me a happy gaze as he crunched it. Then he turned and almost shook his head at Charity as he started for the woods.

Just as he pulled nearly level with Charity's face, he released his parting shot. A big long one, like he'd been saving up gas for a while.

It was hard not to take it as a statement, and harder not to laugh.

So I didn't even try.

Charity coughed and sputtered, flapping her bony white hands and shrieking.

That only made it funnier. I couldn't help myself. I howled.

Murchison had to maintain demeanor, and it nearly killed her: her face went fuchsia and a vein popped out in her forehead.

"Well, I never!" Charity snapped. "That is the most disgusting thing—we should expand moose hunting! What a repulsive creature!"

Suddenly, it wasn't funny anymore. "Not as repulsive as you."

"Pretty sanctimonious for a liberal hussy."

I wasn't going to dignify that. "What are you doing here, besides trespassing?"

"I do not have to account for my whereabouts to you."

"No, and you don't have to be on my land either. So leave."

Murchison coughed and managed to recover her ability to speak. "Come along, ma'am. Don't you have a dinner . . ."

Charity gave me what was clearly intended as a popular-girl glare. "I have better things to do than worry about that antlered monster of yours."

"Good for you." I returned the glare, then turned to Murchison. "Please get her out of here before I have to call the local police."

"We're leaving, Ms. Jordan. I won't bring her back unless she has permission."

"Murchison!" snapped Charity.

"I'm a sworn officer, ma'am," she said quietly, "not your driver. Please get into the vehicle."

For once, Charity did what she was told. As I watched them go, my phone buzzed with the pickup-time alarm. Back to what really matters.

As I got into the car, I caught the tail end of another Spence promo, and realized that I might finally be done with the creep.

It could really be over. What would I do when I didn't have to fight for my life anymore?

Bad choice of words.

I know a little too much about a real fight for life.

*David had a cold he couldn't shake and he was just exhausted all the time. After an unsuccessful run of antibiotics, and a couple of fruitless follow-ups, his regular doctor sent him to an ENT, who took a look, couldn't find anything, and ordered a biopsy on one of his swollen lymph nodes. She said it was probably no big deal but we have to rule out everything.*

*She didn't say what we were ruling out.*

*We didn't ask.*

*By the time the results came back, David was starting to feel a little better, though the lymph nodes hadn't gone down, and we really thought it had all just been some kind of silly misunderstanding. We even took Ryan with us to his late-afternoon appointment, figuring we'd go out to dinner afterward. One of her favorite pizza spots was right near the office.*

*I'm pretty sure I didn't eat dinner that night. I know I never ate Fiori's Pizza again.*

*Most of the next month or so is a blur, of doctors' appointments, frantic online research, and the fear of not knowing. There are dozens of kinds of leukemia and lymphoma, and some of them are still frequently fatal. Others can be knocked down with chemo, and you go on with your life knowing that next year, or the year after—or twenty years from now—it will be back. And some, like what David had, can be cured outright.*

*We didn't realize how fortunate we were until we started going for the infusions. There's a look that tells you somebody is on their last chance, fighting for whatever bits of time they can steal from the disease. In a waiting room with too much of that look, David was the lucky one, the guy who would walk out of there and go on with his life.*

*I tried to remind him of that when it was really bad, when he was sick and exhausted and hating every second of it and every drop of poison pumped into him to kill the cancer. He hated being reminded and he hated me for being the one who reminded him.*

*That was probably the beginning of the end, not that we would have been able to see it.*

*It didn't matter anyway. He still hit the lottery in the only way that counts. We all did.*

*When we walked out of the infusion suite for the last time, Ryan bouncing between us with her sights on the ice cream parlor ten minutes down the road, David sure didn't feel like the lucky guy after six months of brutal chemo. Neither did I.*

*But he was.*

*And we're still lucky, whatever sides of the Connecticut River we sleep on these days. He did the only thing that mattered: he lived.*

Sally was the first person at the door that afternoon, and she gave me a hug and a big smile as we slipped off to the side to get Ryan's stuff. "So?"

"So it's pretty great, but it's also still pretty early." I shrugged. "Did David tell you . . ."

"That he's the governor, of all things? Yeah." She laughed. "Couldn't you just go pick up a nice hot firefighter? You have to get a guy who brings all that with him."

I laughed too. "But he makes great pancakes."

"That makes up for a lot. You should bring him over here to compare notes with Alan."

"Really?"

"One way or another, Jaye, if he's going to stay in your life, he's going to be our family too."

I looked away for a second as my eyes prickled with the start of tears. "Good to know."

"If you decide to keep him. He's not pushing you for anything too serious too soon?"

"No, and I'm not either."

"Very smart." She gave me an approving nod, reminding me why she was such a good family therapist. "There's a temptation to just jump in, but better to take it slow. At least at first."

I nodded. "Everybody says not to get serious about the rebound man."

"That's only if he is the rebound man. If he's just *the* man, it's fine to get serious, as long as you're sure."

"I'm not good at this."

"You'll figure it out. I know a couple of good people over in Windsor County if you want someone to talk to."

"Maybe."

Sally smiled. "Maybe not, too. You're doing fine. As long as you remember to eat."

"Working on it."

She nodded. "Start with something simple. Eat breakfast every day with Ryan. It's good for her, and you won't weasel because she's involved."

"That's really smart."

"About time I got some use from this degree."

We were laughing together as we went to join the others.

# Chapter Thirty-One

## See You in Court

Chief George was right. The DA sent out a release late Sunday announcing the arrest of Spence Lyle and his arraignment Monday in White River Junction court. Apparently, arraignments don't stop even for President's Day, which was more of a break than the creep deserved, not that I minded.

After all, I probably would not have been able to make it up to White River on Tuesday, because we had to be at the sugarhouse to greet everyone for our big remote. While I hadn't covered arraignment court very much when I was still actually a reporter, there was no way I was going to miss this.

Of course, it was the lead on my morning news updates, and a major relief for most of our cast, starting with Ryan, who took in the details while devouring some brown sugar cinnamon oatmeal. I sat down with her for a bit, eating a cherry yogurt and drawing a surprised smile, but no comment.

She, Xavier, and a bunch of the older kids from Kunin were spending most of the day at a Rube Goldberg machine competition at the library.

The other kids would never see those two coming.

"Awesome, Ma," she said as she read Marianne's front-page article. "They got the little dork."

242

I laughed at her description, however accurate, as I got up and buttoned my old black interview-suit blazer over a heavy light gray mock turtleneck, trying for a decently professional look for court. Not so pro that I was giving up my jeans and long parka, though. "Something like that."

"What will happen to him?"

I sighed. I knew enough about criminal justice to know this was the bad part. "He'll probably get bail and go back to Atlanta until trial."

"Will they let him stay on the air?"

"Maybe. Depends on his contract." If Neely was right that the sat service didn't want to promote Spence, the charge would give them a solid excuse to pass over him, but there was no guarantee—and I wasn't counting on it.

Her eyes widened. "Really?"

"Yeah. They may have no choice until he's convicted. If he's convicted."

Ryan shook her head. "But that's wrong."

"It's the benefit of the doubt, honey. It's actually very much the right thing to do."

"It is?"

"Sometimes, the way we treat people who we think have done bad things is about us and not them."

"About us?"

"About who we are and what we think is right." I put my arm around her. "And we believe everybody deserves the benefit of the doubt."

Ryan shook her head. "He's going to be mad now, and out there saying even more bad things about you."

"Maybe. But everybody who counts knows what he is. And what we are."

She nodded.

"And," I continued, stealing that line from Will, "it doesn't have anything to do with you and me and what happens in this house."

"Okay."

I refilled my coffee mug. "Better?"

"Better." She studied me for a moment. "Ma? About what happens in this house?"

"Yeah?"

"How was your weekend with the governor?"

I had told her I was having dinner with him, not spending the weekend, but kids do their own math. "Um, we had a very nice dinner."

"Am I going to get to meet him?"

"He wants to meet you."

"Good. Are you going to marry him?"

Fortunately, I did not have coffee in my mouth. I put the mug down. "Ryan, honey, we've just started dating. Neither of us is seeing anyone else, and we like each other a lot. But it is going to be a long time before I marry anyone, if I ever do."

"Okay." She smiled. "You like each other a lot?"

"Uh-huh."

"And he's not seeing anyone else."

"Nope."

"That's pretty cool."

"I think so. And I think we'll all just wait and see what happens next."

"Okay." Her eyes took on a wicked sparkle. "What do you get for going out with the governor, Ma?"

I stopped mid-reach for the coffee. "What do you mean?"

"Well, he's the governor. He ought to buy you nice stuff or take you cool places."

"That's not why you see someone, Ryan. You see someone because you like having them in your life."

"And because you love them?"

"Eventually because you love them. Early on, it's because you really like spending time with them." I realized I had a knot in my stomach. It was way too early to talk about things like this.

"Uh-huh." She took the last bite of her oatmeal with a big smile. "Maybe I meet your man soon."

"We'll see."

She laughed at my standard mom catchphrase and so did I. "Come on. I have to go straight to White River after I get you and Xavi to the library."

Arraignment court was a relief after the interrogation at home.

Tim was around, handling a couple of his cases, and we sat down by the vending machines for a quick diet soda (poison we'd never drink in front of our children!) and gossip session before Spence's big moment. Seemed Xavier was only slightly less excited about his dad's new gig than Rob was.

During a midmorning recess, I took a second to call the contract engineer and make sure I had everything set for the remote next day. He also told me how to set up the system to run the weekend public affairs shows, which was a lot easier than I'd thought.

I could go see Will and his lake monster whenever I wanted to.

I sent him (Will, not Champ—though I'm willing to believe that Champ has a good mobile plan) a text: *"Good to go for a Saturday night. Pick one."*

*"This Saturday."*
*"Fine by me. What does Champ eat?"*
*"DJs. Beautiful ones with gray eyes."*

I was still chuckling when they brought Spence Lyle in, abruptly ending the fun.

Spence looked like he'd taken over Perry Como's weekend wardrobe: grandpa cardigan, jersey polo, and khakis that bagged at the back, all in strange shades of brown. Don't get me wrong, I didn't want to think any more than I had to about Lyle's posterior, but the saggy fabric was unavoidable.

Below that oddly perfect half-bald hairline, his face was still scrunched up and his lower lip still drooped, and his expression was still defiant. Maybe more than it had been.

"Spencer Lyle, murder, abuse of a corpse, conspiracy, and harassment, the last two as a hate crime." The clerk, a wry older guy, looked up at the judge. Clearly the big ticket of the day.

Judge Amy Clay Glass, a tiny, no-nonsense woman I remembered from my first hitch, when she had been a very slightly taller DA known for winning terrifyingly long sentences for drug dealers, gazed at Spence over her half-glasses. "Ah, yes. You. Counsel?"

"I will be representing myself with the power and majesty of the United States Constitution."

The clerk gazed up at the judge. "Guess that's pro se?"

She did not roll her eyes, but she did let out a tiny sigh. "Plea?"

"I do not acknowledge the jurisdiction of this court and demand to be tried by a jury of my true peers."

"Who might they be?"

"As a constitutional originalist, I acknowledge no amendments beyond the initial Bill of Rights. You therefore have no right to sit in judgment of me, woman."

"The State of Vermont sees it somewhat differently." Judge Glass looked at him as if he were a new species of bug. "And as it happens, all of the amendments you're taking issue with were duly approved by the U.S. Congress and have withstood Supreme Court tests."

"Then they can be tested again." Lyle smiled unpleasantly. "I can wait."

"Well, the justice system of the State of Vermont cannot. I will enter a not guilty plea on your behalf and you can take up the legal issues with your little friends. Prosecutor? Bail?"

A very young African American guy, clearly cutting his teeth in his first job, stood and did his best not to look at the defendant any more than he had to. "People request remand."

"A bit harsh, isn't it, Ellington?"

"Defendant has no ties to the community, lives and works in Atlanta, and has demonstrated contempt for the local legal system."

"High bail contingent on court appearances might well keep him in line," the judge reflected. "Don't you think, Mr. Lyle?"

"I think you stupid woodchucks have no idea what you're dealing with and—"

The judge's eyes narrowed. "Let's stop with the invective, Mr. Lyle."

"Invective is all you liberal idiots understand. I'm trying to bring truth to the masses . . ."

"Right now, you are a defendant in a murder case, and you would do well to treat your situation with the gravity it deserves." She turned to the prosecutor. "Why should I consider remand, Ellington?"

"Defendant has a daily radio show which he has used to foment hate against any number of groups in general—and against at least one person specifically."

"Political theater." Spence smirked. "No reasonable person would take it seriously."

"Some reasonable person sent me a pipe bomb!" I was on my feet before I realized what I was doing, and bit my lip as the judge raised her gavel.

"Ms. Jordan?" she asked. "The specific person, no doubt?"

"Yes, Your Honor. Sorry, Your Honor."

"Don't ever do that in my court again." Judge Glass narrowed her eyes a bit, into a laser glare, just for an instant. Then her face softened a fraction as she nodded. "It's a bit irregular, but I'll allow it. Goes to danger to the community. Clerk, please swear Ms. Jordan."

Which is how I ended up in the witness box instead of the press box. As a journalist, I hated it. As a mother, I reveled in the chance to go after the man who put my kid in danger.

The prosecutor nodded to me. "Have you been targeted by listeners of the defendant's show?"

"Yes, sir."

"In what way?"

"Well, I've been accused of killing Edwin Anger, sent baskets of nasty postcards, had a pipe bomb mailed to me." I took a breath. That should have been the worst. But it wasn't.

"Please continue, Ms. Jordan," Ellington urged.

I realized my fingers were wrapped around my star pendant. "And some fool spray-painted a backwards swastika on my business."

"The incident for which the defendant is charged with harassment as a hate crime?"

"Yes."

"And how do you feel about that?"

"Sickened. Like I'm not safe in my own home. Like my child isn't safe." I turned to make direct, hard eye contact with Spence. "You don't get to tell me I don't belong here."

"Ms. Jordan," the judge cut in. "You're a broadcaster your-self. Do you think that remanding the defendant would unfairly deprive him of his First Amendment rights?"

I kept my eyes on Spence. "Last time I checked, Your Honor, the First Amendment doesn't allow you to incite people to harm another person."

She nodded. "I've heard enough. Thank you, Ms. Jordan. You may step down."

"Thank you, Your Honor."

Judge Glass gave Spence the same glare she'd given me a few minutes ago. Only this time, she held it and magnified it. Even he wilted a little. But he quickly shook it off and forced back the smirk.

"Defendant is remanded."

"I have First Amendment rights!"

"Which do not permit hate speech or threats to other people." She turned the glare up a notch.

"It's a show!"

"It is not a show, Mr. Lyle, when someone sends a pipe bomb to an innocent woman. Or paints a vile symbol of hate on her home at your urging."

"It's my right–"

"Mr. Lyle, this may come as a surprise to you, but your rights are not absolute."

"The First Amendment—" he sputtered.

"Enough. This nonsense stops now. I am tired of hate mongers like you trying to hide behind the Constitution, and it's not going to happen in my court. Remand."

She dropped the gavel. Spence Lyle started keening.

No, really. Howling like an angry little kid. I'd never seen or heard anything like it, even from the most temperamental tod-dlers in Ryan's preschool, never mind an actual adult human.

Everyone stared as Lyle was dragged out. He wasn't saying anything, or even trying to form words. He was just emitting this utterly bizarre howl of rage. The sound continued after he was out of sight, and the next contender brought to the defense table, a sleepy-looking guy facing a drug possession charge, the only person who didn't seem especially concerned by Lyle's display.

I turned to go, and saw Chief George in the back.

"Figure he's setting up for a diminished capacity defense?" I asked.

"Nah. I think he's just angry and mean. That doesn't add up to crazy, even here."

We could still hear the howl, faintly, from somewhere deep inside the courthouse.

"Kinda scary," I admitted.

The chief smiled down at me. "Shouldn't be. Not to you, anyhow."

"Yeah?"

"After everything you've been through—in the last two years, and the last month, you're gonna get rattled by some weirdo yelling? Please. If I ran into that mope on the subway, I'd tell him to yell louder because they can't hear him at Bellevue."

I smiled in spite of myself at the rough New York accent that crept in as he said it.

"Come on, Jaye. It really is over."

"I don't know what to do for over."

"You'll figure it out." He smacked my arm with his newspaper. "See if your man wants to do dinner sometime when he's in town. Alicia wants to make sure he's worthy of you."

# Chapter Thirty-Two

## Thank You, Yogi Berra

R ob, Ryan, and Xavier were in the old reception area checking the remote kit when I got back from court. The kids had a good spring vacation day to look forward to, what with tech'ing the remote for us, then hopefully scoring some sugar on snow before adjourning back to the station for some extra PBS Kids time.

There were a bunch of activities for the rest of the week at the library and community center, and the two of them had planned a full slate of events. I didn't know all of the details—and I didn't need to because Ryan was keeping track like a professional scheduler. All I'd had to do was approve the activity (the field trip to a trampoline park did not pass muster) and write whatever small check she needed.

I wondered what people with less organized children did . . . and once again gave thanks that I didn't have to find out.

When I walked into the station, Ryan and Xavier put down the cables they were winding, and grabbed a trophy from one of the old sales desks.

"Look!" Ryan crowed.

"We won Coolest Idea!" Xavier pointed to the letters on the trophy.

"Awesome!" I hugged both of them, as Rob beamed. "What was your machine?"

"We came up with a machine that makes cocoa," Ryan said.

"With lights, wheels, and a couple of ramps," Xavi added.

"Double-strength cocoa," my girl finished with a grin.

I laughed. "Of course you did."

"Well," Rob said, "tomorrow you can get a little more real-world experience."

They nodded.

"How was court?" Ryan asked.

I shook my head. "Seriously weird. The guy gave the judge attitude."

"Which judge?" Rob asked.

"Amy Clay Glass, the former DA?"

He laughed. "Good Lord, really? Is he in jail?"

"Oh, yeah. Remand for the safety of the community. Screamed like an angry toddler as they led him away."

"Wow."

Ryan and Xavier gave us a funny look.

"He really is crazy," she said.

"Arguing with a judge and screaming in court," Rob agreed. "Yeah, that'll do for crazy."

"Won't be crazy enough to get him off." I hoped.

"Anyway, it's over," Rob said, echoing Chief George. "Over as it needs to be."

"You aren't going to like me quoting one of the hated Yankees," I told him as I shook my head, "but with thanks to Yogi Berra, it ain't over till it's over."

"I always liked him, even if he was a Yankee."

We all turned at the sound of the voice and a knock. Sadie walked in and grinned.

"Getting ready for the big debut?"

"Yep."

"You know you're probably going to get some company."

Rob and I exchanged glances. That had not meant good things in recent weeks.

Sadie shook her head with a smile. "Not that kind of company, kids. Orville, Oliver, probably a few state lawmakers too."

"We can handle that." Rob gave her a relieved smile and leaned in to plant a quick kiss on her cheek. "Looks like we're all good here. I have to get back to dinner prep."

"I may stop by later." Something in her smile strongly suggested she was not going to be alone. Good for Chief Frank.

"See you then." He turned to me. "See *you* at DeLorme's, bright and surly."

I joined his chuckle. "Bright and surly indeed."

The kids took Rob's exit as their cue to head over to Janet's to enjoy their PBS Kids schedule on the bar TV, leaving Sadie and me for a moment.

"Another good weekend?"

"Yep. Took him up to see the moose Sunday."

She grinned. "Does Charlemagne approve?"

"Seems to. He really got a kick out of the moose."

"Bet he gets a kick out of you, too."

I shrugged. "I don't want to get too serious too soon, but I really like this."

Sadie put a hand on my arm. "You don't want any more kids, do you? And Ryan has a very good dad who is strongly involved in her life."

I blinked a little, and then managed: "Yeah, that's about right."

"So there's no real reason to get serious. At least not the moving van, marriage-vow kind of serious."

"I suppose not."

She gave me a wise smile. "It's very nice to have a good partner who is absolutely committed, tremendously supportive . . . and not at your breakfast table every damn day."

"Really?"

"Really. One nice thing about being a grownup. You can manage a very happy and satisfying relationship without feeling the need to tear up your whole life for it."

I knew she was thinking of herself and Chief Frank. I'm ashamed to admit it, but old-fashioned girl that I am, I'd assumed that if I ever got serious again, I'd have to marry the guy. Sadie clearly didn't feel the same obligation.

Interesting thought.

I nodded to Sadie. "Good to know."

"Yep. Anyway, I should head back to the office-"

Office. That reminded me of something. "Say, did you know there were orange survey sticks up on that old brewery land now?"

Her eyes narrowed. "Really?"

"Yeah. Any movement on it that you know about?"

"No." She toyed with her gloves for a moment, contemplating. "It belongs to Mary Carton, one of several parcels in the same general area from the Carton family. She's got to be in her nineties, and could be winding down her properties for long-term care or something."

"So something could be up."

"Could be. I vaguely remember years ago there was a niece who was handling affairs . . . I'll take a look."

"Thanks."

Sadie gave me a sharp glance. "Did he ask you to ask me about the sticks?"

"Yep."

"Told you he was a good one. Smart one too."

"Don't put much past those Knickerbockers."

We shared a smile.

"See you at the sugarhouse tomorrow."

Asking Sadie about the sticks reminded me of Charity's little surprise visit. Maybe she was looking at the property because she was involved in the development effort? She'd been nagging Will about some land use thing after all.

No time to worry about her right now. I raided the old promo closet and came up with a couple of really cute kid-sized rugbies in the same green-white-and-purple late '80s configuration as the fleece I'd been wearing. Perfect for our crew.

I took Xavier's over to the restaurant and scooped up Ryan, walking in just in time to exchange a good-luck high-five with Tim.

"So did it quiet down after they dragged Lyle out?" I asked.

"Courtroom did. He didn't. Last I heard he was still howling in the lockup, and his lawyer was talking about a diminished capacity defense."

"Good luck with that."

Tim smiled a little. "Let 'em try. Nobody messes with Judge Glass."

"I got that impression."

"Not your problem now, anyway, right? He's off the air for a while, anyway, and can't gin up any more trouble."

"You'd think," I admitted. "But with these trolls, who knows?"

"Jaye, honey," Tim said, a very serious note coming into his voice, "sometimes you have to keep telling yourself it's over and you're safe, or you won't be."

"Thanks." I was pretty sure why he knew that. He never talked about the war or after, except when he and Rob told the story of how they got married.

*They'd been best friends all their lives, and that's all anyone on the outside thought it was. Remember, this was before same-sex marriage and* Heather Has Two Mommies. *Hell, when they were kids, it was still years before civil unions, the first real acknowledgment that two men or two women can have as valid, legitimate, and loving a relationship as a man and a woman. So they were friends. They both had a succession of cute and insignificant girlfriends; when I was in Simpson on my first hitch, Rob had been casually seeing a nurse at the hospital long enough that she might have had hopes.*

*Anyway, Tim came back from Iraq, where he'd seen a lot more than he ever expected to see to pay for his law degree, and just showed up at Rob's house one night. Which is when he informed Rob that he'd decided it was long past time to be who he is. And who Tim is, was, and always will be—the man who loves Rob Archer.*

*More to the point, the man who wants to be Rob Archer's husband and the father of his children.*

*The way they tell it, there was a pause. It wasn't that Rob had to think about it, or that there was any real question about what had been going on between them all along—it was that he was so moved and shocked and happy he couldn't find his voice to say yes.*

*The best jock I know couldn't speak.*

*Luckily for everyone, especially Xavier, that didn't last long.*

*I'm not saying David's and my wedding wasn't wonderful. It was. But there was a joy and magic at Rob and Tim's that we just didn't have. I didn't know what it was then, and I still don't. But if you made me guess, I'd say it was that they had to fight through so much to get there that it couldn't help feeling more special.*

*Or maybe they just belonged together and David and I didn't.*

*I don't know if Rob and Tim would have been able to find their way back. I bet they would have a better chance than David and me. I hope they never have to find out.*

"Seriously, Jaye. Sometimes you just have to call the end, and walk past it." Tim patted my arm. "You're surrounded by a town full of great people who want you to succeed, and it's time you put that creep and his friends where they belong. In the past."

"I like it." I really hoped he was right.

"Best revenge is just moving on."

"I like that even better."

Better still was the notice from the governor's press office that Mr. Ten Broeck would be holding the annual maple-tasting news conference at DeLorme's Sugarhouse in Simpson at ten thirty next morning.

I wasn't surprised when my phone buzzed soon after the e-mail.

"Hey, Knickerbocker."

"Jacqueline. Heard you gave the creep what-for."

"It was really the judge—not me."

"Uh-huh."

I was starting to realize that he didn't let me get away with downplay . . . and how much I liked that. "Well, I did state my case rather forcefully."

"That's how I heard it. Well done."

"Thanks."

"This is going to sound like a weird question, but ride with me."

"Oh, I'll always ride with you."

A naughty chuckle. "Hold that thought. Something weird happened today."

"What?"

"Can you think of any political issue with DeLorme's Sugarhouse?"

"No—Ray's a nice fella. Second or third generation in the business." I took a breath and thought. "His family and Rob's are friends. Nothing weird there."

"I didn't think so. Then why would Chad Slater try to stop me from coming down there tomorrow?"

"He did?"

"Came to my office today and said something about I might not want to do the maple newser at that sugarhouse tomorrow."

"Really?"

"Yeah. Seemed to be implying that it wouldn't be good for me."

"I don't know what's bad about celebrating maple season with nice people."

"Me either."

"Does Charity own a piece of a sugarhouse somewhere? I wouldn't put it past her to use the annual event to make a buck."

"I wouldn't put anything past her." He took a breath. "It was weird. Like he really wanted me to stay away."

"Maybe Mommy just wants to swan in and be a star."

"Maybe. Chad's usually doing her bidding, but he's a basically decent human." Will paused again and I could almost hear his wheels turning. "They run in circles I don't, Jacqueline. There's a possibility that he's heard something."

"Heard what?" I did not like the sound of this.

"We've been going on the assumption that Spence acted alone. What if he didn't?"

"Are you trying to cheer me up?"

"Look, it was really weird. And it's hard not to wonder if it had to do with Lyle since he was just put away today. And while I credit you for it—"

"Some folks will blame me."

"Yep."

"Yogi Berra is always right," I said.

"He is." A wry chuckle to match mine. "It's at least possible that it ain't over yet. Will Chief Orr be there?"

"Both chiefs, plus most of town."

"All right. I'll see if maybe Fortescue can get a pal to look in, too."

"Please don't."

A sigh. "Jacqueline, I have resources you don't. Let me see what I can do for my own peace of mind. And yours."

I mumbled something vaguely grateful-sounding and wished him a good night.

I didn't want to talk about my alleged peace of mind. I didn't have any—and might not for a while. Maybe a long while.

By nine, Ryan was in her bed, taking full advantage of relaxed vacation week schedules with a stack of library books, and the show was in full swing. Something special must have been happening in late February of 1980-something, because everyone wanted slow-dance power ballads: "Oh, Sherry," "Almost Paradise," even the incredibly cheesy "Next Time I Fall." Whatever. I played them all, sprinkling in some newer stuff, and Motown to keep the show moving. I was singing the Cookie Monster version of "Call Me Maybe," because that's how I remember it, when Grandpa Seymour called.

He asked for Rosemary Clooney, but I knew he was just checking in and being supportive. So I was really glad I managed to dig up "Hey, There." Not to mention amazed, as was Grandpa, who told me to give his little Rina a kiss and hung up.

I followed the first celebrity Clooney with that spin of "Next Time I Fall" for one of my '80s couples, and was sitting at the board snickering as Peter Cetera and Amy Grant made their cautious and pretty embarrassing efforts at new love when the doorbell lit up.

Maeve.

I hadn't seen her since Friday, and I hugged her. "I know you guys don't go in for exorcisms, but you sure changed the energy."

She grinned. "That's the idea."

"C'mon. I have coffee and rugelach."

"Can I borrow Ryan's grandpa?"

"You have to take *his* dad too."

"Seymour, right?"

"A hundred and three and sassy as hell."

"He should meet my Aunt Patsy," she said as we headed downstairs.

"Really?"

"My grandmother's sister. Ninety-two, lied about her age to serve in the WAVES, married and raised three kids and then started marching and organizing—when she wasn't being a Playboy Bunny or writing feminist erotica."

"No." I topped off her cup.

Maeve giggled. "Oh, hell yes. These days she's leading the climate change protest at the federal building in Rutland every Sunday."

"Man, we have to get them together."

"Think they'd be a match?"

"Well, he just stopped watching the Gadflies because of everything that happened up here." I took a sip of my coffee. "How's she feel about Israel?"

"Golda Meir is her hero. How's he feel about feminism?"

"Grandma Rina was *his* hero. She died twenty years ago. Cancer."

Maeve nodded. "Let's set up a family dinner as soon as the weather breaks."

"Works for me." I giggled. "We are terrible."

"Nah. Be pretty great if it worked. Everyone needs love and companionship, if not sex."

For a long, awful moment we stared at each other, then by silent and mutual agreement, moved right on from there.

"Anyhow, I'll see what the Metzes' calendar looks like if you see when she's going to be in town next."

"I like it." She took another sip. "What's this one?"

"Something from the Ivory Coast. Supposed to taste like cocoa, spice—and maple."

"Kind of does, actually. Even the maple."

"Appropriate, huh?"

"Ready for tomorrow?"

"In so many ways." I joined her smile. "We're a real local radio station again."

But I didn't go to bed thinking about that. I went to bed wondering who else was out there—and how they were going to come at me.

I really wish Yogi weren't always right.

# Chapter Thirty-Three

## Blame It on Howard Dean

Probably the only thing that the knuckle-draggers and I would ever be able to agree on is that it was all Howard Dean's fault. Will, gracious Knickerbocker that he is, would never blame his distant predecessor, and Chief George, being a straightforward cop, simply held the perpetrators responsible. They were both wrong on this one.

The TruthTellers and their ilk blame the good Dr. Dean for all kinds of trendy lefty iniquities that he could not possibly be responsible for, probably up to and including Champ's habit of eating deer.

My beef is a lot more straightforward, and factual, thank you.

If the then-governor hadn't felt the need to drink a glass of maple syrup one March day about a quarter century ago, to prove how safe it was because of a scare over minute traces of lead, syrup tasting never would have become a thing. So some desk jockey genius in Travel and Tourism would not have turned it into an annual tradition, and Will would not have decided to do his duty at DeLorme's Sugarhouse after Rob's and my remote that day. And me without a muzzleloader. So thanks for nothing, Howard Dean.

Cute former governors notwithstanding (not as cute as the Knickerbocker, of course), Rob and I probably had our share of the blame since we'd decided to make a big deal of that first remote. Much of southern Vermont came out to express support, especially in the wake of the whole Edwin Anger cuchifrito. Really simple: WSV is theirs and they're going to stand with us.

Of course, I knew Will was being supportive too by holding his newser right after our show wrapped. It was pretty slick, actually, offering the endorsement of his presence without saying a word that might raise political issues for either or both of us.

We were probably going to have to deal with those if we kept seeing each other, but it was early for that too.

Vermont being Vermont, and northern New Englanders being what they are, as long as Will and I kept it discreet and straightforward, neither making a big deal of our involvement, nor lying and denying it, we probably didn't have much of a problem anyway. It might be an issue if we were still together when (if?) he ran for reelection, or if we made the relationship official in some way . . .

Way the *hell* too early to think about that.

It wasn't too early for a quick hello to the other very important person in my life, though. Will would meet Ryan at the remote, and that felt just about right. I didn't know what the rest of his schedule was for the day, but I suspected he might suggest a little snack and chat before heading back to Montpelier. It would have been a nice low-maintenance way to make acquaintances without going all happy family moments, and I would definitely have signed on.

Instead, we were just glad to end the day alive.

Not because of the remote.

That was wonderful, and fun, exactly like the coming-out party we intended it to be. Rob brought a big tray of muffins, maple-nut, natch! I contributed some really good coffee and found a box of vintage WSV pens and keychains so we could pass out a little swag.

As for the actual on-air stuff, Rob opened with Elton John's "Friends," his and Tim's song, who knew? He sounded like a kid at Christmas as he talked up music, interviewed Ray DeLorme about maple season, and brought on our local worthies as they filtered in. Sadie urged everyone to register and vote in Town Meeting. Orville and Oliver did their brother act, and even Chief George went on the air to remind people to beware of black ice in the slightly warmer weather.

In between, Rob played all of his favorite songs, introduced my newscasts with cool professionalism and teased me about my never-ending hatred for snow and getting up early.

Finally, just before the last song, he thanked everyone involved in getting us back on the air. It was just a minute or so of acknowledgments, but I had a lump in my throat as he started with the people of Simpson, and ended with a shout-out to "Our wonderful and highly qualified crew, Ms. Ryan Metz and Mr. Xavier Archer."

Then, at three minutes to ten, he wrapped up the show with Sinatra's "Summer Wind," another highlight from his and Tim's wedding. Rob and I were swaying at our table, and the kids joined in, grabbing Sadie, and then everyone else came along. We all ended up in this weird but wonderful sort of circle dance, a hybrid of the hora from a Jewish wedding and a group hug. I was between Orville and Oliver, feeling even more like a giant than usual, doing my best not to giggle when I met Rob's gaze.

We were both a bit choked up, eyes a little too bright, for the best possible reasons. Sometimes you have to go through hell to end up where you belong.

And yes, you can be damn sure we hit the satellite service clean at the top of the hour.

We all stayed in our happy family circle for a few seconds, wrapped in the glow, even as the slightly scratchy opening bars of "Don't Stop Believin'" threaded around us. No way I could have asked for, or gotten, that from the sat service, but it was absolutely perfect.

It was the roll-credits moment.

For a few seconds, it really felt like it. But then it was back to reality. We had to go do the epilogue and score a couple of good voice bites from the newser.

See, what you forget when the lights come up after that happy ending is that in real life, you have to pick your stuff and go back to your job and your responsibilities—and your day-to-day afterward. Only thing is, after you get the big warm moment, you hope the day-to-day is better.

You also forget, in the middle of the warmth and fuzziness, that there may still be a lot of bad things out there just beyond your circle of light.

There sure were that day.

Glow or no glow, the first thing we had to do was knock down the remote and get out of the way for Will's setup.

While governor's offices have gotten a lot more sophisticated since Dr. Dean slurped the syrup, newsers haven't. We still have to roll tape (or pixels) and the principals have to walk up to the podium and do the deed. At least I didn't have to haul a big heavy analog tape deck like I had back in the day; a small digital stick recorder did just fine.

Ryan and Xavier were getting into the idea of being crew, though, and they happily took down our mics from the remote, and moved the one compact news mic with a WSV flag to the syrup setup, which was a table with a small podium sound system and mini paper cups of product neatly arranged around it. A tiny, officious, and brittle woman in a green suit (of course), a maple leaf pin, and a lanyard with a name tag that identified her as being from Travel and Tourism, was fussing with the cups.

Chad Slater brought in the little sound system—apparently Mommie Dearest had an event in Chester the night before and it was easier than hauling another one from Montpelier. Travel and Tourism snapped that she hadn't heard about it, but she shrugged and left him to put it in place.

Yes, that should have struck me as seriously weird.

I didn't spend much time thinking about it, though, because Will walked in then, with Fortescue the standard cautious distance behind. Even in governor mode, he still had the Neptune thing, just appearing behind Travel and Tourism with an easygoing hello.

She startled and knocked over a cup, said something that was definitely not Travel and Touristy, and turned. "Governor! That will never do!"

"What?"

"That tie! We're not promoting horticulture today! We're promoting syrup!"

Will sighed. Today's tie was red roses, maybe in lieu of bringing me flowers.

Travel and Tourism scowled. "I would have thought you'd go with nice maple leaves today."

"You are not my mother. You do not get to dress me." He said it with a trace of humor in his voice, but enough steel in his eyes to back her off.

I suspected this was not their first run-in.

"Well, fine. Just talk up the syrup."

"That's what I'm here for." He looked up and scanned the room, seeing me and my junior helpers. "And glad to be. Hello, Ms. Jordan."

"Hello, Governor."

Ryan and Xavier snickered.

"And hello to the crew." He gave the kids a very grave nod, followed by an impish smile.

"Governor Will Ten Broeck," I started with full and exacting protocol, "I'd like you to meet Ryan Metz and Xavier Archer, my daughter and Rob's son."

"Happy to meet you." Will shook hands with both of them.

"Same here." Ryan gave him a very appropriate smile, even though her eyes were dancing.

"Good to meet you, RyansMomsMan." Xavier grinned, even as Ryan smacked his arm. "Sorry. Governor RyansMomsMan."

Ryan looked to me and we shared an embarrassed head shake, but Will just laughed.

"Master Archer, I think that's as good a title as any." He patted Xavi's arm, gave Ryan a warm smile, and turned to his host. "If it's not considered bribing the media, I imagine Mr. DeLorme here would be happy to help your techs find some sugar on snow."

"I think that's a great idea," I observed. "If it isn't any bother."

"No bother at all, Jaye." Ray DeLorme joined the group smile, clearly taking the measure of the situation and approving. "Call it a little vacation week education."

"Sounds good to me."

"C'mon, kids, I've got a batch almost ready to go."

"We need to finish setting up first, Mr. DeLorme," Ryan said with a very professional smile as she took out a cable from the remote kit.

"A couple of minutes?" Xavier asked, studying the podium and the wired-in mic.

"Sure thing. Nice polite kids you and Rob have."

"Thanks. Start 'em in the family business early." I nodded to DeLorme, who made a tiny nod toward Will and let his smile widen a bit. I managed not to blush and reminded myself that this was going to be a typical day as the governor's girl. Will didn't see it because he was crossing the wide room to greet Sadie, who was sipping from her coffee mug and kvelling over the remote with Rob.

"Um, RyansMom?" Xavier called to me.

"What's up?"

"There's something wrong with the wiring here." He was looking at the mic, and Ryan was following the cords, both of them with very troubled faces.

"Wrong?" I looked, not that I would have seen what they did.

"I'm not a hundred percent sure, Ma, but it really looks to me like the wiring is messed up."

"Messed up how?"

She reached up and took the pen from behind my ear. "Here, we can find out."

Ryan touched the pen's plastic cap to the flexible metal stand that held the mic, and that Will would have adjusted without even thinking about it. The crackle made all three of us jump back.

"God—bless America," I breathed, managing to catch the profanity before Ryan heard it, if not before violating my good Reform Jewish principles against taking the Lord's name in vain.

Ryan and Xavier, who'd both heard plenty of slips in their day, just shook their heads at the silly grownup.

"This is seriously dangerous, RyansMom."

"I'll unplug it—"

I grabbed Ryan's hand before she got to the outlet. "No, you won't."

"But—"

"We don't know if the problem is confined to the unit or if someone has tampered with the outlet too." I slipped the shimmery black Knitting Club Special scarf I'd worn for luck off my neck and wrapped it around my hand. Sorry, Mom. "This should give me a little protection."

As it turned out, I didn't need it. There was a tiny fizz from the mic stand as I yanked the plug, but that was all.

"Now what?"

"You two go get one of the chiefs, whoever you can find first. I'm going to go talk to the governor."

"Your man, Ma."

"Go." I didn't even bother with the maternal look of death.

Because it had just hit me. The really dangerous plot here had never been about me or Edwin Anger or even that little creep Spence Lyle. If I hadn't been so busy fighting for my professional life, I would have seen it. Instead, we were now in an entirely different kind of duel to the death.

Charity was trying to kill Will. Probably with her son's help, which was why he'd been so weird at dinner the other night. And he wasn't all in—or he wouldn't have warned Will yesterday.

I didn't know if it was for fun or profit, but it didn't matter right then. Will would be just as dead if we didn't stop her.

Damned if I was going to let that happen.

"It's not me," I said as I crossed to Will. "It's you!"

# Chapter Thirty-Four

## Wicked Witch of the East

Will turned as I came at him with that stunning opener, his eyes wide and puzzled for a moment.

"What?"

"I got drawn off by my trolls—but they're mostly just stupid. Charity Slater really wants you dead."

Sadie looked just as confused as Will for a second, but I could see her wheels turning.

"If something happens to you, she becomes governor," I reminded him.

"So?"

For one horrible second, I was afraid I was wrong—or worse, that he didn't believe me.

But then the rest of it came together.

"She would allow the land use change on Quarry Hill," Sadie said slowly, as she thought it through. "And probably make a ton of money in the sale."

"How?" Will asked.

Sadie shook her head irritably. "I should have caught that. The Carton who owns the land is her aunt, Mary Slater Carton. Damn it."

"No one would—" he started.

"*You* wouldn't, Knickerbocker." I put my hand on his arm, making serious and significant eye contact. "The rest of the world isn't nearly as principled."

"But, Jacqueline—"

"They've been trying for a while." The whole thing just started spilling out, and I had to work to keep my speech at an intelligible pace. "The step at your office that Saturday. The brake problem at the Grist Mill. And I'm sure the CO scare during the storm."

"I don't—"

"And just now, Ryan and Xavier found that someone switched the wiring in the sound system mic. If you'd just adjusted the stand the way you've done a thousand times, you'd have gotten a nasty electrical shock. I'm not sure it would have been fatal, but—"

"A shock? *Electrical* shock?" Will's eyes widened as he added it up. He believed me now.

"That witch," Sadie hissed. "We need to catch her and teach her a lesson."

"Well, hell," Will said, his eyes a lot less cool and wry than his words. "What do we do now?"

Sadie smiled, terrifyingly. "I think we can turn the plot on the plotter."

"You think?" I asked.

"I *know*. Get Orville and Oliver over here and keep everyone else away. And warn Rob." She smacked my arm and turned to Will. "You tip off your guy and the chiefs."

If anyone could do it, it's this crew.

Will gave Sadie a pretty scary smile of his own. "Lead on, Macduff."

Only ten minutes, but what felt like an eternity later, Will, Travel and Tourism (who wasn't in on it, but couldn't be told

271

without risking the game), and the town worthies assembled at the podium. In addition to the civilians, who were ready to spring Sadie's trap, the chiefs, and Fortescue, who was wrapping up a very intense but quiet conversation on his phone, were close and ready with their own contributions, if needed.

Hopefully not.

Charity Slater walked in a minute or so before go time, joining her grubby son and some of the subsidiary officials in the back, the usual protocol anytime the governor is in town. She seemed very tightly wound, but that could just as easily have been my perception.

My audio stick was rolling on the podium, and I'd taken a space near the syrup evaporator because it was a good, unobtrusive spot on the same side of the room as Charity, carefully threading in between a couple of cooling buckets of fresh syrup—no point in spilling the good stuff. Rob was next to me, with only the heads-up that something big was about to happen, rolling video on his cell phone in case we got anything we wanted to post later.

None of the other reporters knew or suspected anything beyond the usual weirdly wonderful maple tasting, but I surreptitiously made sure everyone's recorders were on and doing their thing, good colleague that I am. Actually, I just didn't want to spend the rest of the day fielding requests to share my tape.

"Thank you all for coming," Will started, hands on the podium, not yet touching the mic. "This was supposed to be one event, but as it turns out, we have a very happy announcement to make before we get to the sweet stuff."

I kept my eyes on Charity. It wasn't just my perception; she was humming with tension. And watching Will—and his hands— much too closely.

"Maple season is one of the great treasures of life in Vermont, a reminder of nature's many gifts. And of our duty to protect those gifts."

I hadn't known it was possible for Charity to look more tense, but I could see the sinews in the side of her neck tightening so much I thought they might snap.

"While we're always looking to invite environmentally conscious businesses and good jobs into the state, we also can't lose track of the importance of preserving what we have for future generations."

His eye landed on Ryan and Xavier, and the kids gave him wicked grins. They weren't in on it; they were just enjoying the shout-out.

Charity seemed to be vibrating, her back jaw grinding. I wouldn't want to be her dentist.

"And so," Will said, with a good pol smile to Sadie and the twins, "after careful consultation with Simpson's leaders, we're going to set up a big new open space area out on Quarry Hill Road, enabling us to preserve a known moose habitat from development—"

"You can't do that!" Charity may have intended it as a cool statement, but it came out as an anguished wail.

Will gave her a faintly puzzled look, but continued calmly. Now for some real political theater. "Of course, it's subject to a vote, which Ms. Blacklaw will duly warn and—"

"That's my aunt's land—and it's for—"

"For what?" Will asked. That's when he very deliberately put his hand on the mic stand, keeping eye contact with Charity, who wilted a little as he moved it. "Expecting something?"

"No!" She spat the word, and quickly tried to turn the table on Will. "You liberal tree-huggers can't just come in and—"

Will held up the unplugged cord of the sound system.

Charity went paler, if that was possible. Chad folded a little, like he'd been hit in the stomach. Gut punch.

"We know." Will's voice could have frozen all of Lake Champlain.

"You don't know anything! You can't—"

"You can't put your office up for sale. Or mine."

"I did no such—" She turned toward me, of all things. "This is all because of that crazy liberal deejay you're sleeping with—"

Will's eyes went steely. "Ms. Jordan is an old friend. My private life, and more importantly, *her* private life, are none of your business."

So much for that gambit, Charity. Try something new.

"You're all in on it," she started, turning toward the cameras. I saw the calculation in her eyes, and I glanced quickly at Marianne Manon, glad to see that she did too.

Charity wheeled on me again. Always easy to blame the media.

"Just another evil conspiracy—just like the big media sent her up here to take out Edwin Anger and Spence Lyle—"

That was enough for me. Good thing there were no snowmen or muskets within range.

"I came up here, you mummified moron, because I wanted to find a safe and comfortable place to raise my daughter."

"Some mother you are, letting your precious child live next door to that den of perversion and run around with that little illegal—"

As G-d is my witness, I did not intend to do it. But we all know what happens when I lose my temper.

"Enough. Just. Damn. Enough."

I grabbed one of the buckets of syrup that had been cooling beside the evaporator. It was about room temperature by now, but it would not have mattered. There was maybe a quarter second where I might have stopped myself—or someone else could have stopped me.

But she'd had this coming for a while—and G-d, the universe, or karma, take your pick, had decided that I was the one to give it to her. Nobody, least of all me, was going to stand in the way of that.

So I threw the syrup.

I'm told, by people who are *Wizard of Oz* aficionados, that what happened next was much like the scene where Dorothy killed the witch.

To me, it was like one of those slo-mo disaster videos. The syrup, a good couple of gallons—a terrible amount to waste—flew in a beautiful golden arc, then settled over Charity in a gooey torrent. It flowed over her brittle hair, smoothing it into shimmery waves, and oozed down her face like some bizarre beauty mask.

For one stunned second, she stared at me.

I was just as shocked as she was. I could not believe I had actually done it.

Then she started spluttering. "How dare you!"

"Um, I dare pretty good. You just tried to kill my *old friend* to make a buck, insulted my partner and his family, and oh, yeah, called me a bad mother." I smiled and put the bucket down. "Next time it won't be syrup. It'll be gasoline."

"You heard that!" she shrieked to her trooper. "It's a threat!"

Murchison shrugged.

My smile widened a little. "It's a metaphor. Do you even know what that is?"

Fortescue stepped up then, holding his phone. "She may or may not know what that is, but I bet she knows who this is."

He turned the phone toward her, and me, showing us what he'd been working on for the last few minutes. It was a surveillance video still, showing a small side door at the Statehouse, which I guessed was the private entrance to the governor's office, and a dishwater blond guy pouring water on the steps. Chad's face was clearly visible in the shot. "Easy enough to find once we knew what we were looking for. Got some good video of a couple of bony white hands on the furnace room door before the storm too."

Charity deflated a little under her coating of syrup. "It's a fake! You're all trying to set me up!"

"Mom." Her son tried to put a calming hand on her arm, moving carefully because of the goo. "Stop it. It's over."

Fortescue pocketed his phone and reached for his cuffs.

"It's not—" she sputtered, shaking off her son's hand, and splattering him with syrup.

"We're done, Mom." He literally and figuratively turned on her. "I'm not going to jail for the rest of my life for you."

"You little bastard!"

Chad Slater met his mother's gaze coolly and said his first sentence as an adult. "I prefer son of a b*tch."

There was a lifetime of hurt and angry in that sentence, and we'd never know the half of it.

"After all I've done for you-" She hauled off to slap him, splattering syrup on Chad, Fortescue, and my WSV tee, but the trooper caught her wrist before she connected.

"I'd start using your right to remain silent, Mrs. Slater," Fortescue said quietly. "You're going to need it."

She wilted, suddenly blinking hard, and probably not just because of the syrup dripping into her eyes. He walked her out as if he were escorting her to her next event. Which, I suppose, he was.

Fortescue held her hands gingerly behind her back, and a small but steady trail of syrup oozed from her feet. As everyone watched that scene, I slipped over to Ray DeLorme.

"Bill me," I whispered. "I know that's probably a couple hundred bucks' worth of syrup."

"She tried to get the school board to stop my daughter from taking her girlfriend to prom," DeLorme hissed back, allowing himself a tiny, satisfied smile. "Worth every drop."

The room stayed silent and stunned for what seemed like forever, but was probably only a minute.

Travel and Tourism finally broke in, clapping her little hands and chirping with high-pitched false cheer. "Well, then, people. Who wants to taste some syrup?"

Which just goes to prove that good maple really does go with everything.

# Chapter Thirty-Five

## Never Mind the Maple, Pass the Whiskey

It took hours to sort everything out, calm everyone down . . . and mop up the syrup.

The reporters were understandably more interested in the lieutenant governor's plot against her boss and her sweet apprehension than in helping sell the maple, but like everyone in small media operations, they appreciated coming home with multiple stories. So they were happy to take a couple of bites from Travel and Tourism and the syrup samples along with their breaking news, and wait for the press releases and arrest affidavits from the state police and the DA for the follow-up. Things weren't quite so easy for the rest of us.

Fortescue handed Charity and Chad off to a couple of staties in suits, the really big guns that you almost never see, who were less than amused to discover that their main collar was a sticky mess. Then he returned to scoop up his real charge because Will had to be in Montpelier at three for a legislative conference on—what else—a new land-use bill. The man himself made his apologies to the cast, and motioned to me to walk him to the door.

"Nice job, Ms. Jordan," Fortescue said as we got out of earshot, cleaning his hands with a wet wipe Sadie had produced from her expansive purse.

"It's Jaye, and it was the kids who solved it."

"Len," he reminded me. "And you were smart enough to believe them. And I'm sorry, but I loved the syrup."

"Can I join the mutual admiration society?" Will asked with a little edge in his voice.

"I'll bring the car around," Len said.

Will and I just stood there for a second. It should have been a happy and goofy and relieved moment, but it wasn't. There was something else going on here that I didn't understand. I couldn't explain it. I just knew that while stopping Charity should have solved everything, it hadn't—and might have given us new trouble.

Which made absolutely no sense.

For most of the ninety seconds it took Len to get back with the car, we just stood there staring at each other. It wasn't the time or place for anything, and we both knew it. Finally, Will settled for giving me a reserved, but not even remotely neutral hug and kiss on the cheek before he left, accompanied by the assurance that he would catch up with me later.

I assumed that meant a phone call. Part of being the governor's girl, after all, is understanding that dude has a job, just like I do. And he probably had a world of mess to sort out since he was down one lieutenant governor and up a giant corruption scandal.

I was absolutely fine with that. We didn't need to rush into big stuff that we might regret because of one crazy day.

Maybe that was it. Maybe he was afraid I was expecting him to go all old-school happy ending and whip out a ring like the guys in those awful Regency romances.

He had to know me well enough by now to know I don't play that smack.

Whatever it was, the Wicked Duke would have to wait.

Once the authorities cleared the scene, the chiefs joined the rest of us in adjourning to Janet's because nobody really wanted to go home yet. Nobody had much appetite, either, so Rob just started pouring coffee for the grownups and cocoa for the heroes, and we settled in to sort it all out.

The grownups, that is. The kids took over the bar with their cocoa and popcorn and settled in for the PBS Kids schedule they only get to enjoy on snow or vacation days.

Alicia and Maeve met us at the restaurant, Maeve with the bottle of good whiskey. Maeve took one look at everyone and opened it, adding a wee drop to her own cup, then handing the bottle to Alicia, who followed suit. When it was her turn, Sadie took her own splash, and looked at the chiefs, who shook their heads.

Despite that, though, our first responders knew far better than to argue with their women.

Then Sadie offered the bottle to me, and I added about half as much as the others had taken. It was still hours to airtime, after all, and I needed something to take the edge off just as much as they did.

The four of us clinked cups.

"To maple syrup . . . and stopping the bad guys!"

We all grinned.

"Good health and good luck!"

"All right, now that we're all properly refreshed," Rob said, sweeping us ladies with a pretty significant glare, "how the hell did we get here?"

"Well," Sadie began, "our august lieutenant governor was apparently trying to bring back the brewery project and make a large buck."

Further down the long table, Oliver snorted and pointed to the whiskey. I handed him the bottle and he added a bit to his coffee. Orville took it out of his hand and did the same, sparking more glaring but no bickering—yet.

"She had to know we wouldn't just roll over in the local permitting," Oliver said.

Sadie shook her head. "You know as well as I do if they got the state permit, it would have been damn near impossible to stop it."

Oliver scowled and drank.

"We'd tie them up in court for years," Orville noted, taking a drink of his own.

"Little Brother is right."

Everyone stared at Oliver for a moment, because it was probably the first time those words had ever passed his lips.

"But by then," Alicia pointed out, "she would have sold her aunt's land and made her money, so it wouldn't be her problem anyhow."

"You know the rules a lot better than I do," I said to Sadie. "Would the state permit have been enough for the land sale?"

"And then some." Sadie took another drink. "And sooner or later the damn thing would have been built, unless the brewery people just gave up."

"They might have, eventually," Rob reflected. "But they would have ruined that moose habitat in the meantime."

"She really wanted to kill the Gov?" Maeve asked, cutting to the chase.

"It probably started as an effort to just hurt him badly enough to get him out of office for a while," I began. "The fall from the iced-over steps would probably have meant a head injury and maybe some broken bones . . ."

Everyone was staring at me. I realized my voice had gone gravelly at the thought of Will getting hurt. So much for keeping it low-key.

"Anyway," I cleared my throat. "That would have given her at least a brief handover, and a fair amount of upheaval she could have exploited to sneak it through. Same with the brakes—neither was a sure way to kill. But the CO at the Residence during the ice storm—"

"That was murder. He just wouldn't have woken up."

We all turned to Chief Frank.

"Seen more than enough people dead in their beds." He shrugged, which meant don't ask.

"The podium thing probably would have stunned him a little but not much else," Chief George said, quickly taking attention from his opposite number.

"Yeah," I agreed. "It doesn't make sense after something as lethal as carbon monoxide."

"He doesn't have a pacemaker, does he?" Alicia asked. "My dad—"

Orville and Oliver looked at her sharply.

"That's right," Maeve said. "They're electrical. If he does, a shock *would* have been fatal."

"He's a little young for that," I pointed out, but even as I said it, something pinged in my memory. I reached for my smartphone.

"Young doesn't matter," Oliver put in. "Little Brother had to get one for a while after he had Lyme disease."

Orville squirmed, but I wasn't interested in that right now.

"Lyme. Ticks. That's right." I ran a couple of searches while the others watched. "He *does* have a pacemaker. He got some kind of obscure tick virus at one of those western parks when he was interior secretary, and it caused a treatable heart problem. It's buried in the bottom of an article from years ago."

My stomach twisted a little. I probably knew it at one time, but I sure hadn't remembered until now. And of course, Will hadn't said anything.

"Damn." Chief George shook his head. "I bet most people don't know that."

"I only found it because I knew what to look for in the search," I pointed out, doing my best to ignore the sudden hollow in my gut. "Charity might know because she's in the administration, and maybe at some level they keep an eye on him."

"It's not an issue in your day-to-day." Orville made very deliberate eye contact with me. "Most people eventually heal and don't need it any more. If you do, it's manageable."

"Unless something disrupts the electrical impulses." Chief Frank shook his head. "We're glad for those smart kids."

Everyone looked at the bar, where the smart kids were happily watching a dancing frog demonstrate long division. We were also very glad for PBS Kids.

"Best kids around." I smiled at the chief, and then Rob.

"So what happens to Charity?" Maeve asked. "Attempted murder, right?"

"Well, first a trip to the shower in the lockup," Chief George said, bringing the house down, and causing at least two spit-takes.

Once we calmed down, he nodded. "But yes, attempted murder, plus all kinds of bribery and corruption charges."

"She's going to be playing that horn in the prison band." Tim had a grimly satisfied smile. "And that was the last good syrup she'll get."

"For a long damn time," Chief Frank added.

"What about her son?" Sadie asked.

"Attempted murder for him too." Chief George shrugged. "My guess is he turns on Mom and gets out in time to have some kind of life."

"Not our problem anyway," Alicia put in.

"I'm just glad it's over," Rob said it for us all.

"It really *is* over." Tim gave me a significant look.

"You're right about that," I agreed as we shared a smile that the others didn't understand for a second.

"Well, the bad stuff is," Rob put in, giving me a wicked grin. "Looked like a lot of other stuff was just getting started."

I glared at him. I didn't want to talk, or think, about Will and me right now.

Fortunately, just then, David blew in, with congratulations and cookies for our young heroes. We didn't know it then, but they were about to have all the praise they could handle.

I had about all the stuff I could handle too.

# Chapter Thirty-Six
## Another Night, Another Request

Eventually, a little before dinner time, everyone drifted off to their lives, including David, who had a new blonde.

Mom and Uncle Edgar had weighed in via video call, starting with congratulations for me and Ryan and ending with the continuing fight over Sadie Hawkins Day at Palm Fountains. All normal there and fine by me.

I was just grateful that my mother's need for protection and my need to tend her had never spilled over into the kind of insanity that happened with Chad and Charity . . . and more determined than ever to make sure Ryan stayed a kid.

Grandpa Seymour felt the need to add his praise too, on a conventional landline, calling his little Rina a Woman of Valor, and extending the designation to me, too. With her Hebrew school background, she probably had a better idea how high an honor that was, but even I knew enough to get a little choked up. And to promise to dig out some Bing Crosby for him.

Hopefully we had something other than "White Christmas."

Since it was Tuesday and the restaurant was closed, the kids took Rob and Tim up on the idea of family mac and cheese and a sleepover in the hearth room at Janet's. I thought I might join them once the station was buttoned up for the night, because I guessed there wouldn't be a lot of sleeping on a vacation week night, especially after all the excitement. Rob said sure, but added that he wouldn't be surprised if I made "other plans."

Probably not.

For one thing, it was a work night for me—and him.

Normal was the key here.

So at seven o'clock, I opened the show as always, and started fielding requests. It was like the night of the pipe bombing, only more so. Seemed like everyone in Simpson wanted to make sure I knew they liked having us back, and the only way they could do it was by asking for a really, really bad power ballad.

Except the Marley Dude, of course. He wanted "I Shot the Sheriff," and you can be damn sure he got it. I also managed to dig up The Binger's "Accentuate the Positive" for Grandpa, which seemed like a good message for everyone right about now.

At a bit after nine, I'd just agreed to break my sacred rule against playing "You're the Inspiration" more than once a night when the doorbell lit up. I figured Chief George, even though we'd pretty much resolved everything.

Not the locals.

State.

Will had changed out of his suit, and taken a shower, which I knew because his hair was still a little damp, and even at the door I caught a tiny whiff of that delicious cologne. More, he was wearing the WSV sweatshirt under his barn jacket.

That was a message, too, but he didn't have to bother. The simple fact of his presence made this a very big deal, because even a math-challenged deejay can add times well enough to know it meant something like three hours of driving by the time he got to Montpelier and back. On a work night, yet.

Might have to make it worth the boy's while, and not with merch.

"Hey, Knickerbocker," I said with stunning originality.

But even as he made eye contact, I got that weird off vibe again. Something was still very wrong here.

Despite the undercurrent, he was smiling as he handed me one of those little glass souvenir bottles of maple syrup. "Just in case you need a weapon."

We chuckled together.

"I was provoked." I pulled him inside.

"You were." He kissed me, just a light, friendly hello with no extra spin. "You're also trending again. Alex says there's one with the Wicked Witch edited in for Slater."

"Of course there is."

"Next time, go straight to the gasoline. It's a lot cheaper than maple."

His voice was light, but his face was still tight, and I just couldn't shake the idea that I was missing something.

"I've got about two minutes left on 'You're the Inspiration.' Come downstairs?"

"Sure." He nodded to the holographic-glitter *Love Always Wins* tee that had replaced the syrup-stained one. "Good thought."

"It's from Ryan's favorite website—I bought the biggest one they had."

He chuckled, but then quickly fell silent.

We were weirdly polite and cool as we walked down to the studio and he poured his usual cup of coffee, then sat down in his usual place in the guest spot. Even Neptune just shot him a glance and curled right back up on the turntable cabinet. Normal, I reminded myself. Maybe important for Will too.

If only it felt normal.

He waited quietly, again with that odd reserve, as I set up a couple of long songs, and talked up the first one, another of those six-minute Celine Dion extravaganzas, then turned the monitor down to a hum.

"You didn't have to come," I started, a pretty stupid opener. "But I'm really glad you did."

"So am I. Hell of a day."

"No kidding."

"At least it's over."

"Back to normal." I couldn't finish the last word without a nervous chuckle. "If we even know what that is."

He was quiet for a little too long, and then: "After my mother's last chemo treatment, she said to the nurse, what do I do now?"

So he really did know. I just nodded.

"And Tracy—you know you get close to all of them—said, 'You just go live your life.'"

"That's it exactly."

"She has." Our eyes held over the board for a second, and he smiled. "Ten years out, the walk and the pink ribbon in October, and a look we all understand at family gatherings . . . but she has."

"Good for her. Things aren't the same—but she's here."

"Yeah. She'll like you."

"I bet I'll like her."

He nodded and drank a little coffee, but it still didn't feel right. Like I'd missed something important even as he trusted me with this.

Finally, after I'd seg'd into the next song, one of those loud power ballads from Heart, he spoke:

"You know why Slater tried the electrical thing." It was a statement, not a question.

"Yeah."

"You also need to know that I'm absolutely fine and I'm not going to get sick on you."

It was in his eyes. I sure *had* missed something important. He was afraid that I would run because of David.

The Knickerbocker didn't know me nearly as well as he thought he did.

"I wasn't worried about that." I really wasn't, despite the way I found out about it. I'd had plenty of time to process in the last couple of hours, not that it required a lot of thought. My answer was the same as it had always been: if you care for someone, you take it all. Even the Mean Guy if that's who he becomes for a while.

I've been there now. I know how to handle it. I might even be able to help find the way back.

If the last year and a half had done anything, it had convinced me that there were no guarantees, and only a fool would expect one.

"No?" His eyes didn't waver from my face.

"Not even a little."

"Okay." He took a breath. "I was going to tell you eventually."

"I knew, I just didn't remember it. No reason to."

"All right." Will nodded, but he still didn't relax. "Look, I—I'm pretty sure I was the Mean Guy when I was sick, and I understand if you don't want to be with someone who's capable of that after—"

"Stop."

He did.

"You are who you are. It doesn't change anything for me, and it doesn't change us." My voice wobbled and I stopped for a second and pulled it back under control. "We don't get to see what's down the road. We just have to take our chances. *I'll* take my chances."

Will nodded. "All right."

More silence. More watching each other. More of Heart wailing just below listening range.

Heart. How unintentionally perfect.

"You've got a right to know," he said finally.

"What?" What now?

"I'm doing my damnedest not to say something right now, because I know it's too soon and if I do, you'll have to say or do something about it. Which will probably screw everything up."

For a full chorus, we just looked at each other. If he'd just gone and said it, I would probably have jumped right in with both feet, especially after this day, and he might be right. It might have screwed everything up. Or not.

Don't rush with the rebound man, but go right ahead if he's *the* man. Sally.

Or Sadie: You can have a very satisfying and committed relationship without tearing up your whole life.

Maybe just do me.

Finally, I took a breath. "I'd say it too, and yeah, we'd just have a spectacular mess on our hands."

"Spectacular." A faint smile pulled at the corners of his mouth as he realized what I'd really said.

Enough for now. We've answered the big questions. Everything else is working out the details.

"So," I started slowly, as Heart went into the final fade, slipping a CD into the other player, "maybe we don't talk for a while."

I seg'd into the new song, and after I did, turned up the monitor. The unmistakable creamy contralto of Shana Gilbert, his request from that first night, a lifetime ago now, filled the studio.

Will grinned, a joyful little-boy expression that just melted me.

*"I never saw you coming . . ."*

He stood, and crossed to me, holding out his hands. "May I have this dance?"

"For as long as you want." I let him pull me into his arms.

"As long as *you* want, Jacqueline."

"We can negotiate terms of surrender later. Right now, just shut up and dance, Knickerbocker." I nestled my head on his shoulder and enjoyed the way we fit together as the music came up around us.

*"I never knew I needed you until I looked up and you were there. Now I can't imagine my life without you . . ."*

It wasn't going to be easy. But it just might be worth it.

# Acknowledgments

First thanks go to my agent Eric Myers for not giving up on this story, and to Crooked Lane editor Terri Bischoff for giving it a chance.

Undying gratitude to my family for backing me all the way, both as a broadcaster and as a writer.

About Vermont. I can never thank my friends, coworkers, and mentors enough for everything they taught me. I'm from western Pennsylvania, but I grew up in Springfield.

To my colleagues at 1010 WINS New York, endless respect, appreciation, and admiration. It's an honor to work with you. Every shift. Every time.

Finally, deep appreciation for two of my on-air partners: Bob Flint of WCFR in Springfield, for giving me a chance—even though I forgot my name in the first newscast! And living treasure Jon Belmont of WINS, for teaching the master class in professionalism.

See you all for the next shift!
Nikki Knight